CW01574845

For my boys, my inspiration,
my life's adventure.

Captain Black Heart and the Ghosts of Sea Cove Bay

by:
H. M. Sharpe

MAPLE
PUBLISHERS

Captain Black Heart and the Ghosts of Sea Cove Bay

Author: H. M. Sharpe

First Published in 2024

ISBN 978-1-83538-071-0 (Paperback)
978-1-83538-072-7 (E-Book)

Book Cover Design, Illustrations and Book Layout by:
White Magic Studios
www.whitemagicstudios.co.uk

Published by:
Maple Publishers
Fairbourne Drive, Atterbury,
Milton Keynes,
MK10 9RG, UK
www.maplepublishers.com

A CIP catalogue record for this title is available from the British Library.

INDEX

Chapter 1 – The Chase – The Boy Black 6
Chapter 2 – The First Spine Quiver 12
Chapter 3 – Black's First Enemy 20
Chapter 4 – Introducing Henry Spode 29
Chapter 5 – The Grave 31
Chapter 6 – Pirates into Port 37
Chapter 7 – Spode in Trouble 43
Chapter 8 – A Black Heart – The Promise 47
Chapter 9 – The Legend – Family Secrets 55
Chapter 10 – Coffin Ships 59
Chapter 11 – The Mutiny 70
Chapter 12 – Uncle Joe Dies 75
Chapter 13 – Grounded 84
Chapter 14 – Henry Dreams of Pirates 86
Chapter 15 – Black Heart's Heart 88
Chapter 16 – Summer Holidays 91
Chapter 17 – Spode's Hatred 93
Chapter 18 – Preparing the Search 99
Chapter 19 – The Pirate Death Code 101
Chapter 20 – The Trinket 109
Chapter 21 – Adventure at Midnight 112
Chapter 22 – The Betrayal 123
Chapter 23 – A Secret Pirate Passage 131

Chapter 24 – The Treasure Hunt......134
Chapter 25 – Secrets of Sea Cove Bay......141
Chapter 26 – The Burial......146
Chapter 27 – Fire in Henry's Belly......150
Chapter 28 – Fr. Raphael......152
Chapter 29 – Captive in the Priory......155
Chapter 30 – Ghosts......160
Chapter 31 – Henry Seeks the Treasure......168
Chapter 32 – Virtute et Ventate......171
Chapter 33 – Spode Sees a Pirate Ghost......176
Chapter 34 – Lucy's Keys......179
Chapter 35 – Quarter to Twelve......186
Chapter 36 – The West Tower......197
Chapter 37 – The Golden Candlestick......202
Chapter 38 – No Proof!......203
Chapter 39 – Max, Not just a little brother!......206
Chapter 40 – Grandad Collapses – Pirate Secrets......210
Chapter 41 – The Pirate Curse – The Last Stand......222
Chapter 42 – Police Sirens......234
Chapter 43 – The Wait......240
Chapter 44 – I Hate You Dad!......244
Chapter 45 – The Ceremony – Treasure Re-united......246

MAP OF SEA COVE BAY

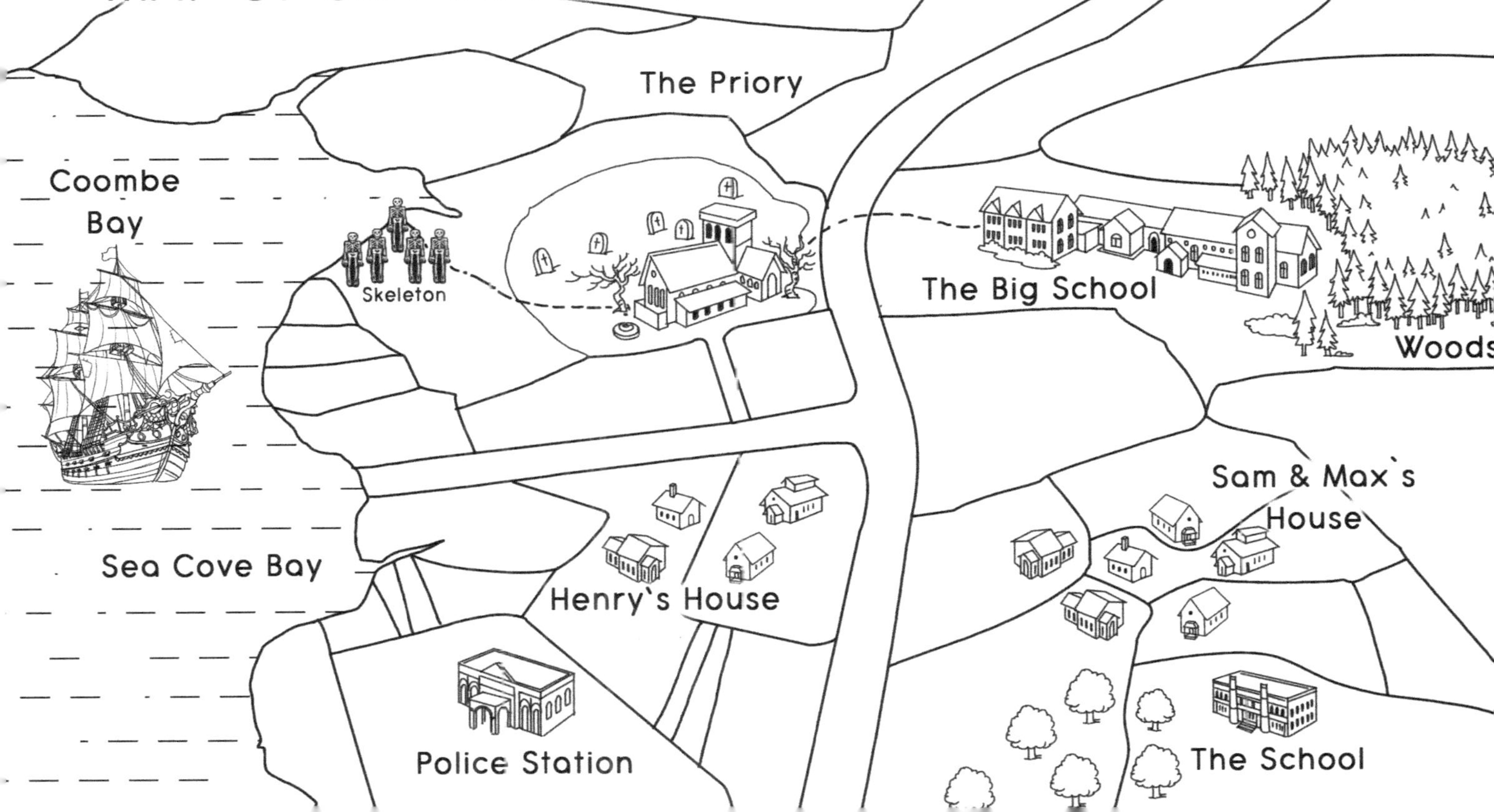

Chapter 1

The Chase – The Boy Black

Captain Sebastian kept the other ship just within sight, allowing it to touch the brilliant blue horizon, without letting it get too far ahead. The plan was for the other crew to believe that they were getting away. The Captain planned on the element of surprise to give him the upper hand. He knew the Onyx could outrun any ship in these waters and he knew his crew would enjoy the chase.

Captain Sebastian was a tall man, about six feet when he stood straight. He was thick set with burly shoulders and, as the years wore on, his black leather belt had been stretched to its last hole to make room for his rotund stomach. He had a thick bushy black beard and a droopy moustache, which he would stand and twiddle when he was hatching a plan.

There was not a cloud in the sky as Captain Sebastian gave the order to speed up. Instantly the crew jumped into their well practised positions and set about harnessing the little wind that there was. The magnificent silky sails billowed majestically.

"Steady as she goes," Captain Sebastian called. "Let's not make this look too easy!" he laughed loudly, a deep bellowing chuckle lifting the spirits of the crew.

"Young Mr. Black!" Captain Sebastian shouted looking up to the crow's nest perched high above the deck. The young boy sitting up in the wicker basket attached to the mast looked down and saluted at the Captain, waiting for his instructions.

Black was a blonde-haired Irish boy with tanned skin and deep blue eyes. His clothes always seemed too big for him, as if he was waiting for his muscles to fill out and his chest to expand. He was sixteen, going on seventeen, and had served happily under Captain Sebastian for the last year. His father had sent him to sea to make a man of him. Black wasn't sure if it was working, but it was a better life than picking potatoes all day, so he never complained.

"Unfurl the flag if you please, boy," Sebastian shouted, "let's show them who they're up against!"

"Mr. Black," the first mate parroted. "Unfurl the flag." Black often responded to being called 'boy', but when he was called Mr. Black, he knew there was serious business afoot. He leaned across to the mast with ease, his long gangly arms making the job simple. As he unhooked the rope to release the flag, a gust of wind blew his long hair into his face where it danced annoyingly in his eyes. He brushed it away and held it back on his head with his other hand. With a flutter, the banner uncurled to reveal the Skull and Cross Bones, the symbol feared the world over. The symbol that meant 'here be pirates, run fast or we will steal all of your gold!' Black gathered himself back into his nest and settled down to watch the battle. This was his first real battle since coming aboard and he could feel the excitement of the crew from up in his perch.

It wasn't long before the ship started gaining on the other craft. Captain Sebastian chuckled as the bow split the waves in front of his ship, leaving curls of white horses dancing in the water in its wake. He savoured the moment. He had been chasing the Captain of the Marylou for years now and following some good fortune in the last port they visited, he had discovered their next destination. Captain Sebastian had planned the attack well. He had dreamed of this. He knew exactly what to do.

They had come across the Marylou, as expected, in the Southern Waters and had stayed on her heel for two hours. The Captain knew Brodie would run and he had looked forward to the chase. The only decision he had to make was when to accelerate the hunt.

As the Onyx sped through the water, the gap between the two ships closed and the sounds from the other ship could be heard faintly on the breeze. Sebastian knew that his plan was working. The flag had clearly spooked the crew and the speed with which they were gaining drove fear into the hearts of the men serving under Brodie. The best part was that Sebastian knew the fear that lay in Brodie's heart after all these years. He could almost taste the dread on the salty air. It was time to reap revenge on the murderous, greedy baron who had stolen so much from those that had nothing.

"Lower the mainsail," Captain Sebastian shouted as they came upon Brodie's ship. "Drop anchor and come up on her starboard side."

"Aye, aye Captain," the first mate replied from the deck. He blew the whistle hanging round his neck and the crew jumped to attention.

Friar didn't really need to use a whistle, the crew would have obeyed him without it, but he was a stickler for good practice on deck. Mr. Friar had been first mate to Captain Sebastian for years and the crew revered him almost as much as the Captain himself. He was a remarkably young man for the position he held. He was small in stature with limp brown hair that hung just below his ears. He kept it tied back with a piece of string that was greasy and brown with use. He wore a brown bandanna over his head and a brown leather waistcoat, which he never seemed to take off, even on wash days! However, his most distinguishing feature was the brown leather patch he wore over his left eye. Nobody knew how he had lost his eye, and no one ever dared to ask. Some rumoured that a jealous girlfriend had done it so that he would always remember her, but Friar kept it secret and would tell nobody what had happened.

"Lower the mainsail, men, and ready the anchor," Friar bellowed. "Bring her about along the starboard side." The men busied themselves hauling on ropes and tying up the mainsail. The man at the helm swung the wheel round hard and the ship turned surprisingly easily for a vessel of its size, coming in close to the Marylou.

A breeze blew across the deck, the salty sea spray raining lightly onto the ship. It was a welcome relief to the men. The crew had been working hard for the last couple of hours. Adrenaline pumped through their veins and brought their blood to near boiling point. What Captain Sebastian hated; his crew out of loyalty and respect hated also. They drew alongside the ship as the wind started to rise.

There was a storm brewing out at sea, at this latitude the weather could change almost instantly. The waves started to roll the ship around a little more, but the crew didn't notice. There was fire in their hearts, and they were ready to fight. Let the sea send whatever foul weather it wanted. This day was the day a great victory would be won.

"Ready to board, men," the Captain shouted.

"Aye Captain," replied Friar, "Ready we are, on your word."

"Steady now," Captain Sebastian called, waiting for the opportune moment.

The noise from the Marylou got louder and louder and the bow of the Onyx scraped her stern. Captain Sebastian noted the screams of panic rising from the other crew. He saw the enemy frantically scrambling across the deck, lowering the rigging and hauling in sails. Then he saw what he had been waiting for, the cannons were being loaded and packed down with gunpowder.

"Ready the cannons," he yelled above the growing roar of the wind.

"Cannons ready, Sir," shouted Friar. "I took the liberty of preparing them earlier, Sir."

"Good man," laughed Captain Sebastian. "Then let's give it to them! Light the fuses, men," he boomed across the deck, twiddling his moustache as a broad smile spread across his face.

"Light the fuses, men," came Friar's immediate response as he wandered down onto the deck. The ship lurched in the water as the waves got stronger. The Marylou was being tossed around more fiercely as the Onyx buffeted her side, the wind aiding the job. The Captain swung down onto the deck to join Friar and dramatically withdrew his cutlass from its sheath. "Victory to pirates!" he screamed as the fire leapt in his belly. He jumped up onto the banister at the side of the ship, steadying himself with a mainsail rope. "Fire, when ready!" he yelled.

"Fire!" roared Friar as he ran the length of the deck and back again to make sure all the men could hear him. His pulse raced and his heart pounded in his chest. "Make us proud, men, send them down." With that the crew ignited the gunpowder that had been packed tightly into the cannons and covered their ears as the guns went off.

The next half an hour was a bloody battle. The guns from the Onyx were far superior to the guns carried by the Marylou. They ripped into the hull as if it were made of matchsticks. The Marylou got a couple of cannons loaded and fired back but they did little damage to the Onyx. Captain Sebastian's plan had worked. Brodie had not been smart enough to think ahead and prepare for battle. He had been caught unawares and ill prepared for such a vicious attack.

As the cannons bedded into the hull of the Marylou, Captain Sebastian returned to his position on the upper deck. He watched with amusement as the other crew scrambled around, desperately trying to load cannons and fight back. He waited for the main guns to be taken out, all the time his fingers working the ends of his moustache, his face a picture of excitement. Explosions erupted violently on the deck only a few feet away from him. The hull splintered and the ship leaned to the port side in an ungainly fashion.

Captain Sebastian scoured the deck searching for the man he hated so much, but he was nowhere to be seen. "Yellow belly," he cursed under his breath. "Let your men fight while you cower in a corner." The crew of the Marylou were desperate. Their leader had disappeared, and men were screaming with fear throughout the ship as the Onyx's cannons ripped into their vessel. Men were dropping like flies, caught in the cannon fire or by flying debris. They watched helplessly as their crew were picked off one by one by Sebastian's men who were swinging across onto the crippled deck. Sebastian's men carried good, strong weapons. Everyone had a short sword and there were usually hidden daggers in boots and belts that came in handy when the hand-to-hand fighting started. The crew of the Onyx swept mercilessly through the enemy, cutting them down where they stood. Some of the men tried to run but they were not fast enough to escape the fearsome onslaught.

Then Captain Sebastian saw him. He bellowed a blood-curdling scream across the deck. "Brodie, you, murderous villain, prepare to fight," then he swung across to the enemy ship, his sword held out in front of him, ready to take care of his enemy. Young Black felt the scream vibrate in his bones. He had never felt such anger and hatred in anyone before. He gripped the basket tightly that cradled him, not taking his eyes off the Captain.

Chapter 2

The First Spine Quiver

Sam was bored. It was one of those really hot summer days where the flies buzzed lazily against the school window. The classroom was hot and stuffy and in Sam's opinion, so was Mr. Clayton, the history teacher. He stretched his legs out under the desk and leaned back in his chair. He loosened the tie around his neck and tugged at his shirt collar. The uniform they wore at school was OK as uniforms go; grey trousers, white shirt and a royal blue tie with red and yellow stripes. Fortunately, in summer the boys were allowed to go without their blazers which was a good thing for Sam as his was now too small, the sleeves only reached half way down his arms.

Sam Forshaw was a tall, slim eleven-year-old boy. He had short blonde hair that was bleached in places by the sun. He had vivid blue eyes and a tanned face from being outside all the time. He was currently daydreaming about the summer holidays that were just around the corner. He longed to be out of this place with a whole six weeks ahead of him where he could do what he wanted and go where he wanted with his mates and of course his faithful Labrador, Jet.

It wasn't that Sam didn't like school; it was alright (apart from History which he hated). He even found himself looking forward to some lessons. Geography was his favourite, because he loved the thought of travelling the world, having the sort of adventures his Grandad was always telling him about.

Sam's Grandad was a dreamer like Sam, and Sam was never quite sure which of his stories were true. Sam knew that his Grandad had done a lot of travelling and had been all over the world. He had brought back some weird things from faraway places with ancient ruins and broken-down temples and stuff. He also knew that his Grandad had a fixation for pirates. When he was younger, he would listen for hours to the stories about a brave warrior of the sea who sounded more like a Robin Hood of the ocean than the blood thirsty cut-throat person Sam really suspected he was. It was strange when he thought about it; pirates used to be the main topic of conversation they had. But these days his Grandad always went quiet when pirates were mentioned. Whenever Sam started a conversation about treasure or galleons full of pirates and the mighty deeds they got up to, his Grandad would look uncomfortable and try to change the subject.

Sam loved his Grandad more than anyone; they had one of those special relationships that only happen once in a while. When Sam was younger he used to spend most of his spare time around his Grandparents' house. His Grandma used to spoil him with chocolates and treats. She would indulge his pirate craving with fayre such as Treasure Chest Trifle, Swash Buckle Stew and pieces of Eight Pie. These days however, he didn't get to see his Grandad as much. Since his Grandma had died three years ago, his Grandad had gone to live in an old people's home, which was about ten miles away from Sea Cove. It was nice enough as places like that go. It was a modern building with large windows for the residents to sit in their armchairs and look out at the gardens. The lawns were always well kept, and the flowerbeds were a riot of colour in spring and summer. His Grandad had his own room, which was plain and simple, just as he liked it. When he'd moved there, he had insisted on taking some of the furniture from his old house as he said he couldn't bear this 'new fancy plastic stuff'. Sam's mum took him through regularly, but it wasn't nearly enough for Sam's liking. Every time he visited him, Sam noticed how he was visibly ageing; he was slowing up and had to use sticks to help him get around. He was clearly lost without Grandma, and the staff at the care home had said they thought he was losing his mind. He would pace up and down the corridors muttering about pirates and the time coming soon and how the truth must be revealed. They thought he was nuts, but Sam knew that he wasn't.

The last time Sam had been through was about a week ago. His mind wandered back to the small stuffy room that his Grandad was always complaining was too cold. It had been a strange visit. Mrs. Forshaw had been going on about the price of shoes these days and how Sam and his brother Max had both needed new pairs. His Grandad had seemed quiet and had just sat in his chair, listening, with his hands steeped in front of him. At one point mum had gone out to talk to one of the nurses who looked after him and Sam remembered how eagerly his Grandad had waited for the door to close behind her, as if he had been waiting for her to leave. He pictured the look in his Grandad's eyes as he turned to look at him and re-lived the conversation that had taken place.

"Here lad," his Grandad had said as he opened an old wooden box that was sitting on the coffee table by the side of his chair, "take this."

"What is it?" he had asked taking the object being handed to him.

"A piece of family treasure," his Grandad said with a twinkle in his eye. "In the right hands, when the time is right, it will bring the owner good fortune." Sam opened the battered brown leather case that lay in his hands and pulled out an old tarnished knife. It had a glossy black handle with a Skull and Cross Bones motif on the side. The blade still looked strong and sharp, even though the rust from years and years of use was slowly taking hold.

"Wow, thanks," hc had said turning the knife over in his hands.

"Put it away now, lad, before your mother comes back, she doesn't hold with such things," Grandad said, leaning round slowly to check the door. Sam slipped the knife back into its case just as his mother came back into the room. He slid it under the cushion he was resting his arm on and slowly moved it round to his back, where he pretended to scratch an itch and slipped it into his back pocket. His Grandad winked at him and said, "I was just telling young Sam here about his great, great Grandfather." Mrs. Forshaw scowled at him. "You know, love, the pirate."

"Yes, I know who you mean," his mother replied curtly, "and you should know better than to go filling the lad's head with such rubbish." His mum glared at him with a 'don't push it' look on her face. Sam looked from his mum to his Grandad trying to work out what was being said, without being said, but neither of them had given anything away.

They left shortly after that; his Grandad hobbled to the door to see them off but pulled Sam gently back as his mother walked out.

"Be on your guard, lad; stay alert," he had whispered, "it won't be long now," but before Sam could ask what wouldn't be long, his mum had bustled him out and was giving her dad a hug and a kiss.

"What did he mean?" Sam thought as he tried to focus back on the classroom.

Mr. Clayton was droning on about something incredibly boring. He drifted in and out of the lesson. He was vaguely aware that today they were learning about the Irish Potato Famine and how Ireland had been hit by hunger and disease sometime last century, Sam couldn't remember when. He heard Mr. Clayton say that acre upon acre of farmland had been covered with black rot which devastated the potato crop and left everyone hungry, ill and dying. Sam stared out of the window, the sun was high in the sky and there was a heat haze coming off the sea. He loved living in Sea Cove Bay. As far as he was concerned, it was the best place on earth for a boy and his dog. He loved being down on the beach messing about in rock pools, clambering over the rocks and throwing sticks for Jet out to sea so that she swam for them. Jet was a black Labrador, she was a little overweight as Labs go. Sam had had her from a puppy, and they were inseparable. As soon as school was over, Sam was planning to take her over the cliffs down by the golf course for a good run. That was Sam's favourite walk. He would spend hour after hour gazing out to sea, dreaming about what it would have been like to be a pirate and live out on the ocean. Sam had the sea in his blood. It was weird how passionately he felt about Sea Cove Bay, he felt strangely tied to the place.

His gaze drifted back into the classroom and something on the wall behind Mr. Clayton's desk caught his attention. He leaned closer and saw it was a map of some sort.

"Funny," thought Sam, "I haven't noticed that before, I wonder if that's been there all term." He looked again and saw that the map was browned with age and ripped over one corner. It looked like a map of the Sea Cove coastline; he could just make out the Isle of Man opposite and the borders of Scotland. There was a strange symbol in the top right-hand corner, which at a glance looked like some sort of gold coin, but as Sam stared closer an image of a skull and cross bones stood out from the paper. Sam felt a shiver go down his spine, but he was jolted out of his dream by Mr. Clayton.

"Sam Forshaw, have you heard a word of what I have been saying?" yelled Mr. Clayton as he stormed over to Sam's desk. Behind him Henry Spode giggled. Sam turned to glare at Henry as Henry mouthed the word 'thicko' at him.

Sam hated Henry. They had grown up together in the village and seemed to have despised each other from the start. Sam didn't really know why, there was just something about Henry that grated him. He was the only person who seemed to be able to get under his skin without even trying hard. Henry was growing bossier as the years went by and was slowly losing the friends he had grown up with. He had started knocking round with a gang of lads that were known troublemakers. Sam looked up at Mr. Clayton who was seething with rage. If there was one thing Mr. Clayton could not stand, it was a day dreamer, and he knew Sam was one of the worst.

"Well!" he said, "would you like to tell the class what happened to the poor farmers whose crops were destroyed and whose children were left dying in the streets? Hmm? Please enlighten us with your wisdom, or don't tell me, perhaps you weren't listening, where were you this time, Sam? Hunting for pirate gold on a secret desert island?" Henry and his gang laughed loudly behind him. Sam felt himself going red.

"No, Sir," he replied meekly, not wanting to make eye contact.

"Please, Sir," to Sam's relief it was Lucy, "they were sent away on coffin ships."

"I was asking Mr. Forshaw, here, Lucy, but as you seem so keen to come to his aid, please feel free to dig him out of the hole he is currently in," said Mr. Clayton angrily.

Lucy was a slim blonde girl that had recently moved to Sea Cove Bay. Sam suspected that she fancied him, but he was way too shy to even talk to her, never mind ask her out. She smiled at him and he could feel himself going redder and redder.

"Well, the rich landowners sent the poor families across to British North America with the promise of food, money and clothing," she parroted, as if reading from a textbook. "But the ships they sent them on were poorly built and unseaworthy. Disease soon spread through them and they became known as coffin ships."

"Yes, well, at least someone was listening!" said Mr. Clayton moodily as he stalked back to his desk in front of the blackboard. "Sam, as you have clearly not heard a word I have been saying, you will write me an essay on the Irish Potato Famine, and have it ready for me first thing on Monday morning, do I make myself clear?"

"Yes Sir," Sam said grumpily. Blimey, if it was Friday today, he only had the weekend to write the stupid thing and how was he going to get that done when he had so much planned?

He heard Henry whisper behind him, "Forshaw, what a divvy!" and he felt his muscles tense in his arm, he was about to turn around and swing at him when his mate, Andrew, sitting next to him, put a hand on his arm as if to say, 'Let it go mate, it's not worth it!' Andrew was always a calming influence on Sam. He had common sense dripping out of him, which sometimes made him a bit boring, but he and Sam had been friends all their lives and they seemed to brush along nicely together. Andrew was slightly shorter than Sam. He had a mop of brown hair that drooped onto his forehead and his face was broad with freckles stretching across his nose.

Sam caught Lucy's eye as he turned back to face the front and mouthed the word "thank you" at her. She smiled and looked back at Mr. Clayton who had started droning on again.

Sam tried his best to pay attention for the rest of the class, but his eye kept roaming over to the map behind Mr. Clayton. There was something about the map that was familiar to him. In some strange way, he knew he had seen it before somewhere, but he couldn't remember where.

The bell rang for the end of school and Sam's misery was soon over. Everyone started packing their books away and there was the usual noise of scraping chairs and loud chattering that signalled the start of every weekend. He shoved his books into his rucksack and stood up ready to go.

"Going out with Lucy Woosey tonight, are you, Forshaw?" came the taunt from Henry behind him.

"None of your business," replied Sam angrily.

"At least someone of the female sex will talk to you, Sam," said Andrew, patting Sam on the back, "unlike our little friend Henry wenry over there, who makes the girls cry when he looks at them." Sam laughed loudly. Henry bolted forwards towards Andrew, making his hand into a fist, when Mr. Clayton appeared looming over the desk.

"Now boys, as you pay little enough attention when you are in my class, perhaps you would all like to stay for an extra bit of revision in detention tonight?"

"No thanks, Sir," said Andrew cheekily, "we were just going!"

"Pleased to hear it," said Mr. Clayton. "Oh, and Sam, I want that essay on my desk first thing Monday morning, do you hear me?"

"Yes Sir," said Sam despondently, "you'll have it."

As everyone filed out of the classroom, Sam caught sight of the map again. "I've seen that map somewhere before," he thought to himself, "but where?"

Chapter 3

Black's First Enemy

Captain Sebastian landed with a thump on the deck of the Marylou and raised himself up to his full height. As he got his bearings, he was shocked to see a sailor hurtling down the deck towards him. The man was wielding his cutlass madly and screaming obscenities as he went. Blood dripped down his arm and his run turned more into a weary hobble, as he approached Captain Sebastian, as if he were running out of steam. Captain Sebastian raised his sword, preparing to make his first kill, but something behind the man caught his eye. He lowered his sword in disbelief as he watched a dark shape grappling a lifeboat into the water, making ready to climb aboard. "Brodie, you scum," Captain Sebastian cried, ignoring the immediate threat in front of him. "Stand and fight, you coward." His voice roared above the noise of the battle, the wind now howling through the rigging. Captain Sebastian went to step round the man in front of him, now much more interested in catching Brodie before he escaped, but the man wasn't about to make the Captain's job easier for him. He seemed intent on giving his own Captain as much time as possible to get away. Captain Sebastian raised his own sword again, angry at the thought that Brodie would desert his men and not stand by them to fight. He looked the man in front of him in the eyes but stopped when he felt a tap on his shoulder.

"Captain," said a deep calm voice in his ear, "go seek your revenge I will take care of the first mate here." It was Friar. He stood next to the Captain, a fire burning in his eyes,

"One first mate to the other," he said spitefully as he drew his sword on the man who was now standing bemused in front of him. "Mr. Blaney isn't it?" he said venomously, "we meet at last."

"You won't get away with this," Blaney screamed, spitting on the deck in front of Friar, as Captain Sebastian bowed at him and danced across the deck to intercept Brodie.

Blaney raised his sword threateningly at Friar and stabbed forwards. Friar jumped backwards, easily avoiding the end of Blaney's sword. "The battle has wearied you, Mr. Blaney," Friar mocked as he ducked out of the way of a second tarry.

"You may have won this battle, but you will not win any others," Blaney yelled. "Before sundown you will be dangling off a thick rope, courtesy of the British Navy."

"Really," laughed Friar. "And what makes you so arrogant in the face of defeat, Mr. Blaney?"

Blaney stood tall, for a moment his eyes blazed, and Friar wondered what could possibly be going through the man's head.

"Look behind you, Mr. Friar," Blaney said, a sarcastic tone to his words. "God has shown us mercy today, has he not?" Friar turned; his sword still outstretched in case Blaney found any strength left to raise his sword again. He could not believe what he was seeing. On the horizon, gaining speed and heading straight towards them were not two, but three British Navy ships, the St. George's cross blowing straight and true in the gale. He spun back towards Blaney, anger bubbling from his stomach. His vision clouded as the red mists of pure hatred descended on him. He raised his sword and was about to take a swipe at Blaney's neck, when he heard a shout from behind him.

"Mr. Friar," the voice said, full of panic and distress. "Mr. Friar, Sir, come quick it's the Captain." The boy, Black, had been watching what was going on from his perch, high up on the Onyx. He had watched Captain Sebastian head off towards Captain Brodie and had feared for him. Driven by his love for the man, and with no regard for his own safety, he had taken the brave decision to follow, to make sure all was well. He had climbed down the mast easily, his bare feet gripping the slippery wood tightly. Then he had crept across the deck and had swung across to the Marylou seemingly unnoticed by anyone. As he approached the place where he had last seen Captain Sebastian, he found a pool of blood that was slowly being washed overboard by the rising waves that were now crashing down on the vessel. A trail of blood was smeared along the deck and disappeared into the cabin a few feet away from him. His heart missed a beat, as he feared the blood might belong to his Captain. He crept closer on all fours and peered in through the window trying to find Captain Sebastian in the melee.

The vessel rocked wildly on the waves as it was tossed this way and that. Black had to hold tight to a large coil of rope to prevent him being washed overboard by one of the ferocious waves that beat down on him in his hiding place. One wave soaked him completely and he struggled to catch his breath before the next wave hit him. He heaved himself up and managed to swing inside the door of the cabin, away from the worst of the waves. He ducked as a set of crockery slid off the table in front of him and crashed to the floor, joining the other table debris of candlesticks, broken plates and glasses. There in front of him he saw a grave sight. Captain Sebastian lay on the floor motionless, blood oozing from a wound in his leg. The other Captain lay face down, an arm's width away from the Captain. Black noticed that there was a large pool of blood seeping from under the man's chest.

Black crawled over to his Captain and bent over to see whether there was any breath left in the man. He felt a faint breath on his cheek, but the Captain was out cold. He looked around desperately for something to stop the bleeding, but finding nothing, he ripped a piece off the shirt he was wearing and carefully tied it around the Captain's leg.

"I have to stop the bleeding," he muttered to himself as he attended the wound, his voice taking on the Irish lilt of his homeland. Once he had finished his makeshift bandage, he approached the other man. He rolled him over to get a good look at him, but Black knew even before he saw the man's face that he was dead. The wound in his chest went deep and had gone straight through the man's heart. Black released his grip on him and stood up shaking with fear. This was the first dead person he had ever seen, never mind touched. He moved back to the Captain and tried to lift him, but Sebastian was a heavy man. "There's no way I can move you on my own!" Black panted as he laid the Captain back down again. "I'll be back, Sir, and I'll bring help." He knew the Captain couldn't hear him, but he felt better talking to him none the less.

Black ran out of the cabin and saw Friar along the deck with a man kneeling in front of him. He also saw what was coming up fast behind them, three large Navy ships that Black recognised instantly.

"This is a set up," he whispered under his breath. "I've got to do something." He danced round some men that were still fighting ruthlessly with swords and daggers and fists. He avoided a sideswipe from one of the enemy and scrambled over to where Friar was looking in horror at the vision behind him.

"Black," Friar grumbled in a deep menacing tone. "Get back to the ship and raise the spinnaker, then get to the helm and take the Onyx out of here."

"But Mr. Friar," Black yelled over the noise. "What about the Captain, we can't just leave him here, he's alive!"

"Leave the Captain to me," Friar replied. "Get back to the ship and start her under way. You know what to do Mr. Black." Friar then grabbed the whistle from around his neck and blew three short blasts. The Onyx crew looked up from their fighting, unaware of the danger approaching from behind.

"Men," Friar bellowed "Take what you can find from the hold and get back to the Onyx. We sail in three minutes." The men looked astonished that their victory was being cut short, but they did as they were told. They dropped the men they were holding instantly, setting off to find what gold and treasure they could carry.

Friar barged past Blaney, knocking him sideways as he went. He strode purposefully down the deck towards the cabin, his goal to rescue Captain Sebastian and return to the Onyx. He was about to duck under the cabin roof when he heard a scream from behind him. He turned to see Blaney running wildly towards him, a dagger having just left his hand and heading straight for him. He dived sideways and rolled helplessly towards a gaping hole in the side of the ship. At the same time, he heard an agonising scream, from where he was not sure. He scrabbled around for something to hold onto, but his fingers couldn't get a grip on anything. He felt himself slipping over the edge and desperately flung around for anything to save his fall. He glanced down at the dark ocean only a few feet below him, the waves clawing at his legs. Then a vision blurred in front of him. He felt a hand reaching his arm and taking hold of his wrist. Then he felt the pressure in his chest as his body was hauled back over the side onto the deck. He looked up into the panting red face of young Black who was stretched flat out on the deck, a heavy rope twisted round his right leg to hold him fast and stop his catch from falling.

"Boy," said Friar, gasping for breath between waves that crashed down on them both, he managed a brief smile, "I thought I gave you an order."

"Yes Sir," replied Black still holding onto Friar with a fierce intensity, his breath short and tight in his chest. "But I knew that scum would try something once my back was turned, so I took the liberty of giving him a little reminder of me, in case we meet again." Friar looked over to where Blaney lay and saw that Black had stabbed the man in his leg. It was not a bad wound but Blaney was rolling around, whimpering, as if his life force was being sucked out of him.

"Good man," Friar said, as he got to his feet. "Now, this time Mr. Black, do as you are told. You have less than one minute to get the Onyx out of here, or we are all scuppered. Do I make myself clear?"

"Aye Sir," Black replied. He unwound the rope from his leg and reached for his sword, just as an almighty wave crashed over the side of the ship. The sword slid towards him and he grasped it fiercely, having no intention of losing his weapon just now.

"I'll get you for this, you, young vermin," Blaney shrieked as he rolled around the deck, fighting the waves that soaked him and clutching his torn leg. "If it's the last thing I do, I'll get you!" Black said nothing, he knew better than to tempt fate. He tightened the grip on his sword and bounded across the deck, taking a flying leap onto the Onyx. He ran straight for the front of the ship where he released the spinnaker sail to allow the wind to turn the boat. He joined the men on the starboard side and helped them to haul in the anchor, muscles glistening in the continuous onslaught of the sea. Then he heaved the mighty wheel at the helm to head away from the approaching ships that were closing fast. The last of the crew were jumping aboard as the Onyx sped past the Marylou. Friar clambered onto the deck with his heavy load just in time to see the defeated crew desperately trying to climb into lifeboats and save themselves. As Black turned the ship into the open waters in front of him, he heard the last creaks and groans as the Marylou finally gave up the fight and went down to her final resting place on the ocean floor. As he watched the ship succumb to the waves, he saw a young man, about his age, clinging onto a piece of the wooden ship wreck. He locked eyes with the boy and a wave of pity and sorrow over took him. He felt an odd sensation that he had never felt before and wondered what was wrong with him, who was the boy and why did he feel such sorrow or was it anger for him. He hadn't noticed the boy on the Marylou but then he had been rather busy, perhaps he was the lookout boy just like him, but the hatred in the boy's eyes made Black look away. He wondered whether Blaney had made it or not, something told him that Blaney was a survivor and that they would meet again. He looked back to where he had last seen the boy but he was gone, probably sunk without trace to the bottom of the ocean, but Black had the strangest feeling that he would also see the boy again somewhere. However, the thought was fast put from his mind as Friar took up his usual position on the upper deck and blew his whistle.

"You, and you," Friar yelled pointing to the nearest crew members, "go and see to the Captain. The rest of you, all hands on deck. Get us out of here with all speed."

"Aye, aye Sir," the crew responded, and they set about raising the mainsail and driving the Onyx through the water at lightning speed so that she skipped across the crests of the waves with ease.

Black wasn't surprised at how easily they outran the Navy ships, but he was surprised at how quickly the Navy gave up the chase. If he didn't know better he would have sworn the ships were just seeing them off, rather than putting up a proper chase. The skull and cross bones worked all sorts of magic in these waters! However, he kept his thoughts to himself and slipped silently into the background, working alongside his crew mates, setting about the task at hand.

It was later the next day that Black was summoned to the Captain's quarters. He left the rope he was splicing and with some trepidation, he followed Friar to the Captain's bedside. He was amazed to see the Captain sitting up in bed looking so healthy and rosy cheeked. He hadn't been able to shake the picture of his beloved Captain lying unconscious on the unfriendly floor of the Marylou. The Captain looked up from the charts he was studying as Black entered and beamed at him.

"Well, well Mr. Black," he said beckoning the boy over. "It looks like you made a hero of yourself yesterday, if what Mr. Friar here tells me is true."

"Aye, Sir, it's all true Sir," Friar retorted in a serious tone. Then he turned and winked at Black. Black was speechless, a feeling of great relief washed over him now that he knew the Captain was going to live.

"It it it was my pleasure, Sir," he managed to stutter, before going bright red from cheek to cheek. The Captain laughed his hearty laugh and Friar joined in. The sound touched Black's heart and he laughed too.

"Let that be a lesson to you, young pirate," said the Captain as he made himself comfortable on his pillows, "never trust a fat merchant whose ship is named after a girl!"

"Right Sir," said Black laughing again. The Captain's laughter suddenly died away and he leaned forward and beckoned Black closer to him.

"Now listen to me, young pirate," he said speaking in a slow, smooth voice. "You keep up the standards you set today and one day this ship could be yours. What do you say to that Mr. Black?" Black found himself speechless for the second time in five minutes.

"Well Sir, I'm sure I'm not worthy of such an honour, Sir," he bleated, looking to Friar for help.

"What you did yesterday was a courageous and brave act indeed!" the Captain went on. "You had the foresight and heart to look after your crew and in doing so you saved not only my life, but the life of Mr. Friar here and half of the crew." Black could feel his cheeks burning scarlet and his ears pulsed with the heat of the blood pumping fast through his veins.

"It's true, Boy," Friar said, holding Black's embarrassed gaze. "You saved my life and for that I am forever in your debt. I will serve under you when the time comes until I can repay your mighty deeds." Black was dumbfounded. He had done what he knew in his heart to be right and nothing more. He thanked the Captain and Friar meekly, then turned slowly and wandered out of the cabin, his mind fizzing with what he had just heard.

"Captain, one day," he muttered to himself. "Me, of the Onyx, wow."

Chapter 4

Introducing Henry Spode

Henry Spode went home from school feeling very smug. He loved it when he got one over on Forshaw. He visualised the look on Sam's face when Mr. Clayton told him off. "Priceless," he thought to himself. He let himself in through the front door and dropped his bag and coat at the bottom of the stairs.

The Spode family house was a small terrace with an unkempt garden at the front and back; tiny in comparison to the Forshaw's which was one of the many reasons why he hated Sam so much. There was no one else in as both his mum and dad went out to work. Henry was used to coming in on his own; in fact, because of how things were with his father, he preferred it that way. He tried to keep out of his father's way as much as possible because he always seemed to be on the receiving end of a clip round the ear or a slipper across his backside. He often thought his mum was nuts for staying with his dad, what she must have put up with over the years he could only imagine. His dad was always so angry, as if he had a volcano inside him, waiting to explode at any moment and these days the eruptions usually happened because of him. His mum seemed to stay out as long as she could, saying she was working late, but Henry suspected she wasn't coming home because of his father. It hadn't always been like this; something had changed about a year ago but he didn't know what.

He headed for the kitchen to make himself a sandwich and as usual, he left a sticky mess as he didn't see why he should have to clean up after himself, then he headed upstairs to his room. He fired up his computer and started killing aliens on the game he had got for his last birthday. After a while he got bored and headed out to meet his mates, not giving the mess in the kitchen a second thought. He found Tezz and Pike in the usual place, hanging around by the bench on the railway platform. Tezz was kicking a coke can into the back of the shelter and Pike was staring into space looking gormless. Tezz was a big lad, overweight, with ginger hair and a spotty chin; Pike in comparison was tall and gangly. His arms seemed to loll by his side as he walked, and he appeared to be all elbows and knees. Both boys had their school uniforms on which looked dishevelled and dirty. After a brief discussion about what to do, they decided to head down to the apple trees at the back of the Priory to nick some apples from old Mr. Willis' orchard.

Chapter 5

The Grave

Sam raced home, wanting to get as far away from school as possible. He flew in through the front door. "Hi Mum," he shouted as he grabbed Jet's lead.

"Hi Son," came the faint response from somewhere upstairs. "Had a good day?"

"Not bad," lied Sam. His mum always made a fuss when he got into trouble at school and he had learned to his peril not to tell her too much about what he got up to. Jet came bounding in from the back garden and jumped up at Sam with hcr tongue hanging out and her tail wagging in sheer delight to see him again. "Hi Jet," laughed Sam. "Get down, you daft ape, we're going out right now, alright?"

"Sam, are you taking Jet out?" came the voice of Sam's younger brother, Max, as he ran down the stairs. Max was three years younger than Sam, with dark hair and a more olive complexion. He was stocky but not fat and his hair was long in comparison to Sam's. He insisted on gelling up the front to try and make himself look older than he was. Max was always trying to follow Sam, much to Sam's disgust. The boys would wind each other up until Sam would punch his brother and he would go crying to his mum about how horrible his brother had been.

In general, though, for brothers, they got on reasnably well, although neither of them would admit it openly. Sam often rushed to Max's side when his brother was about to get into a fight or if someone was bullying him, that was different. But as younger brothers go, he quite often succeeded in plaguing the life out of Sam.

"Yes, I am taking Jet out," replied Sam, "and you're not coming,"

"Mum, Sam won't let me take Jet for a walk with him," whined Max to his mum who was following him down the stairs.

"Oh Sam, let your brother go with you," Mrs. Forshaw said wearily.

Sam always thought it was funny that already, at the age of eleven, he was almost as tall as his mum and it wouldn't be long before he passed her in height. Mrs. Forshaw had long blonde hair, which she usually wore tied back in a ponytail at the back. She had sky blue eyes and laughter lines, now a permanent feature on her ever-smiling face.

"But he always gets in the way," Sam said angrily.

"Fine," said Max, "I'll stay here and go on your bike instead."

"You will not," Sam said, stepping forward and punching Max lightly on the arm.

"Now boys, don't start," said mum. "Sam, go and take Jet for her walk and Max, you can help me get tea ready."

"Oh mum, do I have to?" Max groaned.

"Yes, you do. Your dad's coming home early tonight, and I want a nice family meal in peace, so make sure you're back by six, Sam."

"Alright mum," Sam said as he ran out of the back door with Jet before Max could follow.

He ran down Main Street in the general direction of the beach. The sun was burning down and he soon slowed into more of an amble in the heat.

"Plenty of time, girl," he said as Jet tugged at the lead. They wandered down the road and Jet in her usual style started leading the way. Sam started daydreaming again as he walked. A vision of a coffin ship drifted into his head and he wondered in the heat haze what it must have been like to be one of those poor people stuck on a ship, knowing you were going to die. Then his mind wandered, and he thought about how fantastic it was going to be to break up next week and have a whole glorious summer to spend outside. His feet fell into their usual rhythm as he wandered on and a vision of the map at school came into his head. "Where have I seen that before?" he mused.

He suddenly became aware that everything had gone really quiet, he couldn't hear the birds singing anymore and the insect chirping noises had stopped. He looked up and found himself outside the Priory. The Priory was a really old church, which as far as he knew, dated back to the 1100's, nearly 900 years ago. He remembered the legend told in school of how St. Betha, an Irish Princess, had sailed across the Irish Sea to escape an arranged marriage, made by her father, to the son of a Viking King. The story was full of mystery and drama and Sam had always loved it because somewhere along the line he suspected there was treasure and pirates involved!

"Funny," he thought, "that's the second time Ireland has got a mention today." He took Jet off her lead and she wandered off sniffing the ground, looking for anything to eat. She headed up into the graveyard and Sam ambled after her. He jumped when a large black rook screeched at him on the path ahead and flew up into a tree on the side of the path. "Blimey," he said under his breath, "you nearly gave me a heart attack, you stupid bird," and he picked up a stone and threw it at the bird, not really meaning to hurt it. The bird squawked rudely and flew across to what Sam noticed for the first time must have been a rookery. Large tangles of nest were visible at the top of the trees; they looked dark and cold and had an eerie feel to them, casting a gloomy shadow over the path. Sam shivered and moved along the path, letting Jet go off ahead. His feet crunched on the gravel under foot and he noticed that in places the path was covered in moss that gave it a spongy feel. He came out into a patch of bright sunlight and blinked at the glare of a white gravestone that dazzled him. He walked up the hill, past a few more graves and saw Jet sniffing in the top corner. He continued his climb and sprawled down onto the cool grass, looking back across the graveyard. It was only a small place, but it was very old. Most of the headstones had started to crumble away and were covered in moss and lichen. Alder trees surrounded the graveyard that threw their dappled shade across the graves and a large horse chestnut tree stood in the corner. Sam often used to come here in autumn to collect conkers that blew down in the early storms. An old stone wall ran around the edge marking the boundary to the holy ground. Ivy trailed down, twisting its way along the rocks, strangling the honeysuckle that grew wildly in places. Wild roses also grew along one side, forcing their branches into the cracks in the wall and up onto the branches of the trees. There was a smell of freshly cut grass with a strange earthy smell Sam recognised as freshly dug soil.

His gaze travelled across the headstones until it came to rest on a lumpy patch of earth that he assumed was a grave. As he stared, he had the strangest feeling that someone was watching him. He looked around and heard a snuffling sound behind him, but it was only Jet, routing her way along the back wall. He turned back to look at the grave again and that's when he saw it.

He jumped up and ran over to the grave, he gingerly stretched out his fingers to move away a piece of ivy that had grown down and wrapped itself around the loose stones. As he did, he felt his whole arm tingle, as his fingers touched the stone; it felt surprisingly smooth but cold to touch. "I've never seen this before," thought Sam, "This can't be where I've seen the markings on the map before," but there it was, vividly standing out on the ground; a man's face on what looked from one angle like a coin but if you moved your head slightly, it looked like a skull and cross bones.

"What's the matter Forshaw, Lucy not your girlfriend anymore?" came a voice from over the wall. "Got no mates to play with, so you've started talking to dead people?" It was Henry and his gang.

"Get lost, Spode," Sam said angrily. He knew he could take Henry in a fight; he had always been able to. It was Sam's height that gave him the advantage; that and being sleek and fast. However, on this occasion Sam knew he did not want to be stuck in a tight corner with Henry and his mates as well. He felt strange and lightheaded, so he turned and ran down the grassy slope and out onto the path again.

"Come on, Jet," he called as he heard the boys scrambling over the wall. A crab apple hit him on the back of the head, and he heard Jet yelp as one stung her on her side. Jet came running across to him and Sam clipped her back onto her lead and they both ran back up the Main Street, out of the way of flying crab apples. "One day!" thought Sam, "I'm going to teach that idiot a lesson!" He arrived at his back door panting for breath, Jet wheezing besides him. His head was pounding, and he felt like he was going to be sick.

"Good Lord," said his mum "Are you alright, child?" as she opened the back door to put the rubbish out.

"Yeah," Sam replied as he gasped air into his lungs. Jet padded off to her water bowl and drained the lot in one go. "Just a few restless natives," he said with a smile.

"I see," said his mum, "and would these natives be known as Spode and the gang by any chance?"

"Have you been fighting?" asked Max appearing at the kitchen door.

"No, but I'm not too tired to start on you if you like," he said, standing up and heading towards his little brother.

"Alright, that's enough," said his mum. "Go and get changed, Sam, and have a wash to cool down. Your dad's just rung and he's on his way home."

"OK mum" Sam said and went off upstairs to his room.

Chapter 6

Pirates into Port

"Land Ahoy," came the shout from the crow's nest, "To the starboard, land ahoy!"

"That be the starboard," came the reply from the man at the helm. He hung onto the enormous wooden wheel with one strong arm, his muscles bulging under the strain, the sweat shining on him in the afternoon heat. "Land ahoy, I see it." He heaved on the wheel and the ship slowly turned and headed for port. After a while the Captain emerged onto the deck and climbed to his favourite position on the upper deck. Captain Black had aged a few years, his face lined with a few more creases, weathered from the wind, salt and sea his skin was permanently exposed to. He liked standing there, he could see across the entire deck and watch his crew ably outrun a Navy ship or catch up to a wealthy merchant vessel. They were also extremely adept at bringing the ship neatly into port.

"Lower the flag, men," came the order from Captain Black. "We'll not be pirates tonight, but free men." His voice still held the Irish lilt he had been born with. A familiar whistle blew in the Captain's ear and he waited for the parrot like response to come from the First Mate.

"Lower the flag," came Friar's voice booming over the deck. Friar had also kept his rugged good looks and still had the twinkle in his eye from his youth.

"Aye Sir," came the cheery response from the crew.

"Drop the mainsail and lower the anchors," instructed the Captain. "Bring her about."

"Drop the mainsail and lower the anchors, bring her about," Friar bellowed as he turned to smile at the Captain.

The mighty ship lurched in the water as Captain Black and his crew brought it under control. The rigging whirred and pulleys buzzed, ropes tightened here and there, pulling the sails back into their storage position. The bowsprit, keeping tension over the bow to hold the mast in place went taut and the sound of metal chains lowering the anchors over the side could be heard throughout the ship as they rattled their way down to the seabed. Ropes were fastened and sails were tied, the whole crew seeming to know their job well, having done this drill many times. A bell rang and a cheer went up from the crew. A wave of excitement buzzed through the men. The lights from the local town twinkled in the evening dusk and the sounds of early evening drifted across them. Music played and people were singing and laughing, enticing the pirates to join the party.

"All hands," cried the Captain, waiting for the instruction to be passed on.

"All hands," Friar roared, and more sailors seamlessly joined the men pulling at the rigging. They glided into the channel cut into the thick mud by large vessels and the Onyx came to rest on the ocean floor. A tavern door flew open across the pier throwing yellow light onto the cobbled street. Two men burst out, rolling onto the cobbled road; one still holding his beer jug trying desperately not to spill any. The men swung at each other but with little effect due to the large amount of ale they had already drunk, each making vague attempts to insult the other with words that came out all garbles and slurred. Then a lady in a brightly coloured dress drawn tightly around her waist, giving her the overall shape of a pear with a large frilly hat, came tumbling after them trying to pull one man off another.

"Lawd," they heard her say in a sharp voice, "the shame of it, get up, you, useless bag of bones," and she grabbed hold of the beer tankard held aloft in front of her and poured the contents over the man's head. "To think, my own husband, scrappin' in the streets, what will everyone think?" The crew cheered, enjoying their first taste of action for a long while. The lady looked up and realised she was being watched. She grabbed her skirts indignantly and stomped off in a huff, leaving her husband soaked in beer sitting in the road whilst his fighting partner was rocking on his knees laughing at him.

"Looks like we're in for a wild night, Captain," chuckled Friar.

"Aye, indeed, it does Mr. Friar," replied the Captain laughing. "I'm sure there'll be stories to tell in the morning and no mistake. Right men," he shouted to his crew who had gathered on the deck ready to disembark. "Before you go I want a word." There were some groans from the men and a couple of wolf whistles.

"Hurry up, Captain," someone shouted, "the night wears on and we haven't started drinking yet!"

"Perhaps he's going to tell us to be good boys and be back for midnight," came the thickset voice of another crew member who laughed as he said it.

"Alright you vagabonds," the Captain said, his eyes twinkling in the tavern lights.

Captain Black loved his crew and they loved him. He had grown into a decent, proud and handsome man with it. Many of the men that served under him were Captain Sebastian's old crew, the rest he had chosen for himself. They were a mixture of robbers and thieves and gypsies, but Captain Black had an eye for a good heart. It was said that he would look deeply into a man's eyes to see whether there was good or bad inside. He could tell whether there was mutiny inside, as his stare penetrated into men's souls, or whether there was trust. A Captain needed his crew to trust him, and he needed to be able to trust his crew.

"You, Thompson, you old sea dog," he smiled, swinging himself down from the upper deck with his right arm gripping a rope for balance, his long blonde hair flowing out behind him.

"You're with me and Mr. Friar." "Aye Captain," said Thompson, looking wistfully at the shore.

"Don't worry, Mr. Thompson," smiled the Captain "I'll not keep you long, you too, Mr. Gore and Mr. Hicks. There are provisions to be got and deals to be done. I need my finest men on the case."

"Aye Captain," said the men, standing to attention and saluting.

"The rest of you," said the Captain looking round at the men. "Go, enjoy yourselves, eat, drink and make it a night to keep us in tales until we reach the western waters."

"Aye," cheered the crew stamping their feet and rattling their swords.

"But remember," continued the Captain, "there is a price on each of your heads, so watch your backs. We should be safe here, and we sail at noon tomorrow." There was another cheer from the crew, then as Captain Black stood back with his close circle of friends, the crew lowered the gangplank and clambered across onto dry land for the first time in three months. "God bless em," said the Captain, "God knows they deserve a night off." Then he led the men that were left into the Great Cabin at the other end of the deck.

Black walked across to the large wooden table that was positioned in the centre of the room. It was highly polished with six matching chairs neatly arranged round it. Charts and coastal maps lay piled at one end and a large black quill pen stood erect in its pot of ink. Oil lanterns stood along the large bay window, casting a yellow light into the room. On either side were shelves lined with books and the Captain's personal items.

"Please, sit down," said the Captain pulling out a chair at the head of the table, "there is work to do." Friar took up his usual position at the Captain's right hand with Thompson and Gore to his left. Hicks took up position at the other end.

"Thirty men, the Captain began. "Mr. Friar, if you please." Friar reached into his coat pocket and pulled out a small scroll of paper. He uncurled it and began to read:

"200 bags of flour, 5 barrels of sugar cane, 500 pouches of tobacco, 100 sacks of cabbages, 100 sacks of potatoes, 100 sacks of carrots, 5 pigs, 3 goats, 4 chickens and a cockerel, 10 barrels of gun powder and as much rum as ye can carry."

"Aye men," laughed Black, "as much rum as ye can carry. Make arrangements to have it delivered by noon tomorrow or we sail without it."

"Aye Captain," said the men saluting as they stood up and they headed off to find the provisions as quickly as they could so that they didn't miss too much drinking time.

Captain Black stayed for a while in the quiet of the Cabin. He walked over to the dresser and took up his pipe then he sat back down again and lifted his legs up resting his large black boots on the table. He pulled a pouch of tobacco from his pocket, filled his pipe and lit it. He then leaned back and listened. The sounds of the town warming up for a noisy night of revelry could be heard and he listened to the groaning and creaking of the great wooden beams that held his vessel so strongly together. After a while he reached into his jacket pocket again and pulled out a gold watch that hung on a chain. He rubbed his fingers across the decorated surface and threw it lightly into the air catching it gracefully each time it fell. Then he smiled and slipped it back into his pocket. He looked out of the great window; it was getting dark outside but the beam from the lighthouse shone boldly across the rocks at the foot of the large cliff that marked the entry to the harbour. He patted the watch safely back in his pocket and still puffing on his pipe, moved slowly out onto the deck. The stars twinkled above him and the moon was bright, not quite full, but still bright enough to light up the deck in ghostly white shades. Black headed for the gangplank and went to join his crew.

Chapter 7

Spode in Trouble

When Henry arrived home for the second time that day, his mother's car was in the drive and the front door was open. He went in feeling very pleased with himself. It was rare to get at Forshaw twice in one day and he was enjoying it. He went into the lounge and found his mother sobbing quietly into a handkerchief. She looked up at him and grimaced.

"You wretched child," she said angrily through gritted teeth. "How many times have I told you to clear up after yourself when you've been in the kitchen?"

"Alright mum," said Henry sarcastically. "Don't stress, keep your hair on."

"How dare you speak to me like that," she shouted and lunged at him with her hand trying to slap his face. Henry ducked and ran out of the room before she could reach him. He ran up the stairs his feelings of happiness evaporating with each step.

"And get that room tidied," she yelled, sobbing as she said it. "It's a disgrace; just wait till your father gets home and see what he has to say." Henry slammed the door and threw himself onto the bed in a red-hot temper.

"Why do they always resort to violence?" he thought to himself. "I hate living in this house. I can't wait till I'm sixteen, then I'm leaving home."

Before long he heard the sounds of his mother getting tea ready. The banging of saucepans and the clatter of plates told him that she was still in a foul mood.

"I wonder what the matter is?" he thought feeling hurt and lonely. "A little bit of mess doesn't usually drive her that barmy!" A while later his mother called up the stairs for him. He went down and ate his tea in silence. There was no sign of his father yet which surprised him as he was normally home by this time. His mother just pushed her food around the plate hardly eating a thing. Every now and then Henry noticed his mother would look at him and it seemed to him she almost started to say something, then changed her mind and fretted over her food again. When he had finished he got up without saying a word and went to his room. As he figured it, he was in trouble already and would probably get the slipper from his father later when his mother told on him so why should he bother helping to clean up now? Surprisingly his mother didn't say a word as he left the room. She just got up and started tidying away.

Henry stayed in his room for a while shooting aliens and watching telly. He was just wondering what to do next when he heard his father's car park on the road outside the house. He waited for the inevitable bark of his father's voice to call him downstairs but amazingly it never came. Instead he heard raised voices, first his mother screaming something, then a reply from his father in an angry shout. This carried on for a while, but Henry couldn't make out all of the words, so he crept out onto the landing and crouched down by the laundry basket so that he could hear what they were arguing about.

"I don't care," yelled his father, "anything that man has to do with is no interest of mine. He lost any rights to be part of this family a long time ago."

"But he's your brother," shrieked his mother "I can't believe you are not going to see him under the circumstances. He may only have days to live."

"Shut up," yelled his father, "I am not interested. He can rot in hell for all I care."

"But he's your own flesh and blood," implored his mother. "He's all you've got left."

"I have no family left," replied his father curtly. "Now leave me alone before I do something I regret."

Henry heard the living room door slam shut and his mother breaking down into tears again, crying almost uncontrollably. He wondered whether he should go down and say something to her, but he knew he wasn't much good at things like that, and anyway it seemed that whatever they had been arguing about had taken the attention away from him. He went back into his bedroom and closed the door quietly.

"I wonder what that was all about?' he pondered. Then he heard the door slam and looked out of his window. He saw his father drive away in the car and his mother striding off in the direction of the pub she often went to when his dad had really annoyed her.

"Well I'm not staying here on my own," he said angrily to himself and grabbed his jumper and headed off downstairs. "Uncle Joe," he mused as he pulled his jumper on. "I know dad's brother is called Uncle Joe and he did something when I was quite small that annoyed dad. I wonder what could have been so bad that he cut him off from the family."

He was just about to head out of the door when he saw something peeking out under the front door mat that his mum must have missed. He bent down and picked it up. It was a pale blue envelope. He turned it over and read the front, the writing was shaky and pale. It read: 'Master Henry Spode, 13 Railway Road, Sea Cove.' Henry never received letters of any kind. Not even on his birthday. His mother had no relatives and as his father didn't speak to his brother. The only cards he got were from his parents and one or two of his friends if they ever remembered. He read the envelope again just to check that he was seeing straight then shot upstairs as fast as he could to the privacy of his room, just in case one of his parents returned. He sat on the bed and opened the letter wondering who would be writing to him. He pulled out several bits of pale blue paper and began to read.

Chapter 8

A Black Heart – The Promise

Captain Black walked along the cobbled streets listening to the shouts and laughter coming from behind tavern doors. He stopped in front of one. A large sign swung in the breeze above the door. A picture of a large sweaty brown animal with two large tusks protruding from its mouth snarled down.

"The Boar's Head, I presume," he said to the world at large and headed inside. He was met with a warm welcome. Everyone inside seemed to recognize him. A couple of ladies danced past him fluttering their fans in his face and swinging their skirts. Black took off his hat and bowed theatrically at them giving them one of his dashing smiles. The ladies giggled and scuttled away. Black was a handsome man, tall and strong. He was dressed all in black except for a red silk belt that was tied around his waist. He had a long gold earring that danced on his left shoulder and a short black moustache on top of his lip. A serving girl carrying jugs of ale came over to him and he helped himself to a tankard. He gulped down half of the beer before turning to see what else was going on. It was hard to see across the room for the smoke that hung in the air. A large fire roared in the corner even though it was warm outside. A couple of old men sat close to it putting the world to rights. Large wooden tables were scattered around where the revellers were drinking and dancing and stomping on the tables to loud cheers from the men around them. Ladies wearing brightly coloured dresses danced and flirted with the men. Black smiled to himself and headed off for a quiet corner in the shadows. He sat down and watched as more and more jugs of ale were brought out and placed on the tables in front of his crew.

A lady in a red dress with a tight-fitting bodice and a large flowing skirt moved gracefully over to where he was sitting.

"Evenin' Captain," she said as she sat herself down on his knee. "Is there anything I can be getting you?" She pouted her best pout trying to make herself appear attractive to Black.

"Evening Gracie," replied Black tipping her off onto the floor as he stood up. "You know there's nothing you can do for me except give my crew a good time."

"Oh Captain," she moaned standing up and brushing her skirts down. "You're hard on a girl; I was just after a bit of fun."

"Well, go and have some fun with the lads, there's a good girl, I've brought thirty into port for you; that should be enough."

"But Captain," she said throwing her arms around his neck and smiling. "You're the one for me," and she stood on tiptoe and tried to kiss him.

"Get off, woman," Black laughed as he pushed her aside. "Oi, Mr. Haslam, over here a minute," he shouted over the noise at one of his crew who was dancing on the table slopping the beer from his jug everywhere. "Miss Gracie here would like some company," and he spun the woman round into the arms of Mr. Haslam.

"Hello sweetie," he heard Haslam say as he walked over to the door. "Come and dance with me." Black paused as he reached for the handle and heard Gracie giggle, and then walked out into the warm night again.

He leaned against the wall whilst he pulled his tobacco pouch out of his pocket intending to re-fill his pipe when he heard a shout from farther down the street. "Captain," a muffled voice called, "Captain, come quickly."

"Who's there?" he asked peering into the gloom. This part of the town was not lit like the harbour. Black walked towards the voice and noticed that the houses were a lot more run down and shabby than those that lined the quaysides. Wisps of sea mist blew across the street making it difficult to see anything.

"Captain," said the voice again. "Over here please, come quickly, there isn't much time." Black crossed the road and a shadow detached itself from the wall and ran down the street. Black followed and saw the shape turn a corner. His hand reached automatically for his sword, but he stopped and rested it back in its sheath. He slowly turned the corner and saw the shadow waiting for him outside a house. Then it turned and ducked into the doorway. He strode towards the small hovel, then paused. The person had disappeared inside. He looked about him wondering if this was an ambush but the street was empty, so he ducked under the low lintel and emerged in a gloomy room.

The ceiling was low and the smell of boiled cabbages hung in the air. A fire burned pitifully in the hearth not giving off any confidence of warmth or cheer. The room was sparsely furnished. There was a small, well-scrubbed table in the corner and along the back wall a makeshift bed had been erected upon which lay an old man. Black looked from the man to the shadow person standing in front of him. Realisation dawned on him fast.

"Captain Sebastian," he yelled, a wave of emotion choking in his throat. "Captain, is that really you?" He stumbled over to the bed and looked in disbelief at the dishevelled face of his beloved Captain. Gone was the light in the man's eyes, now his face looked gaunt and pale. His thick black beard had turned silver white and had thinned in places, as had his hair.

"Sir!" he said choking back the tears, "what has happened to you these past years?"

"Ah lad," came the croaky voice of Captain Sebastian. He shifted uneasily on the bed as he turned to face Black. "The years have not been kind." Black looked up at the person kneeling down next to the Captain. He was shocked to see the face of a young woman looking back at him with what he thought was an exact copy of the Captain's face. She was a stunning girl even in this light; Black could see the beauty in her eyes. She reached up and unpinned the bun at the back of her head letting the long black hair cascade around her face and bounce off her shoulder. She smiled,

"Thank you, Captain, for coming," she said in a slow and serious voice.

"This is my father," she said as she caressed her father's face. Her voice wobbled a little as she turned to speak and a tear appeared in her eye.

"He is dying, Sir, he doesn't have long left." Black looked back at the Captain and fear blazed in his heart.

"Do not be afraid, young pirate," the Captain croaked. He tried to lean up on his elbow, but a rattling cough caught in his chest and he retched for a long while. Black took hold of his shoulders and gently laid him back onto his pillow.

"What is it I can do for you?" he asked staring deeply into the Captain's eyes. "You have gone to some trouble to find me; there must be something I can do to help you."

"There is, young pirate," came Sebastian's rattling voice. "I need you to do one last thing for your old Captain."

"Anything," said Black with earnestness. He didn't have the first clue what the Captain was about to ask him, but he knew he would do anything for this man.

"Young pirate, my daughter, Fee here, said you had docked and I sent her to find you." Black nodded his head at Fee as if seeing her for the first time.

"Captain Black," Sebastian wheezed. "I do not worry for her, she will be fine, she has skills; needlework and she cooks. There is a place for her in this town and she will be well looked after. It is my son I need you to help me with."

"Your son?" Black said, looking around him. The man set off with another bone shaking cough. Black waited patiently for the cough to subside. He held onto the Captain's shoulders trying to ease his pain.

"My son," Sebastian said desperately. "They will take him away, make him join the Navy." Sebastian gasped for breath, and then continued , "Captain, he's a good boy but he's frightened. I will not have a son of mine put to work in the King's Navy. He wouldn't last five minutes once they learned who his father was. They're coming for him tomorrow. Young pirate, you must help us."

"What is it you want me to do?" asked Black, but no answer came from the man. He lay still on the bed, his eyes closed, his breathing barely audible above the small crackle of the fire.

"Captain," said the girl, turning to face Black. "My brother is in hiding. He mustn't join the Navy. If they find him they will press gang him into leaving and I will never see him again, they will kill him. Please let him go with you. Take him aboard as one of your crew. He will work hard and learn all he can. I'll take you to him."

"Wait," said Black standing up. "You do not know what you ask of me. I am a pirate, young Fee. This life is no life for a young boy to make his way anymore. There is a bounty on my head and on each of the men that joins me. It is a hard life and I could not guarantee his safe return ever."

"Oh Captain," said the girl breaking down into tears. She grabbed her skirt and buried her face in it. Black looked at the man on the bed. He knelt down again by the man's shoulder and stared at his face.

"Captain," he said choking back the grief he felt. "I cannot do this, please, ask anything else of me, anything, but not this. He would be dead within the year." Suddenly Captain Sebastian opened his eyes and grabbed Black's collar.

"Now you listen to me, young pirate," he said in a loud strong voice. Black jumped at the sudden strength the man had found from somewhere. "I took you onboard when you were barely older than my lad. You were one of the finest crew I ever had, and I have put my trust in you over these last years to look after my ship and treat my crew well. You are not about to dishonour me now, are you Captain Black?" Black was speechless, he stared into the Captain's eyes and felt his heart melt.

"Take my boy," the Captain said. "Train him, let him sail with you. You cannot deny a dying man's wish." Then pulling Black even closer to him he whispered, "Captain Black, I trusted you then and I trust you now. Please, do this for me. Show me you have a heart, Captain Black." Then just as suddenly as it had arrived his strength left him. He released his grip and lay back limp on the bed.

"So, Captain, what's it to be?" said Fee, tears streaming down her face. "Shall I take you to him?" Black slowly stood up and turned to face her.

"Aye," he said staring into her eyes. "Take me to him; I'll not dishonour the greatest man I ever knew." He turned back to face the Captain, "Rest now," he said quietly, then turned and strode out of the room.

It wasn't far. The boy was hiding in the basement of a house farther down the street. Black waited as Fee went in and found him. As the boy emerged into the gloomy light his foot tripped on a protruding cobble and he fell forwards into the outstretched arms of his new Captain.

"Well," chuckled Black, "I am also pleased to meet you, young man." The boy hung his head with embarrassment, as Black looked him up and down. "You're nothing but a skinny pile of clothes, Master Sebastian," laughed the Captain. The boy looked up warily into Black's face.

"It's Joshua, Sir. My name is Joshua."

"Well, Joshua," said Black gently lifting his chin so that he could look into the boy's eyes. "Do not be afraid. I have sworn to your father that I will look after you and we'll start by getting some decent grub inside you. I need strong men on my crew not ragamuffins." The boy smiled.

"I am at your service, Captain Black," he said standing as straight as he could.

"Make that Captain Black Heart," said his sister not taking her eyes off the Captain as she hugged her brother. Then she turned and looked into Black's deep blue eyes.

"Sir," she said. "Please take these, they belonged to my father." She held up two halves of a coin that had each been fastened onto a gold chain. "He made me promise to give them to you if you agreed to take young Joshua." Black took the two talismans, staring intently at them. "They fit together Captain, look," Fee continued, as she showed the Captain how they slotted into each other. "My father said to tell you they are the key to a secret place that he visited once years ago. He said you would find it and use it if your need was ever great." Black stared transfixed at the coin then slowly broke the bits apart again.

"Aye," he said looking up, "I know what these are, and I know the place. I have not yet seen it with my own eyes, but I know a man who has. I feel certain that Mr. Friar will know the way if ever we need to go there." His eyes shone for a moment as he thought of the loyalty Mr. Friar had shown him, and the Captain before him.

"I will use these well." He turned to Joshua who was still standing close to his sister.

"I will entrust one of these into your safe keeping young man," he said in a quiet whisper as he placed one of the chains around Joshua's neck. "Keep it safe and don't tell anyone about it. The other half I shall keep myself," and he slipped the second chain over his head and tucked it inside his shirt. The three stood motionless for a while then Fee bowed gracefully.

"I thank you, Captain Black Heart," she said and turning, she ran back down the street and disappeared into the shadows.

Chapter 9

The Legend – Family Secrets

"*Dear Henry,*" the letter began. Henry shuffled into a more comfortable position on the bed and read on. "*You probably don't remember me; I am your father's brother, Uncle Joe. It is imperative that you keep this letter hidden from your parents. If they find out I have told you the secret they have been hiding from you they will hate me forever. This may not be as bad as it sounds, as I do not have long left. I write this letter from St Gilbert's Hospital where I am dying, so please excuse me if my writing gets poor.*"

"St Gilbert's Hospital," thought Henry looking up, "that's about 50 miles away!" he looked back at the weak writing, found his place again and read on.

"I have been in contact with your mother as I would like to meet my brother again before I die. I am hoping she will be able to talk him round and honour a dying man's wish. I have asked her to tell you what you should know but she has refused so I am left with no option but to tell you myself. I cannot go to the grave with the burden I carry."

Henry looked up utterly aghast at what he was reading. He repositioned himself again and continued reading.

"Henry it is very important that you believe what I am about to tell you. *It will sound like fantasy at first but please believe me. I would not be going to this much trouble and pain if it weren't true. You are the great great grandson of a man called Spode, Jake Spode, a pirate who sailed under the skull and cross bones. When he set out he was a handsome man, virtuous and true. Over the years he fought many a battle and stole plenty of treasure to keep him in a good life. The story goes, however, that his crew mutinied, and he was made to walk the plank. He managed to survive and was rescued by a man named Black Heart.*

They say it took the crew two whole weeks to nurse him back to anywhere near full strength. Once he was able to stand up again he started doing odd jobs around the ship until the Captain took him on as one of the crew. He never spoke openly of what had happened to him except they say, in his sleep. The crew found out nearly all his life history once his eyes were closed at night in his hammock.

Spode stayed serving the Captain for three years but during that time his hatred grew. He saw that the ship he sailed under could one day be his and he meant to take it, disposing of the Captain along the way. The rumour is that he murdered the Captain just before the ship ran aground somewhere near Sea Cove Bay and all of the crew were lost, all except Spode. Spode believed that the treasure on board rightfully belonged to him and he meant to take it for himself, but he never found it.

Henry, I know this must all sound very far-fetched to you, but I have been having some very strange feelings lately. Someone has been trying to tell me something and I think it might be Jake Spode.

There is a legend that pirates used to believe in, that you should know about. It is said that if a pirate murders a pirate, that man has three chances to seek revenge before his soul is lost to the underworld forever. These chances arise every fifty years and it is now one hundred and fifty years since Black Heart died. This is his last chance, because for some reason the other two attempts failed. Henry, Black Heart's spirit will not rest until justice is done and I think Black Heart's spirit has risen and is coming after his treasure, but this time the spirit of Jake Spode has awoken also. I think

Spode aims to make sure Black Heart does not succeed. I've felt his presence in my bones.

Henry, Black Heart will try and come for you, it would have been me, but I am dying, I will be no use to him. You are the only remaining blood relative left alive and I think Black Heart has chosen now to try one last time to revenge his untimely death."

"What about dad?" Henry said out loud to himself. He had a strange feeling in the pit of his stomach.

"I know you are a bright lad, Henry, and you will be wondering why Spode is trying to reach you and not your father. The truth is that your dad is not a blood relative of Spode. He was adopted into our family when he was small. He thinks that you shouldn't know the truth, that it will spoil things, but I need you to know who you are.

Henry, prepare yourself for a shock. You are my son. I held you in my arms when you were born and watched your mother slip away. They did everything they could to save her, but she had lost too much blood and she slowly went to sleep. As she drifted away she opened her eyes and smiled at you, then she looked at me and said, "Do your best for him." I knew that I couldn't take care of you like Sylvia and Charles could, so I persuaded them to adopt you and bring you up as their own. There isn't a day goes by when I don't think of you and I wish with my whole heart that things could have been different. Now as I go to join my darling Rose, I need you to know that you are a true Spode."

Henry felt the sickness rising in his chest. He couldn't catch his breath and he started hyperventilating. He sat up on the bed and tried to calm his breathing down. So, he wasn't his parent's son and his dad was adopted, maybe that explained why he never quite felt comfortable with him and felt there was a barrier between them. His breathing calmed and he picked the letter up again.

"Henry, please don't be afraid. You must be strong, but you must not tell anyone about this. The only way you can stop Black Heart transferring the curse onto you is to find

the treasure he believes Spode stole and return it to him somehow. Otherwise, it will be your soul that will walk in the underworld forever, never finding peace and rest.

There is a problem Henry, because it is said that Black Heart also has a direct descendant, an heir to his pirate legacy. You must find out who it is and get to the treasure first. It is likely that Black Heart's heir will have been contacted already and may already be close to finding the treasure. Henry I'm sorry that I won't be around to help you. Trust no one and Godspeed, child. I love you." The letter was signed *'Joe Spode'* (Uncle Joe) in brackets.

"Oh blimey," said Henry under his breath. He stood up and immediately felt like he was going to be sick. He just made it to the bathroom in time where he threw up vigorously into the toilet then he sat down on the floor and cried.

"The last living relative of a pirate, me! And I'm going to be haunted by someone called Black Heart," he turned and threw up again. He heard the front door go and his mother climbing the stairs. "That was a quick drink," he thought nastily.

"Are you all right, son" his mother asked in a vaguely concerned voice.

"What do you care!" he thought under his breath, but he resisted the temptation to shout it out.

"Yeah, I'm fine," he lied flushing the chain. "I've just got a bad stomach."

"You haven't made a mess in there have you?" she asked grumpily.

"No," he said weakly not believing he didn't even get sympathy when he had been sick. He waited for his mother to go back down and went back to his room.

Chapter 10

Coffin Ships

In the Forshaw household the evening meal went without incident. Mr. Forshaw came home tired and hot from the office. They all ate in relative silence with Mrs. Forshaw doing most of the talking, asking each of them questions about their day, which they all answered in one- or two-word sentences. It wasn't that Sam didn't get on with his dad, he did. It was just that his dad used to scoff at the stories his Grandad told him and Sam hated anyone mocking his beloved Grandad. He knew his dad thought Grandad was crazy so he would often get into stupid arguments that usually ended up with him being sent to his room to cool off. His dad was still taller than him but only just. Everyone said that Max looked more like his dad than Sam did with his dark hair and olive complexion. Max had inherited the stocky build of his dad whereas Sam was the spitting image of his Grandad, tall, slim and energetic.

After dinner Max started playing ball with Jet in the back garden. Mrs. Forshaw started clearing away the dinner things and Mr. Forshaw sat down in the living room with his paper and buried his head in the Sea Cove News. So, with nothing better to do, Sam went up to his room and crashed onto his stomach on the bed. The picture of the markings on the gravestone nagged in his head, he thought about it over and over again. The sounds of his brother and Jet came wafting through the window and he felt himself slipping into a state close to sleep. The room was warm and he could hear his mother chattering away downstairs to his father who made the occasional grunt from his armchair. It was then that he felt a shiver go down his spine and he jerked awake and sat up on the bed. He had that same strange sense that he had had in the graveyard that someone was watching him. He looked around his room, but everything looked in its place. He walked across to his desk and saw his history books poking out of his rucksack.

"Stupid essay," he said under his breath and switched on his computer. "Well if I have to do some idiot homework I might as well get started to get it out of the way," he muttered to himself.

The computer fired up and he settled into his usual slouched position in front of the screen.

"Right, let's see," he thought. "Coffin ships" and he entered the phrase into the search engine and waited for it to bring something up that he could copy into his essay. The computer whirred away and Sam didn't have to wait long before the screen filled with writing and the picture of what must have been a poor farmer crying over a black and rotting potato. He shook his head.

"Oh, the drama!" he muttered and started to read. Surprisingly he found the text in front of him vaguely interesting '*during the famine period, an estimated half-million Irish were evicted from their cottages. Unscrupulous landlords used two methods to remove their penniless tenants. The first involved applying for a legal judgment against the male head of a family owing rent. After the local barrister pronounced judgment, the man would be thrown into jail and his wife and family dumped out onto the streets.*' "Charming," Sam, thought as he read on. '*The second method was for the landlord to simply pay to send pauper families overseas to British North America. Landlords would first make phoney promises of money, food and clothing, then pack the half-naked people in overcrowded British sailing ships, poorly built and unseaworthy, that became known as coffin ships.'* "That bit sounds familiar," thought Sam remembering Lucy coming to his aid in school. He read on. '*Although most of the coffin ships headed for Quebec, Canada, it is thought that some of the ships were blown off course in fierce gales that swept along the Irish coast and resulted in ships landing along the Cumbrian coast.* "Wow," he thought. "I wonder if any landed here."

Just then the phone rang, he heard his mum answer it.

"Sam," she called, "it's Andrew."

"OK." replied Sam and he ran downstairs. "Hi mate, what's happening?" he said.

"Not much," said Andrew. "What are you doing?"

"This stupid essay," he replied.

"Oh right," said Andrew. "Do you fancy heading off down to the cliffs for a bit?"

"Hang on, I'll ask," said Sam. "Mum can I go out with Andrew for a bit please?" he yelled down the hall.

"Where to?" asked his mum.

"Just down the beach. I'll take Jet and I won't be late."

"Alright but be back by nine," she said.

"Cool," said Sam. "Mr. Clayton can stick this essay, life's too short - I'll see you in ten minutes," he said to Andrew picking up the phone again.

"OK," Andrew replied.

Sam put the phone down and ran back upstairs to his room. He picked up his rucksack and walked over to his wardrobe. He pulled out the binoculars he had got for his birthday and slipped them round his neck. He loved staring as far out to sea with them as he could, in case any pirate ships ever came into view. He was about to turn around when he saw the battered leather case that held the old tarnished knife that his Grandad had given to him. He knew it was really old and worn but somehow, he always felt better when he had it with him. He remembered the conversation with his Grandad from a week ago when he got the knife - "in the right hands when the time was right it would bring the owner good fortune."

"I guess you never know," thought Sam and he slipped it into his trouser pocket. He headed off with Jet, much to Max's disgust at being left behind again and met Andrew on the corner.

"Wotcha?" said Sam.

"All right," said Andrew and they headed off down to the beach. The hot afternoon had turned into a warm evening.

"Aren't you hot?" said Sam looking at Andrew wearing a sweater.

"I'm only wearing it till we're out of sight," said Andrew. "Then I'll take it off."

"Oh right." said Sam, he knew Andrew's mum was a worrier and was always bothered about Andrew catching colds. As they walked, they talked about nothing in particular. Andrew had a habit of kicking stones as he walked and they started a game of stone footy as they wandered. They soon came to the beach and walked along the front. "Shall we go up?" asked Andrew looking up at Sea Cove Head.

"Why not?" Sam said. "I only have to be back at nine." So, the two boys with Jet snuffling in front of them started climbing up the cliffs.

The path was well trodden by all the hikers who turned up at Sea Cove every year to walk around the beautiful coastline. It climbed steeply at first over the red sandstone head and then wound its way along the cliff edge for about three miles. The boys were well used to this path; they had been coming up here for years. They climbed quickly, Andrew following Sam and were soon up on the broad grass path that looked out onto the Irish Sea. They fell into step with each other and followed the path as it twisted over the undulating slopes of the sandstone mass. In places the path was bare, and the hot sun had turned the top layer of the soil to dust. Small clouds of dry earth were scuffed up into the air as they walked.

"Do you reckon any of those coffin ships ever landed here?" Sam said to Andrew as they walked.

"What makes you say that?" Andrew replied.

"Dunno," said Sam. "I just read that some of the coffin ships may have got blown off course when they were heading for America and might have landed here."

"OOH!" said Andrew. "Perhaps there are mouldy corpses rotting on the beach to this day," he said in a spooky voice.

"Get lost," said Sam shoving him slightly.

"Or perhaps the ghosts of the potato farmers walk the earth looking for a place to grow their black and rotting crops," he said raising his arms pretending to be a ghost.

"Yeah right," said Sam looking out to sea. Suddenly Sam felt a tingling sensation in his arm again, the same he had felt in the graveyard and he began to feel dizzy and cold.

"You alright, mate?" asked Andrew a little concerned, although thinking it was likely that Sam was having him on.

"Yeah," said Sam sitting down on the grass heavily and he told Andrew all about the map in history and the same symbol in the graveyard and how he kept feeling like someone was watching him and the strange tingling cold feelings he kept getting.

"Weird," said Andrew, "I think you've been in the sun too long."

"Probably," said Sam with a laugh, but all the same he felt as if someone was almost trying to tell him something. They carried on climbing up and round until without realizing it they had reached the old fort that lay in ruins that marked the halfway point to Coombe Bay.

"Here, this would be a good place for your ghost farmers, Sam," said Andrew with a laugh, running over to the fort. He climbed up and threw his arms around his head wildly. "Woooh, look at me," he said, "I am the ghost of a poor starving potato farmer, if anyone dares enter my fort they will be blighted with the same disease that ruined my crops."

"Oooh scary," said Sam and headed off along the path that rose steeply again.

They came to part of the path that narrowed and was nothing more than exposed rock, which they had to clamber over. The late afternoon sun was still warm on their backs as they climbed, laughing and joking, making their way along the path until over the next hill Coombe Bay came into sight. The last part of the path rose steeply.

"Do you think we should turn back?" asked Andrew as he huffed and puffed trying to get his breath back.

"No," said Sam, wheezing, himself, "let's go on, we're nearly there." They headed on and were soon at the deep gully that led down to the Bay.

Over the years the tide and wind had done a good job of etching out this part of the coast. Coombe Bay was a great gorge full of caves and overhanging cliffs. A small stream trickled over the rocks from the hills above making its way onto the beach and back to the sea. There was no sand on this beach, just rocks and stones that the sea threw up every day. Sam and Andrew clambered over the boulders and down onto the broad flat rocks that sculpted the caves under the cliffs. Jet scrambled down following her own route and as usual started sniffing around looking for something to eat; she disappeared out of sight round a cliff edge.

Coombe Bay, it was rumoured, was where long ago pirates would come ashore and stash their treasure before sailing back out to sea to raid some other poor unsuspecting vessel, usually on its way to the Americas. As Sam gazed around him, he could see why this place would be a popular haunt for hiding treasure. The caves were deep and black; they were eerie even in this sunlight. The place had a chilling and somehow sinister feel to it. He sat down on a big boulder that was smooth with age and looked out to sea through his binoculars, scanning the horizon for any activity, whilst Andrew picked up a flat stone and started skimming it out to sea. Sam was staring out, his mind wandering when he heard Jet yelp and start barking.

He jumped up and ran around the corner to where the noise had come from. He looked up and saw Jet above him. She had climbed up onto the rocks above and was balanced precariously on a thin precipice unable to move backwards or forwards.

"You, daft thing," Sam said, starting to climb the rocks to reach her. "How did you get up there, anyway?" Jet was whimpering and Sam could see that her legs were shaking with fright. She was a good way up and a fall would certainly do her some damage. "It's OK," he said trying to soothe her, "I'm coming." He gripped the rock with his hands trying to find convenient hand holds that he could get a firm grip on. He dug his trainers into any cracks he could find between the rocks and hauled himself up until he was level with Jet. Sam could see that she was on a narrow ledge where a large rock overhung what looked like a cave behind her. He planted his feet on top of what felt like a secure rock and reached for Jet's collar. As he did he felt his feet slip and the rock crumbled under him.

He scrambled to gain a foothold, but there was suddenly nothing under him to stand on and he fell heavily back to the base of the cliff. He landed in a heap on the ground and looked up to see Jet carefully picking her way down the rocks as if she had meant to do that all the time.

"Jet, you ape," he said, groaning. He bent double for a minute, winded from the fall trying to catch his breath. He got to his feet and brushed himself down. Then he saw something half buried in the soil. He reached out to see what it was but saw a movement above him. A large boulder that he must have dislodged when he fell started rolling forwards from its resting place. He heard the soil slide down in front of it and larger pebbles bounced onto the ground below. The boulder ground forward with a loud creaking noise. He grabbed Jet's collar and rolled sideways as the boulder crashed to the ground and came to rest a few feet away from his ankle. A by now familiar shiver ran down his spine and the hairs on the back of his neck started to prickle.

"Blimey, that was close," he said letting go of the dog's collar as she strained under his grip. He sat up and looked around him. Jet had wandered over to the boulder and had started digging furiously, scratching the soil and stones away with her paws. "What have you found, girl?" he said pulling Jet away. He saw it again; it looked like half a coin, on a blackened and dirty chain. It shone with a strange greenish hue although in another way it looked dull and tarnished. Jet whined and limped away as if she had been hurt. "It's alright," Sam said grabbing hold of her collar and stroking her. "Let's see what you've found, shall we?" He picked the coin up and as he did he felt the same eerie feeling that someone was watching him. He turned around quickly just as Andrew came running towards him.

"What's up, mate?" said Andrew, a concerned look on his face "I heard Jet, is she OK?"

"I think so," said Sam. "Look at this," he said holding up the coin.

"What is it?" asked Andrew for some reason starting to feel a bit apprehensive. Sam spat on the edge of his t-shirt and rubbed some of the grime off.

"Maybe it's part of a coin or something," Andrew offered.

"Sherlock, you're a genius," said Sam sarcastically. "Of course, it's a coin, the question is - what sort of coin is it?" He managed to get some of the dirt off and there it was in his hand, a man's head on a gold coin that if you narrowed your eyes looked like a skull and cross bones. Sam had a sharp intake of breath.

"Look, it's what I've been telling you about," he said holding the coin out to Andrew in his trembling hand. "It's the same marking I saw on the map and the gravestone."

"Look I'm not being funny," said Andrew, "but I don't know what map you are talking about. I haven't seen anything like it in Mr. Clayton's class, what does it mean?"

"I don't know," said Sam wondering if he was going mad, "but I'm going to find out."

He stood up and started scratching at the surrounding rocks.

"Start looking for any more," he said. Andrew walked a little way off and started pacing slowly up and down looking for more coins. They worked their way along a bit staring at the stone wondering if they would see anything else. Sam remembered the knife in his pocket and pulled it out; he flicked up the main blade and started digging into the spaces between the rocks a bit farther along from Andrew.

"This is stupid," said Andrew after about half an hour, "we should start heading back or we'll cop for it."

"In a bit," said Sam; he couldn't shake the tingling sensation that was sizzling at the base of his spine. "This may sound weird," said Sam, "but I think someone is trying to tell me something and I'm going to find out what it is."

"Come on, mate," said Andrew with slightly more fear in his voice than he would have liked. "This is starting to get creepy, let's get out of here." Sam looked up and saw that the sun was beginning to set; although it wouldn't be dark for a while, they still had miles to go to get back.

"OK," he said reluctantly "I suppose you're right. If we leg it, we'll just get back by nine."

Sam put Jet back on her lead and scrambled over the rocks out of the Bay. There it was again, the shiver down his spine. His hand curled protectively over the coin he had put into his front pocket and without looking round he started climbing back up the cliff and out of the gorge.

"Wait for me," said Andrew moving quickly to catch up.

"Let's get out of here," said Sam. "We'll come back tomorrow when we've got more time to explore."

"Yeah right," said Andrew grudgingly, "we'll both be grounded by tomorrow, next month may be."

They slowly made their way back up the cliffs and over the path to descend into the dusky light that was settling on the village of Sea Cove. All seemed quiet as they reached Sea Cove Head; the streetlights down in the caravan park were slowly twinkling into life as were a few lights in the caravans that were being rented out for the summer. They started their descent when something flew past Sam's ear. It was a barn owl that silently glided past them and landed on a fence post not two metres away from where they were standing. At first the sight gave the boys a start. The bird was larger than you would expect an owl to be. It had beautiful light plumage and turned its large round head to stare directly at them.

"Whoa!" said Sam quietly. "She's beautiful, isn't she?"

"Yeah," whispered Andrew. "I've never seen one so close up before." The owl stayed for a minute twitching its head from side to side, then spread its wings and leaped off the post. It soared out into the dusk heading for some poor unsuspecting mouse no doubt. They watched it go then set off back home.

Chapter 11

The Mutiny

The wind was blowing the sails of the galleon out strong and true. The crew were clustered together at the prow of the vessel. They were chanting and jeering. A ragged bunch they looked. Their faces were weathered and brown. They wore an assortment of bandannas and hats. Several wore thick bands of material wrapped around their waists as if to hold their trousers up. Most wore no shoes: their bare feet gripping the deck easily. Swords were drawn and were pointing at someone.

A smallish man with black greasy hair, his clothes torn and ragged, stood facing the men. He had leather boots on and what looked like a leather halberd. He was inching backwards as the sword tips poked at his jersey.

"You traitorous fools," the man said. "You won't get away with this mutiny, I'll see to that." Laughter rang through the men.

"Aye Captain Spode, we live in peril for our lives," sang the man closest to the lone figure. "Be gone now, you murdering traitor, be grateful we spare your life, God knows you don't deserve it." He darted forward with his sword. The crew followed and moved slowly across the deck their feet stamping in chorus with each other.

"You idiots," Spode screamed at the men. "If I hadn't killed that fool, there would have been no gold for anyone, don't you see?"

"No Captain, I don't see," shouted the man nearest to him menacingly. He was a large man. Muscles rippled over his brown back and across his shoulders as he tensed his sword arm. "Searle was a good man and a friend of ours, and you cut him down without mercy. Now you no longer have any rights to this ship. We will not serve under a man like you."

"Aye Captain," said another of the crew moving in closer, his sword pointed at Spode's heart. "And now there is more gold for the rest of us without a thief like you to take more than your share."

"You, fetid scum," Spode screamed at the top of his voice and with that he jumped away from the men, edging backwards until his heel felt the raised lip of the plank. He turned once to get his bearings, and then stepped backwards down the plank towards the ocean.

"This is my ship," he shouted loudly. "May the Gods know this is my ship," and with that he stepped off the plank and disappeared into the depths below. There was a loud cheer from the crew.

"Now that's done," said the man with the sword, "and good riddance. All crew set sail for the western quarter; all hands to the deck."

Spode splashed around in the water, desperately trying to keep his head above the waves.

"Filthy scum," he yelled at the retreating vessel. He heard the laughter coming from the deck getting fainter and fainter as the ship sailed away, abandoning him in the middle of the ocean. He looked around him, wondering if he could swim to shore, but all he could see was the blue horizon on all sides. Panic set in and he felt his muscles tiring already from his frantic attempts to keep afloat.

After an hour struggling to tread water, Spode looked up to the heavens.

"Oh, dear God," he muttered under his breath, "What have I done?" He felt himself getting weaker and weaker but fought desperately to keep his head up and fill his lungs with air. A couple of times he felt his body getting so heavy that his head immersed in the salty water, then his lungs cried out in agony for oxygen and he kicked his legs as hard as he could to reach the surface again. The sun beat down on his head and he knew that he was fading fast. Even though he was submerged in cold water, his head felt hot and dizzy. Another few minutes passed and Spode felt himself losing consciousness. He closed his eyes, and waited for the world to go black, deeply regretting his actions back on the ship. As he disappeared under the water, again something brushed against his head. He was vaguely conscious that something was floating above him, on the surface. With all his might he kicked his aching legs one more time and reached the surface, barely able to catch his breath and forced his eyes to open. He blinked in the dazzling sunlight and his splaying arms touched something hard and warm. He reached out desperately and found what he was looking for. It was a large piece of driftwood that must have been thrown overboard. He clutched the wood as tightly as he could and somehow, all his strength now gone, he managed to haul himself up onto the wood and lay there exhausted.

Three days passed and Spode lay still on top of his raft. Every few hours he would open his eyes and try to swallow, but his parched mouth sent searing hot pain to his brain and he would close his eyes again and drift into unconsciousness. The sun beat down onto his limp body, burning his skin, sucking any moisture that was left out of his body. In his subconscious state Spode knew he was dying. He couldn't feel his body anymore and his head was full of pain.

He didn't see the vision on the horizon on the fourth day that would have filled his heart with joy. And he didn't hear the shout from the crow's nest of the mighty vessel as it got closer and closer to him.

"Man overboard," the voice called. "There's a man in the water." Spode wasn't even aware of the hands grabbing him and hauling him up onto the deck of the ship. His hands by now were covered in blisters. His face turned an angry red colour from the baking sun.

"Get him inside, Friar," a gentle voice said, "Give him water and bathe his wounds."

"Aye, Aye, Captain," said Friar. Then he carried the man into the Captain's cabin and laid him on the bed. "It's a good thing Captain Black Heart is a decent man." Friar muttered as he set about seeing to Spode's sunburn. "There's not many pirates in these waters would stop to save a half-drowned man." Spode was vaguely aware of hands on him and felt a cool trickle of water fall into his mouth. Then he passed out again with exhaustion.

It took Friar three days of continuous nursing to bring Spode out of his delirious state. He lay on the Captain's bed in a red-hot fever. By the fourth day, Spode was just about able to swallow the water that was offered to him but would spend most of his time in a fitful sleep. Captain Black Heart checked in on his visitor once each day but left the main task of getting the man well again to Friar and his crew. For some reason, he didn't know why, Black Heart felt quite dispassionate about the man he had rescued from certain death. He had a strange feeling in the pit of his stomach each time he looked at the man that he couldn't explain. It left him feeling angry inside which was unusual for Black Heart.

"How's he doing?" Black Heart asked one morning as Friar finished changing the dressings on Spode's hands.

"I don't know, Captain," Friar replied. "His body is healing well, but if you ask me, that man's got something big on his mind. He's carrying a secret that bothers his sleep."

The Captain nodded and pondered what could be bothering the man, aware that he was feeling a strange premonition of something since the man had been brought on board.

As the weeks passed, Spode's strength slowly returned, and he was moved into the crew's cabin. He was able to hold the water canister himself, and he started to eat tiny morsels of food. Friar learned that his name was Spode, but that was all the information he got. Spode never spoke of the reason for him being afloat in the middle of the ocean.

One morning when Friar entered to give him his breakfast, Spode was gingerly standing on his feet. He held onto the pole at the end of his hammock that had been his bed for the past few weeks and took his first step forwards. Friar clapped him on the back and congratulated him for his efforts. But instead of the laughter Friar expected to hear, Spode wriggled away from his hand as if it had scorched him. Spode looked away from Friar not wanting to show him the hatred in his eyes.

"I remember you and your bloody Captain," Spode hissed to himself, "you don't remember me as I was only a boy that day you sunk the Marylou, but oh I remember you! I hate you and your Captain, and I mean to take this ship for my own one day!"

After that his recovery was fast and he soon found that he was being treated as part of the crew. He kept his loathing for Friar and the Captain hidden, knowing that the crew were loyal to them. Each day that passed he plotted and planned, his devious thoughts known only to himself, the plan that would restore him to the position he knew he was entitled to, that being ship's Captain!

Chapter 12

Uncle Joe Dies

Henry decided he would hide the letter under the mattress of his bed. He made sure it was right in the middle so that his mother wouldn't find it when she changed the sheets. He wandered round his room as if in a dream. The knowledge that he wasn't who he had always thought he was had knocked him for six. He found that he couldn't concentrate on anything for long and kept trying to work out whether it was all true or whether it was some cruel joke. He wished he could get on the train and go to visit his Uncle to check things out face to face. He was just debating what to do next when he heard his father return in the car. Almost at the same time the phone rang. He heard his mother answer it, and then his father's voice came on. It seemed like all went quiet for a while then he heard his mother begin to cry. He crept downstairs and found his father sitting in his armchair with his head in his hands, his mother kneeling in front of him caressing his knee.

"What's the matter?" asked Henry nervously as he entered the room. His father didn't look up. His mother stood up and walked over to him.

"Son, we've just heard that your Uncle Joe passed away in his sleep this morning. I know you probably don't remember him. He was your father's brother. Go up to your room now and give your dad some space."

Henry gasped in shock and quickly left the room. He went back upstairs without saying a word, his body feeling numb. He was shocked that his Uncle Joe had gone, and he'd only just received his letter. That was it. He'd gone and his father hadn't been to see him before he died.

"Well," he thought to himself. "I guess I won't get the chance to ask Uncle Joe if it's all true."

He sat on the bed and wondered what it would be like to be contacted by his pirate ancestor. He felt almost excited at the prospect. Then he started to think about Black Heart and that made him feel really scared.

"And who is Black Heart's descendant?" he thought to himself, "I wonder?" He dug under the mattress and got the letter out and read it again. "So, I have to find this treasure before someone else does." He started thinking where it could have been buried. Then a thought struck him. "If Spode was the only one to make it to shore after the shipwreck, which would mean the treasure would have been washed up onto Sea Cove Bay somewhere." Then another idea struck him. "Weren't there caves that ran underneath Sea Cove Head? That's where the tide would have washed debris ashore. I bet the treasure is buried under there somewhere." He was so pleased with himself that he didn't stop to think things through, never mind doing some checking to find out where the ship went down. He was so sure he was right that he almost ran out of his room straight away but he stopped himself as he got to the door.

"No," he thought, "I need to do this properly. I don't even know who I'm up against yet. I'll tread carefully then there won't be any mistakes." He went back downstairs and called to his parents, "I'm just going out for a bit." They both seemed so preoccupied that neither of them answered him. He headed off to the train station to find Tezz and Pike. He would need them if his plan were going to work. Without much persuasion he talked them into going with him and they headed off to the beach.

"What is it you want us to do?" asked Tezz warily. He knew it would involve doing something bad. Not that he minded; he just liked to know what was happening.

"I'm looking to see whether any of these boats are easy to nick," Henry said heading for the right-hand side of the beach. Ten or so assorted rowing boats and dinghies were lying upside down on the rocks just up from the tide line. They were held down with ropes so that the wind wouldn't carry them away.

"What for?" asked Pike nervously. He hated water and Henry's plan clearly had water in it.

"We need to take one," Henry said. "I need to check out the caves under the Head. I think there might be something there that belongs to me."

"What?" asked Tezz looking at Pike warily.

"I can't say yet," said Henry pulling at one of the ropes that secured a small rowing boat. "This one will be fine." He stood up and looked around to see if anyone was watching.

"We're not going now, are we?" asked Pike his voice nervous with fear.

"Yes," said Henry. "Help me untie the ropes." Tezz was used to taking orders from Henry and he immediately got onto his knees and started wrestling with the knot that held it in place. Pike was not as sure. He really really hated anything to do with water, especially the sea that had a tendency to tip boats over. He had capsized a few times in one of the local lakes when he was supposedly enjoying himself with his older brothers. He hated going under the water. He remembered the agony once when his lungs had felt like they were going to explode and the frantic thrashing around that had gone on before one of his brothers had rescued him.

"I have to get back," he said in a whiny voice.

"What's the matter, too chicken, are you?" said Henry nastily.

"No," replied Pike defensively and realising he had no choice, he got onto his hands and knees and started to untie the knots on the other side.

The boat was soon free and, with another glance around to check nobody was looking, they turned the boat over and carried it down to the sea.

"Climb in," Henry ordered. Tezz and Pike dutifully clambered in getting their shoes and socks wet. Henry heaved the boat out with his shoulder until it was afloat. He was up to his knees in water, which was freezing, even though it was mid summer. He cursed under his breath then half climbed, half fell into the boat. It rocked uncontrollably and Pike screamed, clutching each side with a vice like grip.

"Make it stop," he wailed as Henry steadied himself and sat down at the front on the boat.

"All right," he said, annoyed with Pike for being such a wuss. "Take the oars and start to row," he ordered as they bobbed up and down on the waves. Tezz and Pike took an oar each and started hauling on the oars, heading in the general direction of Sea Cove Head.

Henry turned to watch where they were going. As the boat got nearer he scanned the rocks looking for the right sized cave that might be what he was looking for. "Over there," he pointed as a dark cave came into view.

"No way," said Pike physically trembling with fright , "I'm not going in there."

"You can get out here if you want to," Henry said, a menacing grin on his face.

"No thanks," replied Pike. They headed for the cave and found that the tide was pushing them in that direction whether they wanted to go that way or not. Henry carefully stood up planting his feet either side of the centre of the wooden bottom. He stretched up and touched the roof of the sandstone cavern as the boat passed underneath. The tide gently washed them to the back of the cave. He looked around desperately hoping to see the sparkle of jewels and diamonds and the glitter of gold, but there was nothing in the cave but bits of seaweed that had drifted in on the current. There wasn't even a place to land or a sandy area where treasure might have been washed up and buried. He leaned over the side to get a better look at the back of the cave just in case he had missed something obvious. His foot slipped on the wet wood and he tumbled over the side making a huge splash in the freezing water. He spluttered to the surface gasping for breath.

"Grab him quick," came Tezz's muffled voice through the water in his ears. He felt a hand grab hold of his collar and drag him upwards. Henry thrashed around gasping for breath, he felt a second hand, weaker this time, grab his other shoulder. He kept his head above the water and reached up trying to grab the side of the boat. It rocked vigorously and both hands were knocked away as Tezz and Pike tried to steady the boat. Down he went again feeling the air being squeezed out of his lungs. He reached up and connected with Tezz's outstretched hand. Tezz hauled him up whilst Pike tried to steady the boat by hanging onto a rock that jutted out behind him. With an almighty struggle Tezz hauled him back into the boat where he lay gasping for breath and choking up the revolting seawater he had swallowed.

"Are you alright?" Pike fretted as he tried to wipe Henry's mouth.

"Get off me, you idiot," Henry yelled, pushing his hand away. "Just get me out of here," he ordered, leaning himself up on his elbow.

"What were you looking for anyway?" Tezz asked getting hold of the oar again.

"Never you mind," replied Henry getting his breath back. "I'm freezing, just get rowing." Obediently the two boys started working the oars and they battled against the tide to move the boat out of the cave. They worked hard straining against the weight of the water as the tide constantly tried to push them into the rocks. They cleared the cave, but the wind had got up and there was little they could do to move forward. They heaved on the oars but made no headway against the tide. The current was notoriously strong round the Head. They fought desperately to keep moving but it was no good, they were being driven onto the rocks. Henry saw what was happening and pushed Pike out of the way thinking a bit more muscle would help. Pike sprawled in the bottom of the boat and started sobbing.

"We're going to die, aren't we?" he whimpered. "We're going to drown, oh please somebody save us."

"Shut up," yelled Henry against the wind that was blowing fiercely in his face. He looked up at the shore briefly and noticed that the wind was only blowing out here. The trees at the caravan park were standing still not moving a single leaf. "So, it's like that, is it?" he yelled at the wind. "You want me, Black Heart, you're going to have to come and get me." He yanked at the oar. "Heave," he instructed Tezz. Tezz wondered what on earth he was on about but did as he was told. The two boys heaved and heaved but were fighting a losing battle. The front of the boat scraped against the rocks and spun the boat round helplessly. The tide swelled and threw the boat again and again at the rocks. It was then that Henry looked up and saw two figures running down Sea Cove Head. They appeared to stop and look at something, and then carried on their descent.

"Help," he yelled as loudly as he could. "Hey you up there, help us."

"Help!" came the voices of Tezz and Pike as they shouted as loudly as they could above the wind that was now roaring around them. Henry saw the person in front look down.

"They've seen us," he said, battling with the oar. An enormous wave crashed over them and Tezz lost hold of his oar. Pike screamed and the boat crashed again onto the rocks. A loud splintering sound could be heard, and water started pouring in through the rip in the bottom.

"Help us," yelled Henry again desperately not knowing what was happening. The boat spun round uncontrollably as if a giant whirlwind had it in its grip. Just as the three thought their number was up, they heard a voice shout at them over the storm.

"Throw the rope," it said. "For Goodness' sake throw the rope and I'll pull you in." In his misery Henry recognized that voice.

"Oh no," he muttered under his breath. "Not him, anybody but him." He looked up to see Sam Forshaw clambering along the rocks towards them.

"Throw him the rope," yelled Tezz as Henry remained motionless at the bottom of the boat. Then he reached over and threw the rope himself, yelling at Henry to get out of his way.

Sam caught the rope easily and as his fingers curled round it the wind died down and the sea calmed. Jet jumped around excitedly getting under Sam's feet.

"Jet, get out of here," Sam ordered and the dog backed away and started snuffling around the rocks. Sam hauled the boat towards the flatter rocks. Andrew arrived a few seconds later and helped haul the boat into shore. Then holding his arm out, Sam helped Pike, then Tezz, climb out where they sank onto the rocks both crying bitterly from the shock of their experience. Sam stretched out his hand again for Henry to take. He was surprised to see the look of pure hatred that was returned in Henry's stare. His arm wavered but he thrust it out again. Henry took a firm grip and jumped out of the boat onto the rock.

"What on earth were you doing out there?" Andrew asked as he knelt down to check Pike out. He was shaking uncontrollably and was as white as a sheet.

"Ask him," said Tezz jerking his head towards Henry, the anger breaking through his shock. Henry was standing where he had landed, glaring fiercely at Sam.

"So," he said in a cool voice. "It's you, then, that suits me fine!"

"What are you talking about Spode?" Sam replied reaching out to touch his shoulder. "I've just saved your life. What were you doing out there? You could have got everyone killed."

Henry brushed Sam's hand away angrily. "Don't touch me," he said venom dripping from his words. He shoved past him heading for the beach. "Come on, you two, useless idiots," he shouted at his friends. Tezz and Pike got to their feet and sheepishly followed Henry as he made his was up the beach and onto the promenade. Pike looked back and smiled weakly at Sam.

"Thanks," he said looking into Sam's eyes. "He said he was looking for something that belonged to him, but he didn't say what."

"Weird," said Andrew and started clambering back over the rocks behind the others.

Sam turned to catch up with the others when he suddenly felt strange and cold. On the edge of his vision out at sea he thought he saw something. A person dressed in black. It shimmered as if in a heat haze, and then disappeared like a mist blowing away. He turned to stare at the place the figure had been but there was no one there. He felt a shiver run down his spine. He shook his head trying to work out what he had just seen but there were just the waves breaking into white horses as the tide surged in. He headed off up the beach. Henry and his friends had gone out of sight.

Chapter 13

Grounded

Sam crept in the back door. He silently slipped Jet's lead off and hung it on the peg. He crept forward heading straight for the stairs, intending to go up to his room and pretend he had been on his computer for a while. As he tiptoed past the living room door the floorboard creaked and his father's voice came loud and clear into the hall.

"Sam." Sam paused thinking about what he should do or say, he checked his watch. It was ten thirty; he was an hour and a half late.

"Yes," he said trying to keep his voice as calm as possible.

"You have anything you want to share with us?" asked his dad in a sarcastic tone.

"Er no," squeaked Sam.

"No Sam, that wasn't a pleasant way of asking if you've had a good time. That was 'a come in here and explain yourself'." Sam knew the game was up for now and went into the living room to face the music. He hung his head.

"Do you know what time it is?" asked his father.

"Erm 10:30," said Sam dismally.

"Have you any idea how much grief your mother has been giving me, not to mention Mr. and Mrs. Johnson who have been worried sick about Andrew?"

"Well the thing is, dad," Sam began.

"Actually Sam, I don't want to hear it," interrupted his dad, "go to your room and we'll discuss how long you are grounded for in the morning."

"But," began Sam.

"I think not," interrupted his dad again. Sam knew he would get nowhere even if he explained that he had just saved somebody's life, so he turned to leave the room.

"Sorry," he called back hoping that would save him at least one week's grounding even if he did get some stay at home time. As he undressed the sight of a man dressed in black came into his thoughts.

"Who was that?" he mused as he drifted off to sleep.

Chapter 14

Henry Dreams of Pirates

Henry went straight up stairs to his room and took off his wet clothes. Both his mum and dad were out. He found a carrier bag and stuffed his clothes into it. "I'll get rid of them tomorrow," he thought as he climbed into bed. "It's easier than explaining how they got all wet." He climbed into bed, only now realising how tired his body was and he fell into a fitful sleep.

He was standing on the rocks at Coombe Bay. He recognized where he was, he had been here lots of times when he was younger. He had always hated the place. It made him feel weak and small and somehow insignificant. There was a storm raging out at sea. The wind howled and as lightning flashed across the sky piercing the clouds, it lit up the debris of a boat sinking beneath the waves. He saw the hull of what must have been a large vessel disappear as the waves rolled over it. For some reason it gave him a warm feeling inside. He smiled and looked around. In the water making good headway was a lone figure. Someone was swimming to shore, heading directly for him. He watched as the man reached shallower water, his feet slipped over the slime covered rocks, but he slowly managed to scramble his way onto dry land. He was a short stocky man, Henry wondered who he was. He looked familiar. The man stood catching his breath, the full moon outlining his silhouette against the dark rocks. He turned and stumbled off up the rocks that led out of the cove. Henry watched him leave. He thought about following him but something else in the water caught his eye. A second person was swimming to shore.

The passage through the water for this person was not as smooth as the other man's had been. It was as if he was being dragged back by something. Waves washed over his face and a couple of times Henry thought the man was going to drown, but somehow, he struggled on. He got closer and as he emerged from the water Henry could see he had a large sack over his shoulder. A sudden feeling of hatred filled his heart taking him by surprise. He felt cold and hungry for something. He shook his head "What's that all about?" he wondered to himself. The man hauled the sack onto the rocks ahead of him and Henry heard the tinkle of metal. "That's mine," he shouted. "Take your hands off that, it's mine." The man carried on oblivious to Henry's presence. Henry tossed and turned in his sleep. "That's mine," he called out again. Then rolled over and dreamt about gold and hidden treasure all night.

Chapter 15

Black Heart's Heart

Sam tossed and turned in a fitful sleep, he opened his eyes and saw that he was standing on top of Sea Cove Head looking out to sea. He blinked in the half-light and wondered how he had got there. "I must be dreaming!" he thought.

A storm was brewing out at sea, the sky was darkening and the wind was whipping up. He looked down at the murky waters of the Irish Sea and watched the waves rise and fall getting higher and fiercer with each wave. The wind had an icy blast to it, which made it difficult to breathe. He looked out to sea again and saw what looked like two ships heading straight for each other. He watched, as they got closer. He could make out the ship closest to him was an old battered thing. Its sail was torn and the paintwork looked worn and shabby. The other ship looked like a sleek galleon; it was painted black and as it came out of the mist he saw that the skull and cross bones flag flew from the mast. Its silky white sails billowed in the wind. Sam gasped as he saw the name painted in white along the side 'The Onyx'. He watched wide-eyed as the galleon sailed along side the stricken vessel. Two, three, four sailors swung across from the Onyx and landed heavily on the deck of the other ship. Sam could just make out the word 'Izaro' on the side of the boat. Two more sailors jumped across, then another, then another. He couldn't see what was happening. He strained to get a closer look, but the mist rolled in over both vessels.

He opened his eyes again and caught his breath. He was standing in the cabin of a dilapidated ship. The floor was wet with sea spray; there were holes along the side that were letting water pour in. There were ragged curtains at what had once been windows and the rain was coming in through a great hole in the ceiling. Sam lost his balance and fell onto the deck as the ship was tossed on the ocean waves. He rolled around trying to find something to hold onto. His hand reached a rope that was flapping free; it must have been part of the rigging at some stage. It was enough for him to get his balance. "I'm on the Izaro," he thought to himself. He turned and saw a man lying on a mattress full of holes. The mattress was stuffed with straw but most of it had fallen out onto the floor and was being washed away. He heard the man groan. He was wearing a dirty grey robe and he was convulsing with pain. Sam leaned up onto his elbow and saw that the man was covered in sores and red marks. His tongue lolled to one side, but he seemed to be trying to talk, and his eyes were closed. Sam wondered what he should do. Should he help the man? What could he do?

Just then a tall blonde-haired man walked over to the bed. Sam watched him approach, wondering what he was going to do. The man was dressed all in black except for a red silk belt that was tied around his waist and a red bandanna over his head. He had a long gold earring dancing on his left shoulder and a short black moustache on top of his lip. Sam recognised the man from his vision earlier that day and in his sleep, Sam had a sharp intake of breath. The man leant down across the stricken invalid.

"Oh no, don't do it," Sam tried to shout, but the words were lost at the back of his throat. He tensed himself waiting for the vicious blow to be delivered but it never came. Instead the man bent down and kissed the man.

The man opened his eyes slowly and looked up into a face that had struck terror in many a rich merchant's heart, but all Sam saw on his face this time was compassion and grief.

"You will rest soon, my son," he heard the deep cool voice of the pirate say.

"Please," gasped the man grasping the pirate's shirt, "you must take it, please. Don't let him take it back." The pirate gently laid the man back down; he was fighting for breath and had started coughing a horrible rasping cough that made Sam feel sick to the bone.

"Steady," he heard the pirate say, "try not to talk." The man turned his head and coughed up blood and green bile that dripped to the floor.

"Please," he said trying to lift his head gasping for every breath. "Take the crate in the hold, take it and put it somewhere safe, it's all that's left of my farm. He's taken everything else. Please do this, answer a dying man's wish." The pirate smoothed down the man's hair (for what good it would do in this wind) and with his sleeve wiped the bile and blood from around the man's mouth.

"Please," begged the man, the last few breaths rasping out of him, "take it, he must never get it, it belongs to my family, they will claim it when the time is right," and with that he breathed his last breath.

The pirate stood by the man for ten minutes or more in silent prayer. The ocean waves were wild now and he was soaked to the bone. Then he slowly turned, looked directly at Sam and walked away. Sam felt the shiver run down his spine. He couldn't breathe; he gasped for breath and fought to get air into his lungs, the stench from the dead man finally overpowering him.

Sam turned fitfully in his sleep as the dawn slowly approached across Sea Cove Bay.

Chapter 16

Summer Holidays

In fact, both Sam and Andrew were grounded for a fortnight, but far worse for Sam was that he was banned from going on the Internet as well. He had hoped that he could pass the time finding out as much as he could about the half coin he had found and what the symbol on it meant. He thought that maybe it was linked to those poor Irish potato farmers and he knew there were pirates involved somewhere, otherwise why the skull and cross bones?

The next week at school was dreadful. Sam handed his essay to Mr. Clayton who annoyingly showed very little interest in it.

"After all that work," thought Sam angrily, (he had had to finish it using what he could remember from class as he couldn't finish copying it off the net). "And I bet he puts it straight in the bin," he huffed to himself.

It was exam time and Sam had spent so much time trying to write his essay that he hadn't done much last-minute revision. Maths and English were okay and Geography was easy, but history and science were an absolute nightmare. He felt completely drained at the end of these exams, as he had concentrated so hard trying to remember little snippets from the classes he hadn't enjoyed. All through the exams he kept the necklace with him; somehow, he couldn't bear to put it down. He felt much better knowing it was with him. This spooked him a little, but he kept putting the fear out of his mind. "It's only a coin and someone's necklace," he would tell himself as he fell asleep each night.

Term ended and although he was still grounded he felt a sense of freedom wash over him as he stepped out of the gates for the holidays. Just one week of grounding to get through, then he could do what he liked. But that first week of the summer holidays was torture. Sam spent most of his time moping around his bedroom watching Max playing with HIS dog in the back garden. Max being a typical younger brother would remember to taunt him every now and then with stories about what he had seen his mates doing, how cool and refreshing the sea was and how the ice cream was tasting particularly fine down at the beach café. On the Wednesday he was so bored that he sat in front of the telly all day watching Cartoon Network. At one point he was sure that his mum felt sorry for him and nearly lifted the ban, but she held firm and the stay at home continued. By Thursday Sam thought he would go mad and that's when the idea hit him.

Chapter 17

Spode's Hatred

The anger in Jake Spode's belly grew with each passing day. It seemed that every time he laid eyes on Captain Black, he wanted to run at him with his sword held high and stab him though. Each day he told himself to be patient and that when the time was right, he would get what he wanted.

Spode's hatred for Black Heart grew as he learned what a decent man the Captain was; always robbing from the rich to give to the poor. He would never attack a ship that flew under the Irish flag until he was certain it was a merchant ship. Spode had tried to tell him on a number of occasions that there were plenty of gold and other treasures being moved out of Ireland on the coffin ships, but Black Heart refused to attack them, which in Spode's eyes made him weak.

One early dawn, mist hung around the sails of the Onyx, making everywhere dank and miserable. The crew had been woken an hour earlier and had been told to make ready for battle. Half of the crew thought it was Friar's idea of a practice drill, but none the less, with sleepy eyes, they had followed their instructions and had made ready as best they could. It was only as the mist started to curl away that they saw a vessel up ahead. It was clear the crew had no idea they were being followed, hence the Onyx slid silently alongside it before anyone noticed it was there. The Captain gave the order and the skull and cross bones was unfurled as they came upon the other vessel.

It was a smart ship richly decorated with bright billowing sails. The Onyx drew along side and the crew silently made ready to board, clutching onto ropes that hung from the main beam. In their mouths were knives and swords and blades of different sizes. In sudden realisation of what was about to happen, the boy in the crow's nest of the ship screamed loudly, awaking his crew.

"Pirates," the boy screamed, "Pirates about to board." A terrible panic ensued as the crew dashed about trying to load the cannons, and ready the ship for a fight. Black Heart stood proudly on the upper deck of the Onyx, his sword held high in his right hand, his left-hand clutching tightly to a thick rope. He shouted something the other crew could just hear, it sounded like a battle cry, which was enough to send them frantic with fear. Black Heart sang out in a clear voice and his crew responded with a loud cheer, then in one movement they all swung across onto the other ship and started a messy battle with the other crew.

Spode watched as Black Heart's men made a path for him through the crew of the other ship. They cut them down where they stood. Black Heart didn't need to use his sword; no man was left standing in his way. Spode looked to see where he was heading. He saw a large round man in a smart blue uniform turn tail and run through a sturdy set of wooden double doors into what must have been the living quarters of the men. "Well, well," Spoke laughed "My old Captain, Brody, grown fat in his dotage!" There was no love lost there, Spode remembered how he had been left to die, a young boy on his own, after the sinking of the Marylou.

Black Heart strode after him, his hair blowing in the wind, his earring dancing on his shoulder. He turned and watched as two of Black Heart's crew followed the man inside. He was dragged out, kicking and wrestling his captors; they had his arms behind his back a sword pointing in his neck. The man screamed at them and spat in their faces. They forced him onto his knees in front of Black Heart and the man winced in pain as if aggravating an old injury. Then they let go of him, and the man made an attempt to stand up, but Black Heart raised his sword and pointed it at the man's heart. He moved the sword tip under the man's chin and lifted his face so that he was looking at him. Spode saw the man was red with anger. He was a fat man and the buttons on his royal blue jacket were bulging over his large waist. He wore black leather boots with a heel on them, to make himself look taller. His face was round and his double chins wobbled when he moved. He was clearly out of breath from the struggle. He stared into Black Heart's piercing blue eyes.

"So, Mr. Blaney, we meet again," Black Heart said in his deep rich voice. "Many a long year I have seen the evil you have caused. Many a ship I have sent to its end. A mercy on the souls of the wretched farmers you put there." The man spat at Black Heart and one of his crew smacked him across the face. The man reeled and tried to kick the man that had smacked him. He fell in a heap on the floor and there was a loud rip as he split his trousers.

"Too many potatoes perhaps?" laughed Black Heart and the crew standing with him laughed as well.

Spode noticed that the rest of the ship's crew had fallen silent and were standing in a cluster surrounded by the pirate's men, held at sword point. He had remained on the Onyx, pretending to join the remainder of the crew in readying the ship for a quick get away.

"But, no," Black Heart continued, "such rotting poison is not the fare you partake in, is it now Mr. Blaney?" He moved his sword and poked him in the stomach. The crew laughed again. "You dine on the finer delicacies don't you Mr. Blaney? The food put on your table is not black and rotting, is it Mr. Blaney? A fine Captain you have become." He moved his sword back to his heart. "You steal from those that have nothing to feed your fat belly, don't you, Mr. Blaney? You take the last remaining treasures from your father's land and spend it abroad on fine wines and fancy clothes and filling your belly with rich meats, don't you, Mr. Blaney?"

The man struggled again trying to get to his feet but Black Heart held his sword more tightly against his heart. "You are scum, Mr. Blaney, scum." Spode heard the anger rising in Black Heart's voice. "You promise the world to those that are at your mercy and you send them afloat in the full knowledge that you will pick them up later, half starved, racked with disease. You know they will take their worldly goods with them and they have not the strength or the will left to fight you, so you take it all, don't you, Mr. Blaney, don't you?" Black Heart gripped his sword so tightly that Spode could see his fist turning white. He watched with interest wondering what Black Heart would do next. There was silence aboard the ship. A seagull circled high above, some of the men looked up to watch its path but Black Heart never took his eyes off Blaney.

"So, Mr. Blaney," Black Heart said in a cool level voice. "Just how much gold have you stashed in your hold, I wonder?"

"No," Blaney muttered, straining to get free. Black Heart's men were holding him now by his shoulders. His cheeks bulged with the strain and were a purple red colour. He huffed and puffed and spittle dribbled down his fat chin as he tried to stand up again. "No, it's mine, you devil, you thief, you won't touch it. You low down pirate, rot. You leave me alone. It's mine, all mine and I would rather rot in hell than see you lay your filthy hands on it. They didn't deserve it, none of them did. They have made my father's land rotten, not me. They have laid waste to hundreds of acres of my land, the filthy disease-ridden vermin. Let them rot, let them die, they deserve no better."

"You, utter scum," said Black Heart, fiercely, his sword raised against the man's throat. "You do not deserve to live. You are evil, a greedy fat evil man." Spode grinned as Black Heart tensed his arm and waited for the final blow to be delivered.

"Well, well," he thought. "Perhaps the Captain is made of stronger stuff than I had imagined!" Then he spat onto the deck and a pang of hatred flared in his stomach as he turned to watch Black Heart again. Black Heart stared into Blaney's eyes. "May God forgive you, you wretched creature, may he take pity on your soul." Blaney shut his eyes waiting for Black Heart to strike but nothing happened.

Black Heart slowly moved the sword from the man's throat and stood up. Blaney opened his eyes not daring to breathe. Black Heart turned around. "Empty the hold," he ordered, "We take it all."

"What about the men?" asked one of his crew.

"Put them in the hold when it's empty," he said and made his way back down the deck.

As quick as a flash Blaney had got to his feet and had drawn a knife that he had hidden in his boot. He charged forwards towards Black Heart, screaming as he went. He had nearly reached the pirate, his arm raised, ready to stab him. Black Heart turned on the spot and watched as the man fell forwards at his feet, dead from a knife sticking out of his back. He looked up into the eyes of his best friend, John Friar.

"It had to be done, Captain, he was rotten to the core," said Friar as he pulled his knife out of Blaney's back and wiped the blood off on his trousers. Black Heart smiled.

"I am in your debt," he said.

"Aye Captain, once more, and I'll have returned the favour you once did me." Black Heart turned and headed back to his ship.

Chapter 18

Preparing the Search

"Max," Sam called from his bedroom window to his brother who was riding his bike round the back garden.

"What?" said Max looking up.

"Come here a minute, will you?" Sam yelled.

"What's in it for me?" asked his brother.

"Erm, I promise not to beat you up," said Sam sarcastically.

"Get lost," said Max.

"No seriously, come here, will you? I need you to do me a favour; I'll pay you." At this Max propped his bike up against the wall of the house and ran inside to see what his brother wanted.

"Come in, come in," Sam said in an all too friendly voice, for he never ever let Max into his bedroom, "make yourself comfortable." Max sat down on the bed.

"What do you want?" he asked in a sheepish voice.

"I want you to take this message to Andrew for me this afternoon," said Sam.

"You must be joking, what does it say?" he asked desperate to know what the big secret was.

"Never you mind," said Sam, "and Max, I'll know if you've opened it because I've sealed the envelope with candle wax and put my thumb print on it." This was an old pirate trick his Grandad had taught him once.

"What happens if I get caught?" asked Max.

"Why would you get caught?" said Sam. "You're just taking a note to Andrew; there's no big deal there, is there?"

"Well, how much are you going to give me?" Max asked, feeling in a strong position to negotiate terms.

"A fiver and that's my final offer," said Sam knowing that Max wouldn't settle for that for a minute.

"No-way!" said Max. "A tenner and I'll do it," he said.

"Max you're a thieving little toe-rag," his brother said, but he had been expecting this and would have gone to fifteen quid if Max had pushed.

"Right," said Sam. "A tenner it is, you get paid when you get back and don't try asking for half now and half later because you'll get a thick ear." Max jumped off the bed and snatched the envelope out of Sam's hands.

"Consider it done," he said with a smile and ran off down the stairs and out of the back door.

Max came back within half an hour and went straight to play in the garden again. When he thought his mum was well out of earshot Sam opened his window and called down to Max, "Oi Shorty, did you do it?"

"Yes," said Max indignantly. "You owe me a tenner and don't call me Shorty."

"OK Shorty," called Sam and closed the window. Now he just had to wait.

Chapter 19

The Pirate Death Code

All afternoon Sam stayed in his room wondering whether Andrew would be up for it. The afternoon wore slowly on. His mum called him for tea which he could hardly eat in his excitement anticipating for evening to fall and darkness to come so that he could sneak out and find some answers to the questions that had been burning inside him for what felt like ages now. Max kept trying to catch his eye across the dinner table, but Sam kept his head down making out that he didn't feel very well. "He'd better not have read that note," thought Sam. "I'll kill him if he has." He was pretty sure that Max wouldn't risk a hiding from him and put the thought out of his head.

Then the phone rang. Sam's heart skipped a beat.

"Hi Dad," his mum said as she picked the receiver up. "How are you?" His mum turned to look at him and said, "Yes, he's fine." Sam smiled and wondered what his Grandad was saying. His mum carried on. "Yes, of course, you can speak to him, I'll put him on." Sam had a sudden sense that his Grandad had phoned because of all the strange stuff that had been happening. His mum passed him the phone.

"Hi Grandad," he said in a shaky voice.

"Don't say anything about this out loud," said his Grandad in that salty seafarer's voice he had. "Just answer my questions and act normally."

"OK," said Sam looking at his mum to check she wasn't listening too much.

"Have you been feeling strange lately?"

"Yes," said Sam in a stunned voice.

"And have you seen him yet, in your dreams?"

"Erm," Sam said, not knowing how to respond.

"Black Heart, I mean," his Grandad said, sounding irritated, "tall, blonde, dressed in black."

"I.. I.. I.. think so," Sam stuttered.

"Fella would have looked a bit like me," his Grandad continued. Then realisation dawned on him.

"Yes," Sam said in a bewildered tone, "I have." He was starting to get really spooked. Just then the doorbell rang and his mum left the kitchen to answer it. Sam heaved a sigh of relief.

"Grandad," he said in a hoarse whisper desperate to talk before his mum came back in. "What is going on, how come you know how I've been feeling, what does it all mean?"

"Ah, my lad," his Grandad said. "You are going to have to trust me on this one; this is going to sound really strange. I know it did to me when I was told the story by my father. The fact is that you are the direct descendant of a pirate named Captain Black Heart." "What?" said Sam in a voice louder than he wanted.

"Captain Black Heart, he was called," said his Grandad. "He is your great, great Grand Father. They say he was the bravest pirate to sail in these waters. He fought many a deadly battle, he did; always in the name of charity and concern for those whose lives were made wretched by the rich landowners of the merchant lands. He would steal from the rich to give to the poor, a great man and no mistake."

"But what's it got to do with me?" asked Sam, feeling frustrated but excited at the same time.

"It's time to right a wrong Sam" said his Grandad. "It has to work this time or Black Heart's soul will be left wandering the earth for ever."

"What do you mean this time, Grandad?" Sam said feeling nervous.

"Son, it is one hundred and fifty years since Black Heart was murdered. Every fifty years so far he has contacted his family seeking their help to find him the eternal peace that he yearns."

"What are you talking about?" asked Sam, knowing deep down that the answer involved him somehow.

"They say," said his Grandad "that Black Heart's ship was wrecked on the very beach that you play about on everyday."

"What, Sea Cove?" said Sam in surprise; he leaned across the table to see if his mum was still at the door, she was busy chatting to someone.

"The very same," said his Grandad. "The story goes that he ran across a ship filled with starving and close to dead Irish men and their families. He boarded the ship to see if his men could help any of them poor beggars but seeing that there was nothing for him to do: they sunk the ship there and then so as to put those wretched souls to their rest. Only trouble was," his Grandad continued, "they say that Black Heart had a good look round that ship before he put his cannons to it and found a hold full of treasure, the likes of which he had never seen before. He got his crew to load as many canvases as he could find and stole the lot from under those poor blighters' noses, of course they were too weak to do anything about it and he got away with the whole lot."

"Wow!" said Sam, sitting stunned, remembering the dream he had had. "How do you know all this?" he asked.

"The story's been passed down from those around at the time to his son and onto my father, then me," said his Grandad. "Now you listen to me, son," said his Grandad suddenly sounding urgent. "Fifty years is an important number in the pirate world because of the death code. After Black Heart's soul had walked the land for fifty years he called upon his grandson to help him. He tried in vain but couldn't uncover the truth about Black Heart. Fifty years later it was my turn. I tried Sam, God knows I tried, but I couldn't do it. I failed him. The pirate death code states that there are three chances after death to put things right, one chance every fifty years. Sam, fifty years have now passed since I tried. It's your turn. Black Heart needs your help."

"But I don't understand," said Sam tugging at the collar of his shirt feeling hot and flustered. "What does Black Heart need me to do? It doesn't sound like he was a very good person if he stole all that treasure."

"Because, the story about Black Heart stealing that treasure is not true." His Grandad explained. "He was a good man and I don't reckon he would have ever done anything so dastardly. They say Jake Spode, a sailor he rescued, was a wily old bird and Black Heart never quite trusted him not to run him through in the middle of the night, but by all accounts, he was a good sailor and that's what Black Heart needed at the time. Good men were hard to come by and he had to take what he could get. If you ask me I think Spode spread those rumours about Black Heart and stole the treasure for himself."

"What happened to the treasure?" asked Sam wide eyed in disbelief.

"It was never found," said his Grandad. "Black Heart's ship ran aground and there was a fight broke out probably over the gold and jewels on board and they say Jake Spode ran Black Heart through with a silver sword from the stolen loot. They say he's buried up on the hill at the Priory in an unmarked grave, but I could never find it."

"Grandad," said Sam excitedly, "I've seen it, I've seen the grave, it's not marked properly but there's a mark on it like a gold coin. Only when you look again it's the picture of a pirate's head."

"Keep your voice down," scolded his Grandad from the other end of the phone. "Don't get your mother suspicious, she's never liked this story, even though she's got Black Heart in her blood, same as you and your brother."

"You mean she knows about Black Heart?" said Sam in awe at what he was hearing.

"Aye, but she'll deny it if you say anything, I reckon it might have skipped a generation," said his Grandad. "She always was the stubborn sort and it makes her uncomfortable talking about it, probably because deep down she knows the story is wrong."

"What do you think really happened?" asked Sam quivering with excitement.

"I reckon if Black Heart did take that treasure, he took it for a reason. I just don't believe he would have stolen from such poor and needy people especially those close to death's door and the spirit of old Black Heart has one more chance to put the story straight. Sam you are his own flesh and blood. You are the chosen descendant. Black Heart will ask you to rise up and renew his honour; you must set the story straight. You are the last chance." Sam felt a heavy weight in his stomach and his breathing had become shallow and strained. "You must be brave now, lad," his Grandad went on.

"But how will I know what to do?" asked Sam bewildered at what he was hearing.

"You'll know when the time is right," said his Grandad "Haven't you noticed the way you've been feeling strange lately? I've felt it and your brother will have too, your mother probably as well, although she would never admit it."

"Yes," said Sam. "Every time I see that marking I get this weird tingling feeling down my back and I feel cold and sick."

"There you are, then," said his Grandad. "Black Heart is calling you to help him."

"What should I do?" asked Sam, his chair falling over behind him. "You need to find out where Black Heart's ship ended up, you need to track down the treasure, find anything you can, get hold of any records of the shipwrecks off Sea Cove. It's up to you now, Sam. You've got to sort this out, else, Black Heart won't rest and he won't let us rest either."

"Right," said Sam utterly bewildered at what he was hearing.

"But watch your back, son," his Grandad continued. "There is another who will be looking for the treasure as well as you. You must get there first. Do you understand, child?" Sam was about to answer when the phone went dead just as Sam's mum came back into the kitchen.

"Right, see you then, by," said Sam in as chirpy a voice as he could manage.

"Another." Sam mused feeling hot and confused "What did he mean another?"

"That was Mrs. Johnson," said Mrs. Forshaw. "Just came around with that dish I lent her last week."

"Right," said Sam sitting down again. Mrs. Forshaw bustled off to tidy up and Sam pondered what he had just heard. A noise across the table made him look up into the startled face of his brother. Max had been sitting quietly at the table all through his conversation with his Grandad. His eyes were wide open and he looked pale and frightened. Mrs. Forshaw caught the look on Max's face.

"What's the matter, Max?" she asked "You look like you've seen a ghost."

"I, I, I don't feel very well, mum," said Max and got up from the table. "Can I go and lie down?" he said in a whimper. "I've got a headache."

"All right," said his mum putting her hand on his forehead. "You have got a bit of a temperature." Max stared at Sam as he left the room and climbed the stairs to his room. Sam sat in silence, the conversation with his Grandad running through his head. He couldn't eat his tea, he felt nauseous and scared. He pushed the food around his plate until his mother let him leave the table then ran upstairs to his brother's bedroom.

"What's the matter?" he asked Max, barging in through the bedroom door. Max was lying on his stomach on the bed, his face buried in his pillow.

"I heard everything," moaned Max. "I heard Grandad down the phone; I'm scared, Sam. What if the story is true and Black Heart's ghost is haunting us?"

"He's not haunting us in a nasty way," said Sam soothingly sitting down on the bed. "I think he needs our help."

"But what if something terrible happens?" Max asked, visibly shaking under the bed covers.

"It won't," said Sam. "Black Heart doesn't sound the kind of person to take revenge on his own blood relatives now, does he? I think he's been trying to help me find out the truth, that's why my attention was drawn to the map in Mr. Clayton's history class and on his grave at the Priory. Don't you see he's trying to help us?"

"You've seen his grave?" Max trembled.

"I think so," replied Sam.

Well I'd rather he didn't try and help us with anything," Max whined. "I don't like it, I want it all to stop," and with than he threw the covers over his head and burrowed down.

"It's all right," said Sam trying to sound calm. "First thing tomorrow I'll have got some answers."

Max didn't move so Sam left the room quietly and went to his own room waiting for the time to come.

Chapter 20

The Trinket

All was quiet aboard the sleek galleon. The silky white sails rippled above. The decks were newly scrubbed and the skull and cross bones fluttered in the breeze. Someone was breathing thick and fast. There was a young boy cowering behind a great pile of rope. He was hiding from someone and was obviously scared to the bone.

A short, stocky man with his sword raised slowly prowled across the deck. He stopped dead and listened for any giveaway signs. His head twitched as he listened for the slightest breath, the slightest creak of a wooden board under foot. The boy tried to make himself smaller and smaller in the corner, but it was no good, the man was onto him. The man lightly threw his sword from hand to hand as he edged forward towards the boy.

Spode reached the pile of rope and jumped forward suddenly. The boy squealed and stood up looking for a way round his attacker, but Spode had got all the ways of escape covered.

"So, what's it going to be, young Joshua?" Spode asked in a vile oily tone. "Are you going to give me the secret you carry or am I going to have to take it?"

"S.. S.. Stay away from me," Joshua managed to squeak, backing into the cabin wall even further.

"Aw, what's the matter, young pirate?" he said throwing his sword tantalisingly in front of the boy. "Just hand it over and no one gets hurt."

"I.. I don't know what you're talking about," came the weak response. "I haven't got anything."

"Well. then it looks like we'll have to play this the hard way then, don't it?" said Spode stepping closer to the boy. Joshua looked around desperately trying to avoid Spode's clutches. Spode lunged with his sword but Joshua somehow managed to dodge around him. He ducked under Spode's outstretched arm but wasn't quick enough. Spode hurled himself onto the boy and he came crashing down onto the rope that had hidden him a moment ago.

"Right," said Spode kneeling on Joshua's chest as he sheathed his sword. Joshua gasped for breath, his lungs not strong enough to rise with Spode's heavy weight on them. He tried to wriggle free, but he couldn't move, he spluttered and gasped for air. Spode leaned harder on the boy and ripped open his shirt. The half coin on its chain dazzled Spode as the bright sunlight caught an edge. Spode grabbed the coin and tugged so hard that as the chain broke, he fell backwards onto the deck. Joshua lay still gasping for breath. He reached to his neck, but Spode had got what he was looking for. Before the boy could get to his feet Spode was on him again.

"This is between you and me, young pirate," he said grabbing Joshua's collar and hauling him up so that his face was nearly touching his own. "You go running off to Black Heart whining and I will cut you through. Do you understand me, boy?"

"Yes," said Joshua weakly.

"Pardon," said Spode pulling him even harder. "I didn't quite catch that."

"Yes," said Joshua starting to sob.

"That's my good little pirate," said Spode maliciously as he let the boy fall back onto the rope. "You just make sure you stay quiet or it's a sword in the gullet for you."

Spode stood up and was about to turn around but flinched under the harsh grip of a man that had silently appeared from around the thick wooden mast.

"Mr. Spode," the man said.

"Friar," gasped Spode, anger bubbling up once more in the pit of his stomach.

"I think you have something that belongs to the Captain, Mr. Spode," Friar continued, his grip tightening on Spode's shoulder. "Let's not play games now, hand it over and I may just spare your life." Spode glared at Friar; anger blazing in his eyes. He scowled at Joshua then reluctantly handed the talisman over to Friar.

"Why, thank you, Mr. Spode," Friar said smiling. Then he pulled Spode up so that they were eye to eye. "The day has not yet come, Mr. Spode, where you can lay your filthy hands on anything that belongs to the Captain. Do I make myself clear?"

"Perfectly," replied Spode through gritted teeth.

"Pardon," said Friar sarcastically "I didn't quite catch that."

"Perfectly," Spode scowled. Friar released his grip and brushed his hands down his trousers as if he had been touching something dirty. Spode pulled himself together as best he could, trying to reclaim some dignity in front of Joshua, then with a menacing glare, he scuttled away across the deck out of sight.

Chapter 21

Adventure at Midnight

Sam lay on his bed. Hour after painful hour crept past until finally he heard the sounds of Max going to the bathroom followed an hour later by his mum and dad coming up the stairs. He waited until he was sure he could hear the usual snoring coming from his dad and the rhythmic breathing of his mum in the room next door and decided that he couldn't wait any longer.

He picked up his trusty knife and threw open the window to see what the weather was doing. He felt the tingle run down his spine; he had been expecting it. The night air felt chilly so he rummaged in the back of his wardrobe for an old dark sweater that he decided his mum wouldn't miss if it got dirty. Then he stuffed the pillow from his bed down under the covers to make it look like he was curled up asleep in case his parents decided to check on him.

He crept out of his bedroom, across the landing and down the stairs. He had thought about going out of the window but that was a stupid idea, what good would a broken leg be to him? He crept along the hall and into the kitchen. Jet jumped up out of her basket and Sam hurriedly patted her and whispered to her to lie down. She jumped up again, so Sam reached up to the top cupboard and found a dog biscuit, which he threw into her basket. "Be quiet, Jet, you'll get me into trouble," he whispered. "As if I won't be in trouble anyway," he thought to himself. He silently undid the back door and slid outside into the relative gloom slipping the key into his back pocket. There was a bright moon and the streetlights threw their orangey glow onto him. Sam pulled his hood over his face, ducked down and headed out for the rendezvous point.

He checked his watch; it was 10:50, ten minutes to go. He wondered what he would do if Andrew decided it was too risky to come with him. Would he go on his own or would he bottle it and go back home, which would clearly be the sensible option? He reached the corner and hid behind the bush that grew on the corner and waited. The minutes ticked slowly by, five to eleven came and went. Sam checked his watch again. Two minutes to eleven, one minute to eleven. He looked up the street to see if there was any sign of Andrew but there was no one to be seen. He checked his watch and started counting in his head, "One elephant, two elephants, three elephants, four elephants." Five minutes passed and still no sign of Andrew. "If he's not here in five minutes," thought Sam, "I'll go back, I can't risk going on my own." There was still no sign of Andrew. Three minutes passed, four. He sighed deeply and was just standing up having decided that Andrew wasn't coming when he saw a dark shadow moving quickly down the street close up to the wall. Sam held his breath, it had to be Andrew, no one else would be skulking around outside at this time of night.

The figure slowed and stalked up to the bush. "Hi," said a muffled voice.

"Is that you, Andrew?" Sam asked in a loud whisper.

"Guess again," said the whispered reply.

"What? Oh Max you little rat, what the devil are you doing here?"

"I'm coming with you," said Max throwing his hood back to reveal a cheeky grin.

"You are not Max, you're too young, go back home."

"No way," said his little brother. "I always have to miss the good stuff; well, not this time." "For goodness sake Max, you don't even know where we are going," said Sam angrily. "Keep your voices down," said a voice from around the corner. Finally, it was Andrew. "Blimey Andrew, what kept you? I was about to give up on you."

"I had to wait for my dad to go to bed, only it took ages. What's he doing here?" said Andrew looking down his nose at Max.

"He's followed me," said Sam, "You better not have woken mum and dad, Max, or I'll knock you for six."

"Don't worry, I was as quiet as a mouse and Jet was still too busy eating her biscuit to notice me. Good job you gave her a jumbo size."

"You're not letting him come with us, are you?" asked Andrew knowing that wherever Max was, there was usually trouble.

"Looks like we haven't got much choice, have we?" said Sam in his exasperated big brother voice. "You'd better keep quiet, Max, and do as you're told, right?" said Sam taking Max by the scruff of his neck. "Or you are dead meat, comprende?"

"All right, all right," said Max struggling to get out of Sam's grip. Sam let him go. "Right," he said. "Let's get on with it."

"Where are we actually going?" asked Max as he straightened his jumper.

"Coombe Bay," muttered Sam, "and no more questions."

"But that's miles away," whined Max.

"Well you should have thought about that before you decided to follow me, shouldn't you?" Sam said angrily.

"Pack it in, you two, someone's coming." The three boys hid behind the bush again pulling their hoods over their faces.

A man walked past with his dog. Sam recognized him as Mr. Archer from next door; the dog's name was Butch.

"Come on, Butch," said Mr. Archer, as Butch sniffed around the bush, "there's nothing there." Sam held his breath until Butch had been dragged away on his lead. They waited for Mr. Archer to turn the corner.

"Come on," said Sam, "before the sun comes up."

"Yeah right, sarcasm will get you nowhere," laughed Max but kept quiet after that having caught the look on his brother's face.

"We're being haunted by a pirate," said Max smiling at Andrew. "But it's OK because he's a relative," he continued.

"Yeah right," said Andrew looking across to Sam. Sam's face was solemn and grey.

"Shut up Max, you ape," Sam whispered harshly at his brother. "It's not funny in the slightest, I thought you were scared stiff about the whole thing anyway," he said accusingly.

"Well I feel better now; in fact, I think it's quite cool to have a pirate in the family and even better to have the ghost of one."

"What are you two going on about?" Andrew asked mouth open with curiosity. Sam told him all about the conversation he had had with his Grandad earlier, about Black Heart and the treasure he had to find. Andrew couldn't believe what he was hearing, but the look on Sam's face told him not to ask questions at the moment.

They ran down Main Street keeping as close to the houses as they could. Sam glanced back a few times to check no one was following them. The only sound was the noise of late-night revellers as they stayed for a lock in at the two pubs in the square and the sound of a baby crying somewhere in the distance. They reached the turning for the beach and sprinted down as fast as they could. There were no streetlights here, so they were able to run side by side along the pavement. Sam and Andrew, being three years older than Max, started to move ahead.

"Wait for me," gasped Max, out of breath, desperately trying to keep up.

"Move it," said Sam gruffly, but slowed down a little any way. They reached the beach and ran along the front. As they reached the base of Sea Cove Head all three bent double trying to catch their breath. Wheezing, Andrew looked up towards the Head.

"This is nuts," he said, "I'm exhausted already."

"You'll be fine," said Sam gasping to get his breath. "Come on, we'll take it slow." They started to climb and steadily made their way up the steep slope of the Head. The moon was full and seemed to be lighting up the path for them, "Did you bring your torch Andrew?" Sam asked.

"Yeah and some spare batteries, I didn't know what you'd got planned."

"What have you got planned, Sam?" asked Max, trotting next to Sam.

"I need to look at the back of the place where I found this," said Sam stopping suddenly and pulling out the gold coin. In the moonlight the coin glowed with an almost luminous greenish colour.

"What is it?" asked Max, looking transfixed at the coin.

"It's the coin I found under the overhang at Coombe Bay and I think it means something. I saw the same symbol on a head stone in the graveyard at the Priory and the same thing on a map in Mr. Clayton's class at school."

"Wow!" said Max, not taking his eyes off the coin. "It's cool." They continued in relative silence, seeing the coin had seemed to silence Max. Sam was amazed. He had expected twenty questions but instead the three continued to climb up and along the path getting nearer and nearer to the place that he was sure would give him some answers.

They reached the top of Sea Cove Head and started on the undulating path as it wound its way over the land, first Sam in the lead, then Andrew, with Max trailing at the back. They reached the exposed rocks that jutted out into the path but with the moon so bright, all three boys clambered over them easily. On they went in silence until finally they came to the point where they could see Coombe Bay below them.

"What exactly are you hoping to find, Sam?" Max asked as he gazed out across the sea. The moon glistened on each wave making the ocean look full of tiny lights. A warm breeze fanned them and the smell of sea air filled their lungs.

"I don't know," said Sam. "I'll know it when I see it," he said dismissively and walked on.

They reached the gorge that led down to the Bay and carefully picked their way down. The gorge was dark and creepy, the moon blocked out by the great towering cliffs that surrounded the place. Andrew reached for his torch and flicked it on. "Give that here," said Sam taking it off Andrew. Andrew swallowed and followed Sam as he hopped from boulder to boulder. Without warning Sam pulled up suddenly and Max bumped into the back of him.

"Watch out," he cried indignantly.

"Shut up," said Sam. As they had been walking the coin in his pocket had seemed heavier and heavier. He curled his fingers around it and pulled it out. It gave off a faint greenish hue. "Weird," said Sam. "It's not as bright out of the moonlight," and he turned the coin over and over in his hand. They scrambled onto the flat boulders and worked their way along the edge. "This is where we found it last time," said Sam, pointing to a dark cave on his left.

The boulder that had fallen down at their last visit sat alone and looked out of place.

"You must be joking," said Max. "You're not going in there, are you?" he asked with a petrified look on his face.

"Yes, I am, Max, and you're coming with me." Max turned to look at Andrew for some moral support, but Andrew just shrugged and followed Sam into the cave. "Andrew, stay here and keep watch," Sam ordered.

"Aye, Aye, Captain," said Andrew relieved that he didn't have to go crawling about in the dark.

Sam and Max walked in as far as they could get, then dropped onto their knees and crawled until their heads brushed the top of the cave. Sam lay on his stomach and shone the torch into the back of the cave. Suddenly a dark shape detached itself from the overhang and flew towards him with beady green eyes, then another, then another. He flapped his arms around him desperately trying to get the things away from him. Max let out a scream and dropped to the ground sheltering his head with his arms. Several other creatures detached themselves, disturbed by the torchlight and flew out of the cave mouth. As they flew they made strange high-pitched squeaks that echoed off the stone walls. "They're just bats," said Sam when the last one had flown away.

"They're horrible," said Max standing up cautiously. "Stupid overgrown mice," and he brushed himself down trying to shake off the dread that had come over him. Sam looked all around to see if there were any more coins or anything that would give him a clue to the mystery. He wriggled his hand into his trouser pocket and pulled out his knife, then gently working his way across and back he scratched the moss and algae away from the back wall.

"Have you found anything yet?" Max asked by Sam's right ear.

"No, shut up and use your eyes," Sam said irritably. He worked along and back glaring at the back wall almost willing himself to see something. For half an hour he stared and stared at the wall, working his knife along, feeling with his fingers. The cave was damp and smelt earthy. Rainwater seeped down from the vegetation above through the cracks in the rocks to collect in puddles at the back of the cave. Then he felt something; there was something there. It was like the edge of something. He dug his knife in deeper and a smooth round stone sprang out of the wall. He picked it up and shone the torch onto it; it looked like a round piece of granite about the size of a fifty pence piece. He looked back at the wall and scratched more moss away revealing a thin trace.

"I think there is some sort of opening here," he said in a muffled voice.

"How can there be?" said Max trying to get a look.

"Hey, you two," came the harsh whisper of an anxious Andrew who had crawled into the cave to join them. "There's someone here."

"What do you mean there's someone here?" asked Sam moving his head up and banging it on the roof of the cave.

"I mean," said Andrew, "there is a man down on the ledge below."

"Well, what's he doing?" asked Sam getting irritated and trying to rub his head.

"I think he's sleeping," whispered Andrew, "and I think he may be drunk as well, there's an empty bottle of whisky next to him and he's snoring loudly."

"Well, keep an eye on him," said Sam turning back to the wall, "and give us a shout if he moves."

He tried to concentrate on the wall again and ran his fingers along what he was sure was the edge of a large stone that had almost been placed there on purpose. It certainly didn't seem to be part of the cave wall.

"What are you doing?" he said to Max angrily as Max rustled and fidgeted next to him.

"I'm trying to see what time it is," said his brother and with that, pulled out what looked to Sam like an old pocket watch on a chain.

"What have you got there?" asked Sam grabbing the watch out of Max's hand.

"Hey, that's mine, give that back," Max said angrily but Sam held the watch up to look at it in the torchlight. It was a gold pocket watch with a catch on the side. Sam flipped it open to reveal a yellowing watch face with Roman numerals around the edge. He turned the watch over in his hands and rubbed his thumb over the back. 'For use when you need it most' read the inscription on the back and as his thumb rubbed the metal what looked like half a coin gently fell into his hand that had been lightly fastened onto the back of the watch.

"Where did you get this?" Sam gasped, looking up into Max's startled eyes.

"Grandad gave it to me last birthday, he said I would know when to use it and I just felt like bringing it tonight." Sam wondered what on earth his Grandad had got him into. He opened the watch again and stared at the face. An all too familiar shiver ran down his spine and he felt the muscles tense in his neck and shoulders. Then as he stared he felt his other hand, almost with a will of its own, reach into his trouser pocket and pull out the half coin he had put there only a moment ago. Trance like, he brought his two hands together and placed the two halves of the coin together and placed the coin image side down onto the watch face.

"What are you doing?" screeched Max trying to get hold of his watch. "You'll break it," but Sam shoved his brother away and clicked the coin neatly down onto the watch face as if it was a piece of jigsaw fitting neatly into the centre of a puzzle. There was a clicking sound as they slotted together and Sam thought he saw a bright light shine out for a second as the pieces came together.

The watch made a sudden loud whirring noise and like a CD coming out of its slot in the machine , the side of the watch slid out revealing an indented tray with a small glassy stone that looked black all the way through. Sam held the watch right up close to his eye and read the tiny letters that surrounded the stone - "The Onyx".

"The Onyx," said Max staring defiantly at Sam. "What have you done to my watch?" "Nothing," said Sam. "I think Grandad wanted me to find this. I think he wants me to find something."

"You're weird," said Max trying to snatch the watch out of Sam's hands. Sam shouldered him away and with trembling fingers picked the glass stone up and looked back at the wall he had been working on.

He held the stone out and slowly pressed it into the space he had dug out earlier. There was a grinding noise and Sam felt the vibration start in his fingers and work its way up his arm and down his spine. To his screwed-up eyes, it looked like the cave was moving. The floor shook and the back wall seemed to disappear. He felt dizzy and lightheaded as the cave started to spin around him. He shut his eyes tight and reached out for something stable to steady him. His hand grabbed the shoulder of his younger brother who screamed in pain and fell to the floor.

Chapter 22

The Betrayal

The crew slept. Spode had made sure he was on watch tonight. The silver moon threw its light momentarily onto the deck as he steered the ship towards Sea Cove Bay. He knew there was a storm coming. He watched from the helm as big, black thunderclouds rolled across the sky, blocking the moon from view. The wind had been getting up for the last couple of hours and he could feel the chill trying to reach inside his jacket. But Spode had a fire alight in his belly and no cold wind would put out the flames. Tonight, was the night he planned to take what should belong to him. He smiled as he imagined the look on the Captain's face when he realised his ship was about to be wrecked forever on the treacherous rocks of the place he had come to love. Spode wasn't sure, but he had heard the crew talking about how Black Heart loved Sea Cove. He even suspected Black Heart had a girl in this place he was quite fond of.

"Maybe I'll seek her out once I've done away with her fancy man," he smirked.

Rain began lashing down in sheets as the ship headed closer and closer to the unseen perils of Sea Cove Bay.

"Just a little longer," Spode muttered under his breath, hoping none of the crew would be woken yet by the storm. "We need to get closer." His breath grew short, as he knew that soon it would be too late to steer the ship away from certain disaster. He stared out through the darkness and his heart skipped as he saw the first of the treacherous cliffs on the horizon.

"My time comes," he said, his voice oozing treachery. The wind howled round the boat, pulling at the sails and rattling the rigging. Waves started crashing onto the deck and Spode had to hold on for fear of being knocked away from the wheel.

He felt proud of his plan so far. Little did the Captain, or his crew know that he was about to wreck the Onyx on the rocks, barely a mile away. Then he would take the treasure and any crew that survived and steal passage to the Indies where he planned to get himself another ship; bigger and better than the Onyx. He would then lead the high life, launching merciless attacks on any ships he encountered.

The ship was being thrown around on the rough sea. Up onto the crest of a high wave it rose, and then down it crashed with walls of water on all sides. As the bow rose again something moving on the deck caught Spode's eye.

"Well, well, what have we here?" he said, his voice dripping with menace. "Can't you sleep, young pirate?" he took a step towards Joshua who instantly cowered behind the mast. The boy had not forgotten the choking sensation he had felt when he thought Spode would crush his chest.

"What's the matter, young pirate?" Spode continued stepping closer to the boy. "The cat got your tongue?"

"N, No," Joshua managed. He could feel himself trembling, but he knew Spode was up to something and he wanted to prove to the Captain and Mr. Friar that he was an able crew member and not frightened of this bully.

"Well, then," said Spode sounding all too friendly for Joshua's liking. "Come and watch with me, there's a good boy. There's history about to be made."

"W.. What do you mean?" Joshua asked trying to stand tall. His knees felt like they would give way any minute.

The storm had woken him, but unlike the rest of the crew he hated lying in his hammock being swung wildly around. He had decided to get up but had only realised it was Spode on watch as he reached the deck.

"Come, take a look," Spode said putting his arm round the boy. Joshua fought the urge to run away and slowly walked with Spode back to the helm. Spode turned him round so that he was facing the direction they were heading in. Joshua immediately saw the peril they were in. The black cliffs of Sea Cove Bay loomed overhead, and he could see the white horses breaking on the rocks submerged just below the water.

"What are you doing?" he shouted at Spode trying to get out of his grip. "You're going to run us aground." He wriggled and tried to duck under Spode's arm, but Spode held on tightly and laughed.

"That's right, young pirate," he chortled , his evil eyes glowing briefly as the moon appeared from behind a filthy black cloud. The rain whipped at Joshua's face. He tried to scream but the wind seemed to suck the breath out of him.

"I must tell the Captain," he gasped struggling under Spode's grip. He was terrified at the sight he saw. He knew the ship wouldn't last five minutes in this storm when it hit the rocks ahead. "I must warn him." He turned as best he could to face Spode.

"I hate you," he said. "I hate you and what you are. The Captain is a good man and you don't deserve to be part of his crew." The slap that was delivered across Joshua's face stung beyond belief. He felt the tears welling up inside, but it was just the distraction he had wanted. Taking Spode completely by surprise he lashed out with his boot and connected with Spode's knee. Simultaneously he dug his teeth into Spode's arm until he tasted the blood that oozed from the wound. Spode screamed and fell, clutching his bruised knee, releasing Joshua from his grip. Joshua didn't hang about. He dived out of Spode's lashing arms and somersaulted away. He knew whatever happened that he had to warn the Captain and the rest of the crew. He was the only one that knew what peril Spode had put them all in. He tried to get to his feet, but the waves were rolling over the side of the ship now, drenching him. He scrambled around trying to get a foothold and managed to catch a loose rope that was flapping in the wind.

"The bell," he thought desperately. "If I can just reach the bell and sound the alarm." The wind had an icy chill to it now that his clothes were drenched through and he could feel his fingers tightening with the cold. The whirling rain blinded him as he desperately tried to reach the bell that was attached to the main mast. In the noise of the storm he didn't hear the screams behind him as Spode angrily got to his feet and reached for the dagger stashed inside his left boot. He didn't hear the sound of Spode's boots stamping along the deck towards him. His only thought was to waken the crew, what little good it would do now. The first he knew of Spode on him was a cold sensation in his back. He felt his body freeze as realisation dawned on him. He felt the trickle of warm blood seep across his back and felt lightheaded as the blood slowly started leaving his brain to escape onto the deck. He turned and looked Spode in the eyes as a dizzying sensation came over him. He dropped to his knees and felt cold and empty.

"No," he muttered under his breath, "God, no, help me." Spode laughed an evil, dirty laugh and turned to walk back to the helm. Darkness starting to descend over Joshua's eyes as he inched forwards, the pain in his body was indescribable and he knew that he would be dead in seconds. He looked up, the rain driving ice pellets into his face, but he saw what he was looking for. He reached up with the last drop of energy he could muster and fell forwards onto the rope that held the bell. The clanging sound was loud and within an instant the crew began to assemble on the deck, responding to the call for help.

Black Heart was the first to determine what had just happened. He reached Joshua as the light flickered out of his eyes. He picked the boy up and saw the blood dripping from his shirt.

"Who?" he asked softly, leaning close to Joshua's ear. With his dying breath Joshua whispered the word Black Heart had suspected.

"Spode."

Black Heart lay the body of the boy down slowly then reared up an angry red mist descending across his brain. He stormed across the deck towards Spode, his sword drawn, ready to send Spode to meet his Maker.

"It's too late," Spode laughed as he saw the look on Black Heart's face. "It's too late for you all!" Black Heart froze, a sense of foreboding washing over him. He glanced to his right and saw the black line of cliffs stabbing the dark night. He recognised them straight away.

"Sea Cove," he muttered. Then he looked up at Spode and knew that all his fears about the man had come true.

"What have you done?" he said in disbelief at how close they were now to the treacherous rocks he had come to know so well.

"What I should have done a long while ago Captain, show you how a real pirate goes about his business."

"You fool," Black Heart screamed. "I rescued you from certain death, and this is how you repay me?" The anger blazed in his eyes and his grip tightened on his sword.

"Aye, Captain," Spode laughed. "You should have left me for dead when you had the chance." Before Black Heart could respond there was an almighty boom and the topmast came crashing down onto the deck, plunging through the wooden deck. The billowing sail ripped in two and danced angrily in tatters above the frantic sailors. Lightning stabbed down lighting up the ocean as the crew fought desperately to bring the ship under control. Friar lunged at the helm trying to turn the ship away from the looming rocks as Spode drew his sword and advanced on the Captain.

"Damn you, Spode," the Captain yelled as he held his sword aloft. "You'll have us all dead, stay back, you traitor, or I'll be forced to run you through."

"It is not I, Captain, who is the traitor," said Spode's oily voice. "The treasure in these holds is too good for the likes of them peasants you mean to give it to. Share it amongst the crew, we deserve it after all the toils you have put us to."

"For God's sake man," came the angry reply. "The crew knows you would take it for your own, you have run us aground and soon there will be no crew left, no treasure neither, except at the bottom of the sea."

"You, God fearing fool," Spode jeered as he danced towards Black Heart. He thrust forwards stabbing at the Captain, but Black Heart stepped easily away. They fought along the length of the deck; first Spode raining a barrage of thrusts at Black Heart, then Black Heart at Spode.

They reached the Great Cabin and Black Heart danced neatly around so that Spode had his back to the door. Spode's heels clipped the doorframe and glancing quickly backwards he ducked inside and leaped to the chest that he knew the Captain stored at the far end of the room. Black Heart whirled into the room as Spode threw open the chest and reached inside. He laughed a cold, empty laugh as the sounds of the boat splintering into bits could be heard above the angry wind.

"Go to meet your Maker, Black Heart, and good riddance," Spode screamed as he flung himself wildly at the Captain. Black Heart jumped to the side, but Spode had anticipated his move and thrust the thin silver sword he had pulled from the chest, into Black Heart's body.

"May your soul be cursed and never find its rest," he whispered into Black Heart's ear as he twisted the blade deeper into the Captain's chest. The Captain gasped for breath as he clutched at Spode's collar.

"I will come back, Spode," Black Heart muttered through gritted teeth. "Fear me, I will come back," and with that his last breath blew warmly across Spode's face and he sank to the floor. Spode shook the Captain's lifeless arms off him in disgust.

"Call yourself a pirate!" he muttered and strode towards the door, "useless bag of bones." He ducked his head to go back out onto the deck, but a pair of strong hands pushed him back so hard that he fell in a heap on the floor. Friar loomed above him, glowing with rage. He glanced across at the Captain, and then launched himself at Spode. They wrestled each other madly, the storm outside worse than ever. The ship was slowly sinking beneath the waves, but on they fought. Friar was aware of the screams and shouts from the crew as they lost their footing and one after the other fell beneath the black waves, never to surface again. But still Friar didn't let go of Spode. On and on they fought until the floor was completely submerged under water. With an almighty effort Spode pushed Friar down under the water and held him there. Friar wrestled his shoulders out of Spode's grip but instead of surfacing, he swam downwards, a twinkle of something calling him in the murky depths below. Spode waited, watching for Friar to resurface, but there was no sign of him.

"He can't hold his breath for much longer," he chortled, and then allowing himself a smile, he decided Friar would not be coming back up.

Spode struggled out of what was left of the cabin. He had achieved his goal. Black Heart was dead, so too was Friar and the Onyx was sinking below the waves, out of sight and mind. The Onyx gave a last groan; then disappeared. Spode leapt into the ocean and began swimming with all his might to the shore. He was frozen to the core and he knew that he had to get dry and warm. His only thoughts now were about his own survival. The treasure would have to wait.

Chapter 23

A Secret Pirate Passage

Sam opened his eyes and saw that a small opening had revealed itself in front of him. "What the?" said Andrew as he looked at Max lying on the floor.

"I don't know," said Sam looking up into Andrew's concerned face. "Is he alright?" he asked feeling the fizzing sensation leave his arm.

"No thanks to you," said his brother's voice, "that hurt."

"I only reached out to steady myself," said Sam trying to work out what had just happened.

"Hey, you lot, what's going on in there? Trying to steal my worldly goods, are you?" came a gruff voice from outside the cave, "Can't leave a fella to be king of his own castle, can you? Want some of me treasure, do you?"

"Oh no, it's the tramp," said Andrew. "Let's get out of here."

"Like where to?" asked Max starting to panic.

"In here," said Sam pointing to the entrance he had just somehow opened.

"Are you mad?" said Max. "I'd rather take my chances with a stupid drunk tramp than go in there."

"We don't have any other choice," said Sam angrily. "If he sees us he'll start ranting all over the village that he saw us messing about up here. That's Old Billy, I wondered where he hung out these days."

"Where does it go to, do you think?" asked Andrew panic starting to rise in his voice. "There's only one way to find out," said Sam and he wriggled feet first into the black hole, torch between his teeth, arms up above him to give him some support. He felt around with his feet. "It's some sort of passage," he called back.

"Hurry up," said Max, "that nutter's coming." Sam found that behind the initial small entrance was a large passage. He stood up and shone the torch back to allow Andrew and Max to clamber through.

"Get back here," said the gruff voice of Old Billy. "Think you can just disappear on an old timer that easily?" He clambered heavily up onto the ledge and rolled himself uncomfortably into the cave. Sam switched the torch off and the three boys held their breath standing as still as statues.

"Bloody hell," said the old tramp. "That must have been a good bottle," and he rubbed his head trying to work out whether he had actually just seen anyone or not. He looked around the cave, the darkness keeping the entrance a secret. "I'm giving that stuff up," he said, grumpily, putting what he had seen down to just another nightmare. He climbed back out of the cave and settled down in his pile of rags again and in seconds was snoring the noisy sleep of the very drunk. When the boys were sure Old Billy was not going to be a problem, Sam switched the torch back on and they set off down the passageway.

The tunnel was dark ahead and the torch made eerie shadows dance around them. The walls looked like they had been roughly hacked out and water glistened as it dripped through the ceiling and onto the stone floor. It smelled of damp caves, the kind you went on for a school trip.

"Where do you reckon this leads to?" asked Andrew in a shaky voice.

"It looks like we're heading back to the village," said Sam. "I expect we'll come out in a drain somewhere."

"What happens if the end of the tunnel is blocked and we can't get out," said Max, his fear spilling over into his voice. "You know I don't like closed in spaces."

"It'll be alright," said Sam trying to sound more confident than he felt. He was eager to see where the tunnel went. It might reveal something that would help him.

Chapter 24

The Treasure Hunt

Spode reached the stony shore of Coombe Bay and collapsed with exhaustion onto the pebbles. He lay there for a while catching his breath, then turned onto his back and stared at the moon. The storm was subsiding; the bay sheltered him from the remaining gusts of wind. As he lay still, thinking about what had just happened, he laughed, quietly at first, but then louder and louder. The noise echoed round the cliffs, resounding off the rocks. He laughed until his whole body shook. Then as the laughter subsided, he rolled onto his knees and dragging himself forwards, started the slow climb out of the valley. The treasure would wait. And as he was the only survivor, he planned to come back for it some other time.

Meanwhile, Friar felt in the dark for what he was looking for. His fingers became entangled in what felt like fronds of some strange sea creature, fanning in the current, and he knew he had found him. Black Heart's long hair had been wafted out in front of him. Friar caught hold of his jacket and hauled him up to the surface. His body was a dead weight, but there was no way Friar was going to leave him down there to become fish food. As he rose to the surface he tried desperately not to make too much of a splash. He suspected Spode would have survived the shipwreck and he had no intention of letting him know that he was alive. His lungs filled with the air they craved as he drew breath; once, twice, three times. Then carefully scanning the shoreline, he waited, treading water for what seemed like an age, Black Heart's body held just below the surface. As he watched the shore he saw Spode start to crawl forwards and then make his way slowly up the cliffs and out of the Bay.

Friar felt drained, he was frozen and utterly exhausted. He had not been there when it mattered the most and he had let his Captain down. Now a sense of deep remorse filled his heart, and repositioning his hands under Black Heart's shoulders, he turned onto his back and swam as best he could to the shore. The waves were easing now, and he felt they almost helped him onto dry land over the last few hundred yards. He felt the slippery stones of the Bay under his feet and hauled Black Heart's body up out of the water and lay next to him, panting for breath. But he didn't wait long. He knew Spode was not far ahead and he did not want to risk being seen. He dragged the body up under an overhanging cliff and sat down to think.

He looked up to the moon and the tears welled up inside him. The grief he felt at the loss of his Captain was almost too much to bear.

"If only I'd been there a minute earlier," he reprimanded himself. Then putting his head in his hands, he wept and wept for his dead Captain. For ten minutes Frair wept, not knowing what to do next. Should he go after Spode? But remembering the pirate death code, he allowed himself a brief smile.

"He'll get you, Spode, you double crossing murderer. It might not be today, but he will revenge his death, mark my words." The thought seemed to trigger something in Friar's head as he gazed out to sea. Then making sure Black Heart was well hidden in the cave, he headed back out to sea.

"I couldn't save him," he muttered as he caught his breath from the icy cold water, "but I can carry out his plan. I'll rescue the treasure and hide it somewhere safe so that one day it can be returned to its rightful owner." And with that he plunged into the murky depths in search of the Irish farmer's treasure.

His task was made more difficult by the debris of the Onyx that had started floating up to the surface. Three times he came up for air taking huge gulps before diving into the blackness again. He swam down as far as he dared, the visibility non-existent. He desperately groped around in the darkness. Finally, his hand felt something hard and the touch of the rough hessian sack that held the treasure told him he had found his goal. With both hands clasped around the loot, he hauled it off the seabed and fought his way back to shore. This time the journey was far harder. He wasn't sure of the exact contents of the sack, but he knew there were some gold candlesticks, some priceless jewellery and some religious artefacts, all weighing him down, trying to suck him back to the ocean floor. His head went under the water several times, but he pushed on, driven by the desire to carry out Black Heart's wish.

With a last kick, he felt his feet gain contact with the shore and he dragged the sack onto the rocks. The contents clattered and banged in protest as they arrived on English soil for the first time. Friar knew what he needed to do. The treasure had to be buried well before morning in case Spode came back.

"I'm sorry, Captain," he said kneeling down beside Black Heart's body. "But I'm going to have to leave you again." He took Black Heart's limp hand and kissed it.

"But I'll come back for you, Sir. I won't leave you here." Then he opened Black Heart's shirt and pulled the half coin off the leather necklace that he knew hung there and rummaged in the Captain's shirt pocket and pulled out the gold watch he so often used.

"One more piece to the puzzle," he whispered under his breath, and felt inside the pocket of his own trousers for what he was searching. His fingers curled round the cold metal object, which shone in the moon light as Friar held up the other half of the coin he had taken from Spode on the day he had helped young Joshua. But something else had caught his attention that was poking out of the top of Black Heart's jacket pocket. Friar reached down and lifted it up. He knew instantly what it was. It was the Captain's own logbook from the ship. The tight leather binding seemed to have kept most of the sea water out so that it was still legible. He put it into his own pocket, and then he looked up at the cliffs above, slung the sack of treasure over his shoulder, and started to climb.

He knew the entrance wasn't far. He had only been here once, when he was a young lad, serving under Captain Sebastian. But he knew exactly what he was looking for. He hauled himself forwards, his fingers numb with the cold, until he came to a dark cave with a large overhang on the right. He dropped the sack and crawled forwards on his hands and knees to the back of the cave. Turning to use the small amount of moonlight there was, he opened the watch and pressed the two halves of the coin together. Then taking a deep breath, he fitted the coin onto the watch face and pressed down firmly. The watch made a whirring sound and out of the side came a small tray with a black stone laid neatly inside. He carefully lifted the stone and brushed at the back wall of the cave, looking for the place to fit it. He found the place easily and fitted the Onyx crystal into the hole in the wall, then stood back waiting for the stones to stop grinding. The cave wall moved slowly back to reveal the dark entrance to the hidden passage. Taking one last look out to sea, he picked up the treasure and headed off into the dark.

His feet trudged along the passage, his boots catching sometimes on the roughly hewn rock. He knew this place had been dug by smugglers years ago, but nobody knew this place existed anymore except him and Captain

Sebastian. He didn't know how Sebastian had come across the watch and necklace's halves in the first place, he had never asked. All he knew was that where this passage led would provide him with the safe repository he was looking for, safely away from Spode's thieving fingers. He walked blindly along; there was no light in the tunnel. He kept his shoulder against the wall as best he could so that he didn't bang his head; the loot on his shoulder growing heavier and heavier. He was tempted several times to stop and rest, but he knew the bag would only feel heavier if he did, so he trudged on. Soon he came to the part where the passage widened and the floor was littered with empty boxes and bottles. He ignored it all and still he kept on, focussing his thoughts on the way ahead. His body was starting to feel numb and his wet clothes stuck to him uncomfortably, chilling him to the bone. On he went; first up slightly, then down but always in the same direction. Finally, as his back ached and he felt he couldn't take another step, he saw a faint glow up ahead.

He placed the sack down as quietly as he could and looked up through the black grate into the Monastery Chapel above; the tunnel led straight into the Monastery in Sea Cove Bay. He strained to listen, not knowing what time it was. The last thing he needed now was a prayerful monk to interrupt his plan. But the coast looked clear, so picking up the treasure again he headed on down the passage. Another two hundred yards and he was there. He was directly under the main part of the monastery now. He found the second iron grate he was looking for and placed the loot down underneath it. He reached up and took hold of the metal, hoping beyond hope that the monks had not had the foresight to seal the opening shut. The grate moved slightly, so getting his back behind it, he heaved with all his might, until it lifted enough for him to crawl through. Once inside he looked briefly around him, and then reached back down for the treasure.

"Please God," he muttered under his breath, "let everyone be sleeping." He needn't have worried; the place was deserted. He had emerged in a large stone room. Six great stone pillars stood to attention around the room and were joined at the top by large curving arches that pointed heavenwards. Lanterns were hanging on the walls that gave a dim light, casting eerie shadows across the floor and walls. He was in some sort of anti-chamber, but this was not the place he needed. He stood on the spot, trying to get his bearings. He forced his mind back to the last time he had been here with Sebastian. Then as if he had known the way all the time, he headed across the stone floor and into a much smaller room on the left. Moving directly to the far wall, he bent down and ran his fingers over a groove that ran in a square shape across the floor. The treasure in the sack tinkled as it rolled off his shoulder and he cursed himself for not being more careful. He stood for a moment to make sure the noise hadn't woken any of the monks, then bent down again and set to work. He withdrew the dagger that he kept in his boot and dug into the floor an inch around the square edge. Then having loosened the dirt, he dug the knife down and jerked it up suddenly. There was a rush of air and the stone lid to the small hole moved. Friar got his fingers underneath and shifted it out of the way. He smiled as he looked down into the hole. There was an old wooden crate, sitting squat on the floor. A black skull and cross bones were painted on the side with the word 'Onyx' painted underneath. He remembered Sebastian's orders last time: to lay the treasure inside the crate to stop any mice and rats from nesting inside.

"Fat lot of good that did," he chuckled. Then with great reverence he placed the treasure inside the box and reattached the lid as best he could over the top. He knelt for a minute, his mind returning to Black Heart. Then he heaved the stone lid over the box and carefully spread the soil back over to leave no trace of him having been there.

He silently made his way back to the grate and climbed back into the dark tunnel.

"Now for the important bit," he said , his face becoming pained and haggard at the thought of his Captain and he felt his chest tighten as he coughed a loud rattling cough. He took a minute to steady himself, suddenly feeling a lot weaker, and plunged back down the passage. The journey back to Coombe Bay was a lot faster. He emerged into the gloomy night and went straight across to Black Heart. He picked the body of his beloved friend up and slung him over his shoulder. Then turning back towards the entrance, he walked slowly inside again. This time he knew he had to seal the passage in case Spode came snooping around as he more than likely would. He reached back outside and gently removed the Onyx crystal from its resting place in the wall. The stone ground its way across as Friar brought his arm back inside. He was thrown into complete and utter blackness as the cave re-sealed itself. He took a deep breath and re-positioned Black Heart on his shoulder, then started the long trudge back to the monastery.

Chapter 25

Secrets of Sea Cove Bay

The boys trudged on in the gloom for what seemed like ages, Andrew following Max following Sam. The tunnel weaved around a little, but the floor seemed remarkably smooth with a couple of grooves running either side of the centre.

"It's almost as if things have been dragged or wheeled up here," said Sam trying to look ahead to see if there were any clues, but the tunnel continued; one minute gradually climbing, the next gently falling but all the time heading back towards Sea Cove. The boys' legs began to ache, and the tunnel was getting cold.

"We must have gone miles," said Max as he stumbled and bumped into Sam. "Sam, my legs are killing me, can we stop and have a rest?"

"Aye, alright," said Sam. "It looks like the tunnel widens up ahead. Let's take a look."

They staggered on until the tunnel did indeed open up into more of a cave. Strewn about the floor were old oak barrels some standing upright some broken and lying in pieces. There were upturned crates stacked on one side of the cavern a couple of which were standing loose on the floor. There were several empty bottles lying around. Sam picked one up and read the label 'Jamaican Rum 1784'. He shone the torch around the side of the cave and saw that there were brackets hammered into the walls that he assumed were for holding a lantern of some sort.

Suddenly Andrew gave an almighty scream and jumped backwards into Sam.

"Oh crikey," he said his voice trembling with fright. "There's a skeleton over here." Sam gasped as his torch shone on the bones, as they lay strewn across the floor. Fragments of clothing still clung to them, but all the flesh had gone to leave the shiny white bones behind. The skull had rolled slightly onto the shoulder bone and the right hand was pointing on down the tunnel. Max came over to have a look. He stepped over to the crates to get a better look and his foot kicked an old tin of lamp oil that had been discarded in the shadows. All three jumped as the sound echoed off the walls.

"I really don't like this," said Max sitting down heavily on one of the upturned crates. "I want to go home."

"Well, that will teach you not to go around following me all the time, won't it!" said Sam getting altogether sick of his little brother.

"Well I didn't know you were coming on some weird treasure hunt miles and miles away to go crawling around in some stupid cave with skeletons and bats, did I?" said Max struggling to hold back his tears.

"What did you think; we were just popping out to MacDonald's!" he shouted. Max started sobbing onto his sleeve.

"Pack it in you two," said Andrew trying to calm things down. "Having a go at each other won't help anyone will it?" He sat down next to Max and put his arm round his shoulder. "Come on Max it can't be far now. You know I reckon smugglers used this place. I reckon this is where they stopped to have a rest from hauling all that loot and that poor beggar is probably one of them," he said throwing a glance over at the skeleton. "Maybe he was even a pirate," he said trying to get Max to smile. Max like his brother was fixated with pirates.

"Look, I say we carry on," said Sam dragging his eyes away from the skeleton. "We've come this far, let's at least see where the tunnel ends. I think you're right, Andrew. I bet you we come out near the pub or something. If smugglers were shifting drink what better place than to stash it in the cellar of the Wild Boar, that pub's been there ages. We can take a look and sneak out through the back door or something. I bet there's still a lock-in if we hurry."

"What about him?" asked Max pointing to the skeleton.

"We'll just have to leave him," said Sam holding out his hand to pull Max onto his feet. "If we ever get the chance we might be able to tell someone about him one day."

They turned and headed on through the tunnel again. No one spoke, they were each lost in their own thoughts about the skeleton they had disturbed. Who was he and what was he doing here in an under-ground tunnel? How had he died and did anyone know he was down here? After about half an hour's slow trudging Sam said,

"It's getting lighter up ahead and I can feel a breeze on my face."

"Can you see where we are yet?" Andrew asked peering around Sam's shoulder to get a closer look.

"No, keep quiet just in case." They crept forward and found the tunnel started to rise more steeply for a short while. It then flattened out again. The light was coming from a grid up ahead in the ceiling. Sam switched the torch off and crept forward.

"It doesn't look like a pub cellar to me,' whispered Sam. He spread himself flat against the wall and Andrew and Max automatically did the same. They edged closer to the grid and looked up. It was made of what looked like cast iron that had originally been painted black, the iron criss crossed in diamond shapes to make a firm lid over the tunnel.

Sam gasped and jumped with fright. The torch fell from his hands and clattered noisily on the stone floor.

"What is it?" whispered Max, barely able to contain himself anymore.

"It looks like a church," said Sam groping around on the floor for the torch. "I think we're inside the Priory. There's a great big crucifix hanging on the wall, it gave me a shock for a minute there." His groping fingers found the torch and he switched it on again, but it was damaged from being dropped and wouldn't work.

"Can you see anything else?" asked Andrew.

"Hang on," said Sam edging closer again. He stood on tiptoe to see if he could see anything else. "There are a couple of candles burning near a statue, but I don't think there is anyone around," he said straining to see through.

"I think I can get up," said Sam. "Andrew come and give me a hand." The two boys grabbed hold of the grid and pushed to see if the grate would move. It didn't budge.

"Put your weight behind it," Sam suggested tensing his shoulder against the iron. "On the count of three, ready, one, two, three, push." They pushed and pushed with all their might and the grate very slowly lifted slightly.

"Is it on a hinge?" asked Andrew.

"How the hell am I supposed to know?" panted Sam. "Max, make yourself useful and give us a hand," he said straining to hold the grate open. The three boys gripped the iron bars as best they could and heaved and heaved until eventually they felt the grate move upwards.

"It is on a hinge," said Andrew. "We just need to push it up enough for one of us to climb through, and then they can shove something under it to hold it open for the other two.

"Max get ready to go through," panted Sam, his face bulging under the pressure. "Ready Andrew, heave."

The grid moved and Max clambered up through the side using his brother as a ladder onto the hard-stone floor at the front of the Priory.

"We're right in the middle of the place," he said in a loud whisper standing up and looking around him.

"Find something to put under the grate, Max," said Sam gruffly. "We can admire the statues in a minute." Max found a wooden chair nearby and forced the front legs under the grate leaving just enough space for someone to crawl through. He hung on as best he could to try and make the opening wider.

Andrew started to climb through. "Wait," shouted Max. "It's too heavy, it's slipping." He lost his grip and the chair slid backwards and banged against the wall. Max tried his best to hold onto the grate, but it was just too heavy for him to hold on his own. It slid out of his hands and smacked down onto Andrew's leg as he tried to pull it out of the way. Andrew screamed in pain and gripped the grate to try and get his leg free. It wouldn't budge.

"Help me Max," he screamed in pain, "help me."

Chapter 26

The Burial

Friar's chest hurt as he strained under the dead weight of his Captain. Every few steps now he had to stop to allow the rattling cough to escape his lungs. He trudged slowly, step after step, slowly making his way back, desperate to see the glimmer of light ahead. He reached the part of the passage where it widened out and rolled Black Heart's body off his shoulder, where it slumped onto the ground. He lay motionless, utterly exhausted from his quest. But he had to go on. He would not abandon his Captain again. Heaving the Captain up again, he went on until his vision blurred and he could not feel his back and legs anymore. The dim light appeared above, and he dropped Black Heart again, less reverentially this time from sheer exhaustion. He braced his back against the first grid now and heaved with all his might. As the grate swung open it clanged back onto the stone floor of the chapel above. Friar grabbed Black Heart and hauled him up through the grate and onto the floor. Not stopping for breath, his task too important, he carried the Captain across the floor and out into the gloomy night.

He headed round the back of the chapel and up to a grassy slope, where he lay his charge down, hopefully close to reaching his journey's end. As he stood in the moonlight, he looked across at the small graveyard that lay before him. There were several newly dug graves, the earth still fresh looking piled high above the burial site of somebody. Friar slowly walked through the graves and found what he was looking for. He picked up a shovel and moved to the edge of the graveyard, then without looking up, he started to dig.

After half an hour, he stood back, the pain in his chest making it hard for him to breathe now. But he had done it. He walked over to the Captain and as gently as he could carried him over to a freshly dug grave and laid the body inside. Then he carefully replaced the earth, mounding it up on top of his friend. As he shovelled the final bits of soil back into place, he fell to his knees and leaning on the shovel for support, he wept.

"Captain," he said. "Please forgive me, I have failed you. But at least now your body will lie at rest." He looked around him, hoping that the monks would not notice the grave in the morning. He knew there were so many people to bury from the coffin ships that arrived from Ireland, that one more grave would hopefully go unnoticed. With one last look at the grave, he headed back down the slope and into the monastery.

There was one last task he had to do tonight before he could rest. He had to make sure that the treasure could be found again. He stalked back into the great stone building once more and crept through the different rooms looking for what would pass as the bursar's room. He had to get the watch and necklace to the only person he knew would keep it safe, Black Heart's son.

Black Heart never spoke openly about his son, but once shortly after young Joshua had come aboard, Friar had come across Black Heart looking wistfully out to sea. Friar smiled as he remembered the Captain telling him about the girl in Sea Cove that had captured his heart and how he felt so at home there. Then Black Heart had gone on to say that he had a son that he loved dearly but knew that he would never really know him or his girl, the pirate life being no place for a woman and child. Friar felt another pang of guilt as he realised the lad would never know his father.

He found a small room at the end of the monastery that looked like it dealt with the less religious matters of sending messages and dealing with the monastery finances. Piles of scrolls were tied up at one end of a large wooden table that sat in front of a high stained-glass window. He reached down and took a quill from on top of a parchment and dipped it in the inkpot on the right. With shaking hands, he crafted a note for the monk that would hopefully see it in the morning and carry out a desperate man's request. To send the watch and necklace to Master Black of Sea Cove, and to hide the precious logbook somewhere safe, so that nobody would ever find it, except the person that was meant to. He laid the items on the desk, and then stopped. He picked up the logbook again and began to write:

'There is not much time. I know I am a dying man. I am parched and I can feel my strength leaving me, but I have done it. I have hidden the treasure where Black Heart said. God rest his soul and curses on the one who sent him to his early grave. As for this log, if my last wish is carried out it will be well hidden, until the rightful heir finds it. Then all will know that Spode was a double-crossing murderer and Black Heart a good man. May the entire world know that Spode killed Black Heart in cold blood and ran the Onyx aground. Black Heart's body will rest for now, but his spirit will not be at peace until the pirate death code is enacted." Then he signed it '*John Friar, first mate and last remaining friend of Capt. Black Heart.*'

His task completed, Friar turned and slowly made his way back through the monastery, to the iron grid that lay open in the first anti-chamber. He knew he was fading fast now. His vision was continuously blurred, and his head pounded. His lungs burned with a fire that he knew would kill him. Each step he took caused his body to writhe in pain. Friar knew where he must go, his end was not far away now, and he could sense it. The most important thing was for Spode to believe he was the only survivor of the shipwreck; that way his greasy hands would not defile the treasure and Black Heart's body. Friar half climbed, half fell into the secret passage beneath the chapel and heaved the iron grate down on top of himself. Then he lumbered in the darkness back to the chamber farther along. His strength now virtually vanished, he lay down on the cold ground and closed his eyes. He felt himself drifting into a deep sleep from which he never awoke.

Chapter 27

Fire in Henry's Belly

Henry Spode slept, but his dreams were haunted by a strange vision. He felt as though he couldn't breathe and was aware of a claustrophobic sensation washing over him. There was a stench coming from somewhere. He looked around and saw he was in a dark stone passage. There was a flickering light coming from up ahead. He forced his breathing to calm down and gingerly stepped forward. He slid silently towards the light. As he got closer he saw a man huddled against the wall. His clothes looked more like rags, and he had a barking cough that racked his body every time he tried to move. His hair was hanging dankly down his back and over his face and his chin was covered in thick black stubble. Henry stepped closer and saw that the man had an eye patch over his left eye.

The man looked up moving a piece of hair that had flopped across his face. His lungs wheezed and his body shook as he coughed again. He turned his head to the side and threw up green bile onto the floor next to him. He clearly didn't have the energy to move so the sick trickled over his leg and ran down his trousers. Henry wondered why he didn't feel pity for the man. In some horrible way he knew the man was going to die and he was pleased, although through his dream the feelings shocked him. The man was mumbling something incomprehensible through his parched lips as the fever burned through his body. Henry strained to hear what he was saying.

"Captain, please forgive me Captain, I have failed you. Oh, Black Heart, I was supposed to be your best friend," then he was silent and moved no more.

"Black Heart," thought Henry "Now I understand."

Henry felt the fire grow in his belly. The anger was tangible in the air. He hated this man. He stood frozen to the spot watching, as Friar lay motionless in the cave.

Chapter 28

Fr. Raphael

Fr. Raphael rose early as he usually did and slowly made his way to his study before morning mass. He wrapped his cloak tightly round him feeling the chill of the stone reaching into his bones. He winced as his back ached and steadied himself on the wooden desk, trying to gain control of the pain. He was getting on in years; he would be seventy at his next birthday and he had kept the same morning routine ever since he had joined the monastery as a young boy: accounts, mass, small breakfast, prayer, then accounts again. Fr. Raphael was gifted with a head for numbers and he had quickly risen through the ranks to become the head bursar for the Benedictine monks that lived together in the small community at Sea Cove. He was a simple man. He never ventured outside the monastery walls preferring to spend his spare time in prayer to God in the small chapel that had been built by St. Betha all those years ago.

This morning when he entered his domain, he instantly knew that someone had been there before him. He cast his eyes around looking for anyone that might be still there, but he was alone. As usual he hobbled over to the wall on the right-hand side and genuflected as best he could. Then his raised his eyes to the crucifix hanging on the wall and kissed the feet of the man hanging there. His veneration complete, he turned to his desk and sat down heavily in his chair. He sat motionless for a minute staring at the objects that lay in front of him: a gold pocket watch, two halves of a necklace and a small leather-bound book. He cast his eyes up to heaven as if looking for some divine inspiration, and then slowly took hold of the scroll that lay neatly next to the watch. His eyes clouded momentarily as he squinted to read the scrawling writing:

'May who ever finds this letter take pity on a man close to death. I have done some bad things in my life and for that I am sorry, but I have prayed to God and I trust that he will help me in my hour of need.' Fr. Raphael glanced up to make sure nobody was coming. He had a strange sense of foreboding as if somebody's future lay in his hands. He read on:

'There has been a terrible deed done this night by a treacherous villain. He has taken the life of a good man and for that I curse him. He must never lay his filthy hands on the things in front of you. Please, if you can find it in your heart, send them on to one that will know what to do with them.' Fr. Raphael noted the address scrawled across the page: 'Master Black, Sea Cove, Cumbria'. He sat for a minute deep in thought, and then turned back to the parchment.

'One more bold request, if I may,' the note continued. *'Please, hide this logbook somewhere safe, somewhere that will keep it unseen until the time comes for it to be found. I am a desperate man and I fall heavily on your wisdom and grace. Please help me with this task.'* The note was signed *'John Friar'.*

Fr. Raphael sighed. He had learned when to ask questions and when to keep quiet. For an instant he thought about telling the Abbot of his strange discovery and the note pleading for help, but he knew that it was not necessary. He slowly took up a parchment and wrapped the watch and necklaces inside, tying the package up with sisal. Then he carefully wrote the name of the person he would send it to on the front. 'Master Black, Sea Cove,' and placed it in the pile of mail that would be collected from his office later that morning. Turning to the logbook, he picked it up in his tired fingers and felt its weight for a moment in his hands. Then, as if making a decision, he turned to the brown leather account book sitting on the desk in front of him and slowly released the back page from its cover. He slipped the logbook inside and pressed the page firmly back down. Then closing the book, he stood up and hobbled out of the room towards the chapel, the sounds of mass already drifting towards him.

Chapter 29

Captive in the Priory

Andrew screamed again. “Get it off me, Max, please.” Tears streamed down his face. Max took hold of the metal again and gritted his teeth. He hauled with all his might some how finding hidden strength that he didn’t know he had. He leant back using his body weight to move the iron and slowly it raised enough so that Andrew could pull his leg free.

“Are you alright, mate?” called Sam from below. All he could hear were the muffled cries of pain coming from Andrew who was rolling around the floor holding his leg.

“My lcg, my lcg,” cricd Andrew, “I can’t walk on it.”

“Get me out of here, Max,” cried Sam, panicking that his best friend had done something serious to himself.

“I can’t hold it,” said his brother wailing, tears running into his mouth and blurring his vision. Sam reached up through the grate and grabbed his brother’s hand.

“Try Max,” he said staring into his brothers’ eyes “I can’t help you or Andrew if I’m stuck down here can I?” Max took hold of the grid once more.

“Help me!” he muttered under his breath hoping some one would give him strength from somewhere.

Sam heaved with his shoulder and slowly a gap appeared at the side. Sam pulled himself up and squeezed through rolling out onto the stone floor. As Max’s grip loosened, the grate fell back into place with a muffled boom that echoed round the stone pillars of the old church.

"Thank you," he heard Max mutter. Sam stayed on his knees for a minute trying to get his breath back then rolled over to Andrew.

"Do you think it's broken?" he asked wondering how on earth he was going to get Andrew back home with a broken leg. He would just have to go and call for an ambulance and accept the consequences. Andrew rolled onto his knees and tried to stand up.

"I don't think it's broken," he said wincing with pain. "I reckon I'm just going to have a really good bruise there in the morning."

"Can you walk on it?" asked Sam putting his arm under Andrew's shoulder for support. "Just about," Andrew replied. "But you'll have to help me." Sam pulled the chair forward and helped his friend sit down. Then he walked over to where Max was sitting, crying, on the floor.

"It's alright, Max," he said trying to console his brother. "He hasn't broken it, come and give me a hand and we'll try and think of some story to tell his mum about how he got such a big bruise in bed."

Max wiped his nose with his sleeve and walked across to help lift Andrew. "Now to find a way out of here," said Sam as he and Max helped Andrew to stand up. "Wait here while I check the doors. Aren't these places supposed to be open all the time? It seems a shame to have to break a window, they're all stained glass." He ran down the main aisle silently keeping to the carpet that lined the way. The main part of the Priory was fairly small with adjoining chambers having been added over the years. The ceiling was low for a church, which gave it a cosy atmosphere, even in the middle of the night. There were a few statues dotted along the walls with wooden pews on either side that led up to a small stone altar at the front. At the back a space had been left where people met after a service to chatter and have a coffee. There was a table on the left full of brochures and leaflets.

Sam tried the big black handle of the main entrance, the door was imposing and looked large and strong; it was locked, so he went up the side aisle and tried the door on the left. It swung open with a loud creak. Sam hoped the noise wouldn't alert anyone outside. "Here we are, boys," he said trying to sound cheerful. "People usually try and break into these places, not break out," he said as he went back to help the others. With Sam one side and Max on the other supporting Andrew's weight, they slowly made their way out of the door, closing it as quietly as they could as they slipped into the night.

"What I want to know," said Sam when they had moved into the shadows away from the light above the door, "is why a tunnel would lead all the way from Coombe Bay to the Priory?"

"Maybe they were smuggling something holy," said Max, still sniffing, trying his best to support Andrew's weight.

"Maybe," said Sam not knowing what to think.

They slowly made their way back up Main Street trying their best to keep to the shadows. If anyone had seen them they may have thought it was two friends trying to get someone home who was the worse for wear with drink, as long as they didn't see their faces and realize they were only eleven, eleven and eight. Fortunately for them no one was around and before too long they came to Andrew's house.

"Will you be alright?" whispered Sam knowing full well that they probably wouldn't get away with this.

"Yeah," said Andrew "My leg's feeling better, I'll just say I fell out of bed onto my roller blades or something."

"Do you want any help getting upstairs?" said Max, praying the answer would be 'no'. He felt his legs would give way any second if he had to carry Andrew another step.

"No, I'll be okay from here," Andrew said and silently hobbled round the back of his house disappearing into the darkness.

Sam and Max turned up the hill and walked in silence back to their house. Sam slipped the key from his back pocket into the keyhole and silently undid the lock. They crept inside and Max hung the spare key he had taken earlier back on its hook. Jet opened her eyes and stared at the boys but, before she could get up, Sam reached up and got her another biscuit to keep her quiet. They silently glided past and crept up the stairs.

Sam never really knew how they both made it back to their rooms without getting caught. He stepped out of his clothes and slipped his pyjamas over his head then he climbed into bed and lay staring at the ceiling, the events of the night running through his head. He turned to his alarm clock to see what time it was - 05:05am. He turned back and closed his eyes knowing that in a couple of hours' time he would hear his dad getting up for work and his mum would start banging around the house.

"Oh well," he thought, "two hours' sleep is better than none," and with that he fell into a deep sleep.

The sea tossed the mighty vessel this way and that. Waves crashed overboard and swamped the deck. Rain lashed down and the wind whipped up a spray that bit at the faces of the crew desperately trying to steer the ship away from the rocks. There was an almighty boom and the topmast came crashing onto the deck, plunging through the floor. The sail ripped in two and fluttered in tatters above the deck.

He could just make out the sound of an argument above the ferocious wind.

"Damn you, Spode," he heard a voice scream. Sam knew in his dream it was the voice of Black Heart. "You'll have us all dead. Stay back, you traitor, or I'll be forced to run you through."

"It is not I, Captain, who is the traitor," said Spode's oily voice. "The treasure in these holds is too good for the likes of them peasants you mean to give it to. Share it amongst the crew, we deserve it after all the toils you have put us to."

"For God's sake man," came the angry reply. "The crew knows you would take it for your own, you have run us aground and soon there will be no crew left, no treasure neither except at the bottom of the sea."

"You, God fearing fool," Spode jeered. Sam tried desperately to see what was happening, but he was suddenly unable to visualise Black Heart in his dream. The next thing Sam heard was the sound of a sword being drawn and a guttural scream of pain. He writhed around on the bed, almost as if the sword had been driven into his own heart. He woke suddenly, sitting up with a jerk.

"Black Heart," he whispered under his breath. Then he felt the surge of anger well up inside him. "Henry Spode," he said through gritted teeth.

Chapter 30

Ghosts

Sam became slowly aware of the sounds of his father leaving for work. With a massive effort, he dragged himself out of bed and went to wake his brother. Max was buried deep under his covers, as if dead to the world.

"Max," he whispered, "wake up, it's me. We've got to pretend everything is normal."

"Go away," replied his brother snuggling tightly into his duvet.

"Max, you have to get up, it's important," Sam responded, and he pulled the covers cruelly away from his sleeping brother.

"Sam, you rat," Max said blearily as he sat up and rubbed his eyes.

"I'm sorry," Sam said tousled his brother's hair, "but we don't want to get mum suspicious, do we?"

"Suppose not," said Max slowly standing up and stretching. "What time is it?"

"Time to find another clue," said Sam as he turned and headed downstairs.

After a hurried breakfast both boys kissed their mother trying to hide their tiredness and went outside with Jet in tow.

"Be good," called Mrs. Forshaw after them.

"We will," the boys chorused.

"Right," said Sam taking Jet's lead off Max. He felt tired and angry following last night's dream. He was more determined than ever to solve this mystery knowing now for certain that Spode had killed Black Heart.

"First, we'll go for Andrew, and then we'll see if we can get to the bottom of this mystery." They ran down the hill and knocked loudly on the front door of Andrew's house. Andrew limped to the door with a bandage on his leg, an apple in his hand and a rucksack over his shoulder.

"Hi boys," he yawned as he stepped over the doormat. "All set?"

"I didn't know whether you would be up yet," said Sam feeling a pang of guilt as he looked at Andrew's bandaged leg.

"I didn't have much choice," his friend responded. "My folks make that much noise once they are up, there's no point staying in bed."

"What about your leg?" Sam asked concerned that Andrew might have given the game away.

"Oh, I blagged it," he said looking smug. "I told mum I fell out of bed onto my rollerblades. She took pity on me and had it bandaged up before I got out of bed."

"Cool," replied Sam with a smile.

"Where are we going to anyway?" Andrew asked as he took a bite of his apple.

"To the library," said Sam starting off.

"The library!" said Andrew and Max together.

"Have you gone mad, Sam? Max whined. "We're on holiday remember!"

"I know," said Sam. "But we've got to find some stuff out." So, giving an exasperated sigh Max followed his brother and the three set off in the direction of the library. As they walked Sam stared into the distance.

"I had a dream last night," he said as they crossed the road.

"What about?" asked Andrew keeping level with him.

"I saw Black Heart's murder. It was Spode, the evil traitorous vermin." Andrew saw the anger flash in Sam's eyes and reeled at the intensity of his words.

"Talking about yourself are you, Forshaw?" came a voice from across the street. It was Henry with Tezz and Pike. "Off somewhere nice, are we?" he said in a nasty voice.

"None of your business," said Sam gruffly. "That's all we need," said Sam quietly under his breath. "Not a word about this until he's out of sight."

"Maybe you're off to meet your girlfriend, Sam, what's the matter. Haven't you seen her for a day, are you missing her already?" Henry taunted from across the street.

"Lucy is not my girlfriend," said Sam starting to get angry.

"Who ever mentioned Lucy?" whined Henry as his friends started to laugh. "She must be, if she's the first person that came to mind, ah how sweet. I think Sam's in love."

"Shove off, Spode," said Sam crossing the street menacingly. "Or I'll give you a thick ear."

He faltered as he stepped forward. "Spode," he thought to himself. "This worm has to be a relation to Jake Spode who double crossed Black Heart." Sam had already made up his mind that Black Heart was a hero not a thief, and was going to prove to everyone that he was right.

"Ooh, I'm scared," said Henry standing up straight, his cronies stepping closer to his shoulder. "Get lost, you little worm," said Sam anger blazing in his eyes. He felt Andrew and Max stand closer to him, staring menacingly at Henry. His eyes locked with Henry's and they held each other's stare, trance like, for what seemed like ages. He felt an anger bubbling up inside him and he felt like he wanted to lash out and really hurt Henry. A strange feeling was stealing over him. Was it Henry standing in front of him or was it someone else? He held Henry's stare and it seemed to him that Henry was somehow taller with darker hair and his eyes seemed to change colour.

"Spode," Sam whispered through gritted teeth, "Jake Spode." He felt his head start to spin and something brushed against his leg. It was hard and seemed to be weighing down his belt. He felt his fingers twitch as if they wanted to take hold of it. What was it? A sword maybe, yes, that felt right. He reached down and took a firm grip of the metal handle clearly hanging from his belt. He tensed his muscles ready to unsheathe the sword and drive it through Spode's heart when he became aware of someone shaking his arm. He blinked and shook his head; Henry Spode was standing larger than life in front of him.

"It's Mr. Clayton" he heard Andrew say through clenched teeth. He turned and watched in a dream as Mr. Clayton strolled down the street towards them.

"Morning boys, enjoying the holidays, are we?" he asked in his usual patronizing voice. "Yes Sir," chirped Andrew knocking into Sam slightly. Sam turned and it seemed to his friend that his eyes were almost glowing, and his face was haggard and looked older than it should have.

"Glad to hear it," said Mr. Clayton walking past without a glance back. Andrew stared at his friend.

"Are you all right mate?" he asked not wishing to believe what he had just seen. Sam didn't answer he stared down at the pavement looking at his feet.

"Sam, Sam, mate, are you OK?" Andrew asked again looking to Max for some help.

"One of these days Forshaw, I'll have you," said Henry menacingly, "and when I do your little brother won't be around to save you."

Sam looked up feeling lightheaded and cold.

"I'll look forward to the day," said Sam holding Henry's stare again. Then he looked away. "Come on," he said to Andrew and Max. "We've got better things to do than waste time with these losers, let's go."

The three boys crossed back over the street and headed up the road. They stopped as soon as they were out of sight and peered around the corner to check Henry and his mates had gone. They were walking farther down the road. "It looked like they were off to the beach," said Andrew. "They all had towels with them."

"I hate him," said Sam, shocking himself with his anger.

"Steady on," said Andrew patting Sam on the shoulder. "You sounded quite scary then." "Right," said Sam, feeling his cheeks go red. "Come on." They walked in silence until they reached the village Library.

"I can't believe you are making us go in here on such a beautiful day," moaned Andrew as he resigned himself to going inside.

"It won't take long," said Sam.

"What are we looking for anyway?" asked Andrew.

"I don't know," said Sam. "Anything that looks unusual."

"Where have I heard that before?" said Andrew, smiling.

"Start with the sea journals, look for any reference to Black Heart, he must have sailed at the same time as those Irish potato farmers were being sent away." Sam tied Jet's lead to a post outside and the three boys went inside.

The library was in the Village School. It was a modern building with pine shelving. A few orange plastic chairs were dotted about and a pine table sat squat in the middle of the floor where Ms. Mablethorpe, the librarian could usually be found stamping her books lovingly. They spread out and started ferreting through all sorts of books and ledgers. Ms. Mablethorpe came in carrying a large book and smiled at the boys over her half-moon glasses, then buried her head again in her book and kept on walking to the shelf where it belonged. She carefully slotted it back onto its shelf and disappeared again through the door she had just come through.

After what seemed like ages searching, Max said,

"This is rubbish; I can't find anything about pirates or shipwrecks or anything."

"Me neither," said Andrew who was growing equally bored.

"Keep looking," said Sam desperate to find anything that might give him a clue. Andrew looked at Max and shrugged, then turned back to the task at hand. Another half hour passed, no one else came into the library. Ms. Mablethorpe popped back once or twice but she seemed oblivious to the boys' presence; she was too interested in the books under her nose to care about anything or anyone else.

Eventually Max stood up, his back was aching from crouching down to get to the low shelves.

"I'm going," he said loudly. "I've had enough."

"But we haven't found anything yet," said Sam the hope fading in his voice. Just then Ms. Mablethorpe came back in.

"What is it you are looking for, boys?" she asked peering over her glasses.

"Erm, we were looking for something about shipwrecks," said Sam quickly before Max could tell Ms. Mablethorpe everything. "Anything to do with ships that might have gone ashore at Sea Cove."

"Doing a local history project are we?" asked Ms. Mablethorpe in her broad Scottish accent, beaming at them. She was a small thin woman with wild gangly brown hair that she tried to keep tidy with some flower hair clips but bits got free and wafted across her face. Being so small and thin she always put Sam in mind of a field mouse.

"Yeah, something like that," said Sam weakly smiling as best he could.

"That's what I like to see, young ones taking an interest in the local vicinity, but unfortunately you've come to the wrong place for that sort of information." The three boys looked at each other and Max rolled his eyes. "No, the place you want is the other School Library, my dears; they have records going back centuries. I spend as much of my spare time as I can up there, oh its wonderful, the books, and the ledgers - the information stored there is second to none."

"Right, er thanks," said Sam moving towards the door. "We'll just be going then." In his opinion Ms. Mablethorpe was a bit batty but harmless none the less.

"Oh, do enjoy yourselves boys, I'm sure you will find Mr. Hawksclough, the librarian down there, is a great source of inspiration."

"Good, erm, thanks again," said Sam who then turned and scurried out of the door.

"Yeah, thanks," said Andrew and Max in unison.

"My pleasure boys, always a pleasure," and she scuttled back into the room beyond, probably to stick her nose into more books.

"Should have thought of that," said Sam as he untied Jet's lead. She had been sleeping in the shade of a nearby bush. "Come on, girl," he said, and they set off down the hill to the big school as they called it.

Sea Cove School was a really old place built of red stand stone that was common in Sea Cove; after all, that was the local stone. It was built way back in the 1500s and had grown bigger and bigger through the centuries and was known to the boys as 'the public school'. It was a boarding school to boys from all over the country, boys whose fathers had been there and their fathers before them. From the outside it looked kind of churchy with a central tower and wings going off to the north, south, east and west. Sam always thought that it reminded him of an abbey or a monastery, with its big arched windows and stone floors, wooden benches and lots and lots of history.

"Are we just going to walk right in?" asked Max staring up at the grand entrance. The door was a massive oak structure with black studs and around the arch at the top fierce looking gargoyles leered down at anyone daring to cross the threshold.

"Don't see why not," said Sam. "I'll tie Jet up over there," he said walking across to a shady part of the grounds.

"This place is creepy," said Andrew, "and it's broad day light, I wouldn't like to come here at night." He looked up at the frightening stone carvings looking down at him. "Hopefully we won't have to," said Sam. "Come on I'm sure it'll be fine."

The boys stepped gingerly up to the great door and pushed it open. Sam peered his head round. "No one's here," he whispered.

"Do you know where the library is?" asked Andrew, also whispering.

"No idea," said Sam. "Shall we split up and meet back here in fifteen minutes?" he suggested. "No way!" said Max. "I'm not going off by myself in this place."

"Let's stay together," said Andrew feeling relieved that Max had said what he was thinking.

Chapter 31

Henry Seeks the Treasure

Henry was feeling frustrated. His Uncle Joe, or rather his father, had told him he was the great, great Grandson of a pirate who would be contacting him soon, helping him to beat that idiot, Forshaw. But so far, he had felt nothing. A mixture of emotions had been rolling around inside him since he had read the letter. He had started loathing his father more than ever. Keeping a secret like that from someone, in Henry's opinion, was as low down as anyone could get. He now knew why he didn't fit in, why he was always at logger heads with his parents. His hatred for Sam had also grown; knowing he was the person he had to beat made him keener than ever to find the treasure. As he reached the beach with Tezz and Pike in tow, he gazed out to sea hoping for some sort of inspiration to hit him, but nothing came. He dumped his bag down on the sand and watched as Tezz and Pike stripped off and ran into the shallow water, splashing around like kids.

The tide was on its way out, which meant the rocks around Sea Cove Head were slowly being exposed to the sun. He could feel the warmth of the sun's rays on his back as he pulled his t-shirt over his head, revealing his chubby pink stomach and arms. He flashed his friends a disgusted look as they messed about, then wandered across to the rocks and sat down heavily on a large flat boulder to think. He tried to piece it all together, but nothing made sense. He knew that Sam was closer to finding the treasure than he was, and a familiar anger started to burn in his belly.

"He doesn't deserve it," Henry muttered under his breath, "that goody two shoes needs to be taken down a peg or two. If only I could find the gold, then he would be sorry." He looked up, staring directly at the sun. "Then they would all be sorry. I could leave home and never see those two idiots who call themselves parents, again." Feeling angry and confused he stood up and wandered off around the rocks.

He found himself clambering over the rocks in front of the caves where he had nearly drowned the other night. A glimmer of hope arose in him as he headed into the darkness of a cave adjacent to the one he had searched. The rocks were slippery, but he trod carefully on the sand that was now exposed between the rocks. He headed to the back, hoping beyond hope that he would stumble on the hoard he was so desperately seeking. He knelt down and started digging into the sand, working feverishly, anxious to find something, anything. His hand touched something hard and for a split second a smile crossed his face. He dug down further and got his fingers under the thing he had found. With all his might he heaved it out from its resting place, a wave of excitement taking hold of him. But as he drew the piece of driftwood out of the sand, his heart sank, and he yelled loudly with pent up frustration.

"No, this cannot be happening." He turned the wood over in his hands and did a double take as he read the words painted on the side, it was still legible after all these years, although there was no shine or varnish left - 'The Onyx'. Henry hurled the wood at the cave wall where it splintered and fell back to its resting place in the sand. Henry was mad. He kicked the sand under him and stamped his feet, but nothing would ease the pain he felt inside. With a last look at the back of the cave he turned and headed back to the beach where Tezz and Pike were still prancing about. He headed over to them and flopped down in the wet sand, letting the shallow waves roll over him. Pike went to say something, but Tezz had seen the look on Henry's face and motioned to Pike to keep quiet. Instead they joined Henry in silence and let the waves roll over them in the sunshine.

Chapter 32

Virtute et Ventate

The boys crept through the entrance hall of the school staring wide eyed at the tapestries that hung on the walls. There was a suit of armour in the corner and a huge shield with the school motto in Latin written in swirly writing underneath. It read '*Virtute et Veritate.*'

"I wonder what that means," Sam said as he stared at the coat of arms on the shield. There was a boar's head in the top right with sheaves of corn on one side and a meandering river on the other. "Weird," he thought as he tried to work out the relevance to Sea Cove. They headed for a smaller oak door at the other end of the hall and tiptoed through.

"Are we allowed to be here?" asked Max trying to stay as close to Sam as he could.

"It's just a school," said Sam, "I can't see how a school can be out of bounds completely." But he felt nervous all the same. They silently stalked through the next room; it must have been some sort of common room. There were leather chairs and settees placed in small groups around old wooden tables. A large fireplace took centre stage along the right-hand wall and several deer's heads were stuffed and hung from the wall.

"Obviously someone's trophies from way back," said Andrew in a disapproving voice. "They would look better alive," said Sam. He hated the thought of people hunting for fun.

They carried on through another set of double doors and came to a large staircase that wound its way up into what Sam assumed must be the tower. A red patterned carpet ran up the middle of the steps.

"Up here I guess," said Sam. He gripped the worn wooden handrail and started up the stairs. The other two followed. Group pictures in black and white lined the walls.

"1938, 1939, 1940 - these must be the old boys," said Andrew stopping to take a closer look at the boys in their uniform smiling at the camera. As they reached the top the corridor led off right and left.

"Which way?" asked Max but the direction was obvious. A sign hung from the ceiling pointing to the classrooms one way, and the library and reading room the other.

"To the right," said Sam, heading off in the direction the sign pointed. As Sam pushed open the heavy oak door that he hoped would lead to some answers he had a great intake of breath and whistled under his breath. "Wow!" he said, "look at this place, it's enormous."

There were stacks and stacks of books reaching high up to the ceiling. An old wooden handrail ran around the top as a gantry gave access to the higher shelves. A black cast iron staircase spiralled its way up to the gantry.

"Phew!" whistled Andrew as he walked in. "Well, you wanted books, Sam and now you've got them." He was awe struck at the sight that lay before him. There was a musty smell unique to libraries the world over.

"Where to start?" said Sam as he gazed around him, but before he could say anything else the door creaked open behind him and in walked a tall, skinny man carrying a pile of books under his arm. He had a black gown on with a square mortarboard on his head and gold tassels hanging down at the back. Sam noticed that he had a hearing aid in his ear and he looked like he was about the collapse under the weight of the books. He must have been about seventy-five and his wrinkled face was pale and sallow, probably from spending too much time indoors.

He glared at the boys over the top of his glasses.

"Must be a librarian thing," whispered Max to Andrew as he nudged him with his elbow.

"And what exactly are you three doing in here?" the librarian asked in a raspy voice.

"We 'er, we were just looking for some information," said Sam returning the librarian's stare.

"Well this is a private library and you are not welcome here," he said. "Are you one of the new boys?" he asked in an accusing voice.

"No," said Andrew. "We don't come to this school."

"Come to have a sniff around, have you?" said the librarian suspiciously.

"No," said Sam in a defiant voice. "We just wanted to have a look at some books."

"Well, get out of here, all of you, before I call the police," said the librarian stalking towards them. Before they could move he had grabbed Max by the scruff of his neck with surprising strength and was marching him towards the door. Max squirmed under his grip; for an old man he had a grip like steel.

"All right," said Sam. "You don't have to get stroppy," and he took Max by the hand and pulled him away from the man. "Come on," he said, "this place is obviously not the place for the likes of us, we'll just have to come back another time."

He bolted out of the door and down the stairs, Max following closely behind, Andrew hobbling as fast as he could. They ran back through the common room and through the entrance hall not daring to look back until they reached the front door.

"Stupid old fart," said Max as they emerged into bright sunlight.

"Sam," said Andrew following Sam over to untie Jet. "What did you mean we'll come back another time?"

"Tonight, we'll come back when it's dark and no one is around, then we can search the ledgers in peace."

"Oh no," said Andrew, "not another midnight adventure. I only just got away with the last one. My leg still aches and you know we were lucky not to get caught."

"We've got no choice," said Sam. "That stupid fool will be looking out for us and will probably have already warned the Headmaster, it's the only way."

"And how do you propose we get in?" Andrew asked, thinking that he had foiled Sam's master plan.

"Aha," said Sam "I've been thinking about that. I've had an idea."

"What sort of idea?" said Max catching up with the boys as they headed off.

"Don't you worry about it," said Sam. "Just take Jet back home and tell mum I'm having lunch with Andrew alright; I'll be back this afternoon once I've sorted things out."

"What are you up to Sam Forshaw?" Andrew asked; he wasn't sure he was going to like this.

"It's alright," said Sam. "I'm just going to see a friend of mine who I'm sure will help us out with a key to the place."

"Which friend?" Andrew asked suspiciously running through the people he knew Sam was friends with, in his head.

"Some one whose dad happens to be Sports Master at the school," said Sam with a smile. "Lucy," said Andrew, a grin spreading over his face. "You're going to get Lucy to get you a key so that you can break in and steal a book."

"I'm not going to steal a book," Sam said his voice sounding hurt. "I will find all the answers I need up there, I know I will."

"And what makes you think Lucy will help you?" said Andrew. "No, don't answer that, she'll do anything to get the gorgeous hunk, Sam Forshaw, to talk to her won't she? Silly me." Sam blushed; he knew Lucy liked him a lot. Was this mean to get her to do something that could well land her in trouble?

"Well sometimes," he thought, "a boy's gotta do what a boy's gotta do."

Chapter 33

Spode Sees a Pirate Ghost

Jake Spode clambered over the cliffs towards the village of Sea Cove exhausted but feeling smug and self satisfied. He was eager to get the treasure, but he was keener to find shelter and some warm clothes, maybe even something to eat. As he walked, he relived the moment he had driven the sword through the Captain's heart. The only problem was he couldn't stop the nagging doubt in his head following what the Captain had muttered with his last breath. 'I'll get you for this, maybe not today but some day.'

As he descended into the village, he became conscious of how he must look. He was drenched from head to toe and he was chilled to the bone. He headed for a small shack that stood just back from the beach and climbed over the fence. Who ever lived there were obviously sound asleep and nobody stirred. He ran across the back yard and under the clothesline that still held the washing from the day before. He snatched a pair of trousers and a shirt and quietly stripped off and dressed in the warm, dry clothes. Then he headed to the small chicken coup at the bottom of the field adjoining and crept inside. He settled himself down, much to the disgust of the roosting birds and fell asleep.

He was woken a few hours later by the cockerel singing his rather late dawn chorus loudly, just in case the farm was not yet awake. Feeling refreshed, Spode silently slipped out of his hiding place and crept up behind a fat, brown, unsuspecting chicken, he carefully wrapped his hands around the bird's neck and squeezed tightly. The bird flapped its wings, trying to wriggle itself out of the steely grip that was squeezing the breath out of him. Squeezing tighter, Spode planned to cook the bird later after he had recovered his hoard. The bird struggled and squirmed but it was no use, the life force slowly ebbed away, and with small red bulging eyes, the chicken sagged its head and became lifeless. Spode threw the bird over his shoulder and carried it by the neck as he disappeared silently back down to the beach. As the sun was coming further up the horizon, he stashed the chicken under a boat and untethered a second small rowing boat that was tied up just above shore level and clambered aboard. He rowed out around Sea Cove Head and on round to Coombe Bay. He smiled to himself as he went.

"I'll have the treasure in no time," he told himself smugly, "then put some food in my belly, then to make a new life somewhere hot." As he approached the scene of last night's shipwreck, he could see the floating debris bobbing up and down on the waves. A lot had already been washed up into the Bay where it would stay rotting until someone decided it would make good firewood. He shifted his position in the boat and stared down into the black water. When he thought he was about over the place the treasure would be, he threw the small anchor overboard and slid silently over the side. The water was freezing and Spode felt his toes and feet numb instantly. He took a deep breath and dived under the waves in search of the loot. Even with the sun up, the visibility was poor. He scrambled around the wreckage until his breath had gone, then re-surfaced to fill his lungs. Down he went again trying to work out which part of the ship he had found and where the treasure was in relation to it. His hands came up bare each time. Time after time he filled his lungs with air then dived down to search the depths. After half an hour he started to get angry. He knew he had found the Captain's

Cabin, but the treasure was nowhere to be found. Down he went again, the fire in his belly driving him on. A renewed hatred for Black Heart swirled in his chest as still he was unable to find anything. An hour passed and Spode could feel himself getting weaker. His body was frozen to the core but still he kept on. Down he pushed forcing his body to endure the cold. He didn't notice that each time he came to the surface now he was finding it harder to catch his breath. His chest was beginning to feel like a red-hot poker was stabbing his heart. Still he stayed in the freezing waves, desperate to find the treasure that would see him to a new life, but still he could not find it. The anger in his heart kept him from realising what was happening to him. Such a force drove him that he blocked out the pain that was racking his body. He ignored the stabbing sensation in his head and chest until it was too late. As he took what would turn out to be his last breath on the surface he submerged under the waves. He was vaguely aware of the darkness approaching over his eyes, but he was hypothermic, and all sense and reason had left him. He kicked desperately with his tired legs, but they were no use to him now. His arms flailed above him, frantic to reach the surface, searching for something to hold onto to stop him drowning, but the weight of his body pulled him down. He had no recollection now of where he was. His body stopped moving and he sank down under the waves. As he felt the life leave his body he had a final vision. It was of a handsome man dressed all in black with a red silk scarf tied around his waist. The man smiled at him, and then Spode saw and thought no more.

Chapter 34

Lucy's Keys

Sam watched Max and Andrew walk up the road with Jet; he didn't want either of them to hear the conversation he was about to have with Lucy. He hoped she was in. He turned and walked out of the school drive and across the road to where there were some small cottages standing in a row. Lucy's family lived in the end one. They looked very idyllic in the late morning sunshine, all painted white with pretty hanging baskets and neat front gardens. A red climbing rose wound its way up the drainpipe of Lucy's house. He took a deep breath and walked up to the door. He raised his hand to knock.

"No, I can't," thought Sam, "it's not fair." Sam was quite a shy person to start with where girls were concerned. The thought of speaking to one for very long filled him with dread, but especially Lucy. He really liked her but never in a million years would he ever admit it. "But I have to," he told himself, "it's the only way." He argued with himself on the doorstep for five minutes or more. Finally, he reached up and drummed his fist against the door.

He heard footsteps and the door opened to reveal a tall blond woman. "Wow!" thought Sam, "I know where Lucy gets her good looks from." He could feel his cheeks burning.

"Hello, Sam, isn't it?" said Mrs. Collins.

"Erm, hi Mrs Collins," Sam stumbled out "Erm, is Lucy in please?" he looked down at his feet feeling his ears burning red.

"Yes," said Mrs. Collins with a smile, "I'll just get her." She went back inside, and Sam took a deep breath and ran his fingers through his hair. A moment later Lucy appeared. She was wearing blue jeans and a pink crop top. As she stood in the doorway the sunlight lit up her hair and it almost burned a silky gold colour.

"Hi Sam," she said, "How are you?"

"Erm, I'm fine," said Sam trying to act cool. "Erm I just wondered if you wanted to come for a walk with me?" This time Lucy blushed.

"Yeah, sure," she said in what she hoped was a not too enthusiastic voice. "Mum," she called back into the house. "I'm going for a walk, see you later."

"OK," came the reply.

Lucy stepped out and joined Sam on the path; he had his hands in his pockets and was suddenly lost for words. He hadn't planned this, it just sort of happened and now he was going to have to make conversation with her, and he could feel himself getting more and more embarrassed.

"So where shall we go?" Lucy asked, breaking the silence.

"Don't know," said Sam, "how about the beach?"

"Okay," Lucy replied. They set off walking next to each other; Sam kicked stones that lay in his path.

"So," said Lucy trying to fill the painful silence. "What have you been up to?" she chirped in a high voice she had hoped would have sounded cooler.

"Oh, this and that," said Sam. Should he tell her what he had been up to or not? He wasn't sure she would understand or take him seriously, so he decided not to say anything for the time being. "How about you?" he asked sheepishly.

"Oh, this and that," she said with a smile. Sam laughed and they fell into a rhythm with each other and started chatting about how good it was to be on holiday and what they were each planning to do. Sam didn't say a word about Black Heart or his Grandad or the trip to Coombe Bay, and he couldn't yet bring himself to mention needing a key to the school.

They reached the beach and sat down on the stone promenade wall. The sun was high in the sky. There were loads of kids with their families splashing about in the waves and the seagulls circled high above looking for any abandoned ice creams or crisp packets they could devour. Sam took a deep breath. "Might as well get this over with," he thought to himself. Lucy gazed out to sea.

"Isn't it beautiful?" she said looking at the waves curling onto the sand.

"Yeah," said Sam turning to look at her. "Erm, Lucy," he said. Lucy turned to look at him. "What is it?" she asked, a moment of concern showing on her face.

"Well the thing is," Sam started. "Well I need a small favour," he said feeling the familiar redness starting in his cheeks.

"Is that what this is all about?" she asked putting her head to one side.

"What do you mean?" asked Sam trying not to look guilty.

"This going for a walk business," she replied. "I thought it was strange you wanting to go somewhere with me. I know you don't really like me," she said and turned her head away.

"No," said Sam. "That's not true, I do like you, I like you a lot." There he'd said it. Lucy turned back and smiled at him.

"Do you really?" she asked.

"Of course," said Sam turning away, this was starting to feel way out of his league. "I wouldn't say it if I didn't mean it, would I?"

"Well you might," said Lucy. "It depends what this favour is you are after."

"You might not like it," said Sam, giving Lucy a sheepish look.

"Try me," she said.

"Well, I need a key to get me into the big school and I know your dad will have one, so I was wondering if you could get me one," he paused, "tonight."

"What on earth do you want to get into the school for?" Lucy asked in a shocked voice. "You're not planning anything dodgy, are you?"

"No, no," said Sam quickly, "I need to get into the library to check something out. I tried to go this morning, but that daft old librarian guy kicked us out."

"You mean Mr. Hawksclough," she said. "He's not daft; he's just a bit deaf. Did you have permission to go in?"

"No," said Sam. "I didn't think I needed it."

"Of course, you need permission," scolded Lucy. "There's some valuable stuff in the place, they don't just let anybody in, you know."

Sam could feel himself getting cross, he hated the thought that some people thought they were better than others. "I'm not just anyone," he thought to himself. "I am the great, great grandson of a pirate, Captain Black Heart none the less."

"Look," he said trying to stay calm, "I need to get into the library. I need to look something up, but I don't want anyone knowing about it. I can't tell you anymore yet, but I will, I promise."

"So, you want me to steal a key from under my dad's nose and get it to you somehow so that you can go skulking around the school in the dark?" Lucy said angrily.

"Well, yes," said Sam. "I promise, I'm not going to nick anything or do any damage, I just want to go to the library," he said in what he hoped was a meek and mild voice.

"And what if you get caught?" she asked.

"I won't," he replied. "Look I'm not asking you to come with me," he said.

"No," said Lucy, "I'm not doing it."

"Oh, Lucy please," pleaded Sam, "I really need your help on this one. Look if you promise not to tell a soul, I'll tell you what this is all about, and then will you help me?"

"It depends," she said folding her arms and moving away slightly.

"Promise you won't tell?" he said looking her in the eyes.

"All right I promise," she said getting shirty.

"Right," said Sam. "It started in history the week before term ended," Sam started to explain.

For the next twenty minutes Lucy sat in silence as Sam told her all about the map and the grave at the Priory, about Coombe Bay and finding the coin. About sneaking out at night with Andrew and his brother following, about the stopwatch and the talisman and the tunnel and where it led, about the skeleton halfway along and the phone call he had had with his Grandad. About the strange feelings he had been getting since it all started, and how he believed what his Grandad had said about needing to help Black Heart's spirit find peace by getting to the truth about the stolen treasure.

"So, you see," he said finally looking back into Lucy's wide eyes, "I need you to help me, I have to find the truth."

Lucy sat in silence and turned back to look at the waves lapping onto the beach. She seemed to reach a decision.

"All right," she said in a quiet voice, "I'll help you, what do you want me to do?"

"Oh, thanks Lucy," Sam said giving her a sudden hug. "You're a star." Then, realizing what he had done, he moved away again. "Meet me tonight at midnight at the end of your row with the key. I'll go on in and get what I need and bring the key straight back to you."

"I have a bad feeling about this," she said as she jumped off the wall.

"It'll be okay," said Sam jumping down to catch up.

"Ah look," came a sinister voice from the grassy slope above the promenade, "it's love's young dream Forshaw and Collins, how sweet."

"Beat it, Spode," said Sam in as threatening voice as he could manage.

"What's the matter, Forshaw, hoped no one would see you kissing and cuddling, did you?" said Henry's whiny voice; he was naked down to the waist with water dripping from his trunks.

"We were not kissing and cuddling," shouted Sam angrily.

"It's alright," said Lucy "Let's just go."

"Kissy kissy kissy," Henry shouted as they walked past. Sam felt the anger rise up inside him and he headed towards Henry ready to punch his lights out.

"Don't," said Lucy grabbing his arm. "He's not worth it."

"Get some clothes on, fatty," he yelled and turned and walked away; he knew that would do more damage to Henry's ego than any punch in the nose would. They walked back in silence until they came to Lucy's house.

"So, see you tonight," said Lucy looking into Sam's scowling face.

"Yeah," said Sam trying to smile, "midnight at the end of the row, and wear something dark."

"Right," said Lucy as she turned and walked up to her front door, "see you tonight."

Sam went home in a bad mood. Henry had thoroughly embarrassed him, and he hated that feeling. "One of these days," he thought to himself as he walked up the road. As he passed Andrew's house, Andrew was waiting for him in the garden.

"Well," he said a broad grin across his face. "Did you get what you wanted?" he asked cheekily.

"Yes," muttered Sam without looking up. "She'll do it; she's going to meet me at midnight with the key."

"Right you are," said Andrew. "See you later."

"You don't have to do everything I do, Andrew," Sam said with a spiteful edge to his voice. Andrew shrugged and said, "Suit yourself, mate, just trying to help."

"Sorry, Andrew," Sam replied instantly. "I ran into Henry Spode at the beach and he wound me up. If you want to come then come, I'll see you later," and he stomped off to lick his wounds.

Dinner came and went, in the Forshaw household. Sam found he couldn't eat anything again and went to his room as soon as he had finished. He lay on his bed watching the minutes tick by. The room was hot and stuffy from the day's heat and his eyes felt sleepy. He closed them for a moment just to rest them and without wanting to, fell sound asleep.

Chapter 35

Quarter to Twelve

Sam woke up suddenly, someone was shaking his leg.

"Wake up!" said a whispered voice.

"What what's happening?" said Sam through Max's muffled hand.

"Be quiet!" said his brother. "You'll wake mum and dad."

"What time is it?" asked Sam, shoving his brother away.

"Quarter to twelve," said Max, "you must have fallen asleep. I thought you were just waiting until it got close to midnight but then I heard you snoring and figured I better come and wake you up."

"Right, thanks," said Sam swinging his legs out of bed. "Max, how did you know I was going out at midnight?" he whispered trying to get his shoes on silently.

"Come off it," said Max. "The Forshaws are out to redeem their long-lost pirate relative on a secret mission at night. What other time would you be going?"

"Right," said Sam with a smile.

"Anyway," said Max, "I for one don't want the ghost of a pirate hanging round me, thank you very much. I think we should get this sorted then everything can get back to normal. It freaks me out all this stuff about Black Heart."

"I know what you mean," said Sam pulling on his sweater with the hood. "Let's go." Sam stuffed a pillow into his bed to make the familiar sleeping shape in case his parents went in and then crept downstairs with Max hot on his heels. Jet was given her biscuit 'keep quiet treat' and they slid out the back door as silently as they could. Once outside they ran down the road to Andrew's house. Sure enough, there was Andrew hiding in the bushes in front of his house.

"All set?" he whispered, and he fell into step with the others.

"Yep," said Sam. "Now for the guest appearance; I hope she hasn't bottled it."

They ran on down Main Street trying to keep in the shadows as much as possible and rounded the bend to Lucy's row of houses. They crossed the street and ducked behind a fence that marked the garden of the last house.

"Where have you been?" came the harsh voice that belonged to a not too impressed Lucy. "I've been waiting ages," she scolded.

"Sorry," said Sam. 'I fell asleep' didn't sound very impressive at this point. "We got held up," he said. "Have you got the key?" he asked hoping above hope that she had.

"I could only get the key to one of the back doors," she said, "I think it's the fire escape door to the gymnasium but once we're inside we should be able to work our way through to the library."

"Oh no," said Max. "We're going to get lost in the posh school, aren't we?"

"Don't worry," said Lucy, "I'm coming with you; I know the way."

"No, it's too risky with four," said Sam "You stay here, we'll be fine."

"I've come this far, Sam Forshaw," said Lucy in a very school marm voice, "I might as well help you get what you're looking for. Anyway, I can get you there quicker."

"She's right Sam," said Andrew. "And you know what they say, four heads are better than three for looking at books in the middle of the night!"

"All right," said Sam giving up, "but everyone keep the noise down, especially you, Max." With that they crossed the road and disappeared into the shadows of the great school. Lucy led the way as they skulked round the back. This part was not lit so they were able to move quickly through the bushes. They came to an area that was even in this light clearly a more modern part of the school. The wall was made of normal bricks and there didn't seem to be any windows.

"This is it," said Lucy in a loud whisper. She pulled a small silver key from her pocket and slid it into the lock.

"Is this place alarmed?" asked Andrew in a concerned voice.

"Yes, but it's okay, I know the code and the control panel is in my dad's office."

"Very handy," said Andrew, rolling his eyes at Max.

"Wait here," she instructed and disappeared inside.

After a few moments she came out again. "Right," she said, "the alarm's off, you can come in now."

They walked into the gym, which was dimly lit with emergency lighting. It cast strange dark shadows about the place.

"Blimey," said Max, "this is bigger than our whole house." He wandered across the highly polished wooden floor. There were floor mats piled up in one corner and a horse bench next to them. Further along were some climbing ropes that hung from the ceiling. They were gathered together and held securely in place by a metal chain drilled into the wall. It was a large gym, much bigger than the one the boys were used to at their school. Sam looked up and saw that the ceiling was made of white polystyrene squares with small round lights inset into them. It had that gymnasium smell, almost rubbery, and every noise made was echoed off the walls, floor and ceiling. Max wandered off to have a look around.

"Max," yelled Sam in as loud a whisper as he dared. "If you screw this up! Get back here and don't say another word."

"Yes boss," said Max doing as his brother said.

They made their way across the floor, their outdoor shoes squeaking as they walked. Lucy crossed to a small door and fetched a smaller key from her pocket. She undid the lock and poked her head through, just to check no one was around. When she was sure no one was there she beckoned to the others to come.

"I think she's enjoying this," Andrew whispered to Max by his side.

"Right," said Max, grinning.

The door led onto a classroom. The boys could just make out the tables and chairs in the gloom. They crossed it quickly and came to another door. Lucy turned the handle and found this one unlocked. She turned to look at the boys and smiled. She went through, the boys followed and arrived at the bottom of the grand staircase that led up to the library. Dark shadows danced around them as they made their way through.

"Virtute et Veritate," Lucy muttered under her breath.

"What?" said Sam turning to face her.

"Virtuet et Veritate, that's the school motto, it means 'by virtue and truth'."

"Right," said Sam shaking his head, "I might have known it would be something honourable like that." Lucy caught the look on his face.

"Don't mock," she said looking insulted, "this is a very cultural place. Up there" she said further pointing up the stairs.

"I know," said Sam looking up, "we made it here before" and he started to climb the stairs, two at a time.

The others followed and they reached the top just as Sam disappeared into the massive library. Some emergency lights that looked completely out of place in such an old room dimly lit the shelves.

"So," he said as he pulled his rucksack off his back. "Remember we are looking for anything to do with pirates sailing in these waters. Black Heart might be mentioned himself, otherwise it's shipwrecks, smugglers anything like that." He reached into his bag and pulled out four torches all different sizes. "You and you," he said to Andrew and Max pointing across to his left, "start looking over there. Lucy, you start looking over here. I'm going up the top. If anyone finds anything, whistle. We'll rendezvous here in twenty minutes."

"Now who's enjoying himself?" Max whispered to Andrew. Andrew grinned and walked off to his allotted section. Max followed him and walked up and down the aisles shining his torch on the rows and rows of books stacked neatly on the old wooden shelves. Lucy went to the other end and started her search - for what she was not really sure. She still had a warm glow inside her from the afternoon spent with Sam, especially the bit where he had said he really liked her.

Sam climbed the spiral stairs trying to step as quietly as he could. He set to work on the first set of shelves he came across. The library fell into silence; the only sound was the occasional flick of a page. No one spoke, no one made a sound. Sam put down the fifth book he had tried and picked up the next one. He was starting to get restless, but he was also starting to feel strange again. He turned around, suddenly sure that someone was watching him, but no one was there. He turned back and out of the corner of his eye he saw something glisten at the end of the row. A shiver went down his spine and he had a sharp intake of breath.

"What is it?" he muttered under his breath. "What is it you want me to find?" He walked slowly to where the light from his torch had fallen. There on the shelf third from the left was a large red leather book. He reached out his hand and touched the now familiar marking that was embossed on the spine. His fingers tingled as they traced the outline of the man's head on a coin, then moved slightly and traced the outline of a skull and cross bones. He took hold of the book with both hands and lifted it effortlessly off the shelf. He carried it over to the window and placed it carefully on the wide stone ledge. Hands shaking, he opened the heavy cover and read the inside page, it said:

'Ledger XVII – Shipwrecks off the Cumbrian Coast.' Then in smaller letters underneath it said: "Contents of the Holds" and underneath that it read: *'Names of those lost to Davey Jones.'*

"This is it," thought Sam excitedly. He turned the next page but just then felt something brush against his shoulder. He jumped and turned suddenly staring into his brother's beaming face. "Have you found it?" his brother asked excitedly.

"Blimey Max, you nearly gave me a heart attack," he said, "don't go creeping around like that."

"Sorry," said his brother, "but I got this shiver all the way down my back and my hair started standing up so I figured you must have found something." Sam turned back to the book.

"Black Heart showed me," he said fixing his eyes on the old text.

The pages were yellowed with age and some of the ink had run over the years.

"Shine your torch on it, Max," he instructed his brother. Max obediently held his torch so that his brother could use two hands. Sam flipped through the pages searching for something, anything that seemed relevant. He ran his finger down each page looking for the words Black Heart or pirate or anything that might give him a clue. Page after page he turned hoping beyond hope that something would jump out of the page at him. He was three quarters of the way through when the shiver ran down his spine again. He felt his brother jump and turned to look into his face. Without saying a word, he really didn't need to; he turned the next page and started to read:

'Thirteenth Day of September in the year 1854 – The Onyx – Shipwrecked off the Sea Cove Coast – Debris found washed onto the beach Sea Cove and Coombe Bay.

Vessel Captain: Black Heart: sailed under skull and cross bones (body never found)

Contents of Ship's Hold: Never found but believed to include stolen hoard from McClinty coffin ship:

- Gold candlesticks - matching,
- Silver goblets - plain;
- Silver goblets embossed with rubies;
- Three bags of gold doublets;
- One brass chest of assorted jewellery;
- Seven gold signet rings;
- Three diamond rings;
- One ruby encrusted necklace.
- One gold plated Crucifix.
- Three gold Coronets;
- One silver sword;

– Leather bound Ledger- Ship's Log

The Onyx Crew Members:

Black Heart (never found), Sharpe, Hicks, Gore, Thompson, Winkler, Carruthers, Partridge, Fairweather, Caracus, Woods, Woods, Sharpe, Winter, Galley, Cook, Nancy, Brode, Brook, Tyler, Leek, Tuck, Read, Lucus, Friar (never found) & Jake Spode (never found).

Sam read the page again, something nagged at the back of his head - "one gold plated Crucifix" - he whispered to himself. "Coronets, leather bound ledger – Ship's Log; leather bound ledger- ship's log" he mouthed the words. "That's it!" he said louder than he should have - "the ship's log, we need to find the ship's log."

"Why?" asked Max.

"Because, dear brother, the ship's log is the place that Black Heart would have written down what happened, what really happened, don't you see?"

Hearing a shout Andrew and Lucy came running up the stairs.

"Have you found something?" Andrew asked, out of breath from taking the stairs two at a time. Lucy came up behind him.

"I think so," said Sam solemnly standing aside to show them the page he had been looking at. "It's the contents of the hold from Black Heart's ship, the Onyx, and it says that there was a logbook. I reckon if we find that we will have found the answers to what really happened."

"Black Heart's ghost is here helping us," said Max watching Lucy's face for a reaction. "Where?" she said, predictably, looking behind her.

"We both felt him," said Max, shaking with excitement. "He showed us where to look and which page and everything."

"Shut up," said Lucy, getting upset. "I don't like it; it's creepy enough in here as it is. Sam, make him stop." Max chuckled to himself having got the reaction he was looking for. Sam clipped him round the ear and he let out a yelp of pain.

Just then the library door swung open and Mr. Hawksclough walked in with a torch in his hand.

"Who's in here?" he said in a gruff voice. Sam pulled Max down onto the ground and put his hand over his mouth so that he wouldn't give the game away. Lucy and Andrew followed suit. They held their breath not daring to move. "I know you're in here, you devils," said Mr. Hawksclough in a raspy voice. He moved along the aisles of books shining his torch high and low. "It's you, interfering kids, from this afternoon, isn't it?" he said, straining as best he could to look around the corners. "I'll find you, you little rats, and when I do it's the police for you." He headed across the library and stood at the foot of the stairs. Sam risked looking up and saw shadows dancing across the walls where Mr. Hawksclough's torch was casting its light. He peered over the edge of the balcony just as the torch light swung up. He pulled his head back sharply. He heard Mr. Hawksclough start to climb the stairs, his shoes slowly scraping the metal with each footstep. Sam pulled Max up but kept a hand over his mouth. He motioned to Lucy and Andrew to get up. He felt a tingle run down his spine and felt his brother jump as well. "If you're going to tell me something, Black Heart," thought Sam, "now is the time." He backed away until his back was against a shelf loaded with books. Andrew and Lucy did the same, and then in horror he realized he had left the ledger out on the window. He whispered into his brother's ear:

"Don't move and for goodness' sake be quiet."

He crouched down and slowly crawled across the floor in the dark shadows trying to keep as small as possible.

He edged closer to the window and reached his arm up to the cold stone windowsill. His fingers made contact with the book and slowly raising his other arm he took hold of it and lifted it as quietly as possible. The ledger was heavy and it scraped across the window ledge as he tried to move it. "Damn," he thought, but Mr. Hawksclough's footsteps didn't seem to get any faster. He clutched the ledger to his chest and crept back to join the others in the dark shadows at the end of a row of ancient looking books. Mr. Hawksclough reached the top of the stairs.

"I've got you now," Sam heard him say as he swung his torch down the aisle. He pushed Max back hard against the wall and pressed his hand over his mouth so that he couldn't speak. Andrew and Lucy followed in a split second just before the light swung to where they had been standing. Sam felt an anger rising inside him. He was close he could feel it, but this silly old man was slowing him down. He was almost tempted to knock Hawksclough down, but the thought shocked him and he remained motionless.

The friends edged their way along the wall with their hands behind them feeling the wall as they went. Sam clung onto the ledger that was getting heavier and heavier in his arms. They reached an indent in the stone wall that was covered by an old tapestry of some famous battle or other and Sam felt the familiar shiver run down his spine.

"What, what is it?" he felt like yelling. Mr. Hawksclough's torchlight was getting closer as he shuffled along the shelves. The tapestry reached to the ground. Sam risked shining his torch and peeped behind the hanging wondering if there was enough room for four people to hide behind. With no other options he ducked behind the tapestry and held it out so that the others could follow. Then Max gave a cry of pain and the wall behind the four friends revolved. Before they knew what was happening they found themselves in complete darkness.

Chapter 36

The West Tower

All four stood stock still blinking in the darkness trying to get their eyes to work in the pitch black. A tiny window high up on the wall let in a very small amount of dim light from the bright lights that lit the outside of the school. Max bent down and rubbed his ankle.

"That hurt," he whispered in a harsh voice.

"Shhh," said Sam not daring to turn on his torch yet. "Nobody move." There was a feeling of space in front of them. They heard Mr. Hawksclough shuffle past and heard his faint voice.

"I know you're here somewhere," he said, "it's just a matter of time before I find you." They heard the faint sound of police sirens. "Aha," they heard Mr. Hawksclough say "here come reinforcements, you won't get far, you little devils." Then they heard him shuffle off again round the next set of shelves.

"Where are we?" whispered Lucy.

"Stuck in a dark hole by the looks of it," whispered Andrew sarcastically.

"What did you do, Max?" Sam asked, switching on his torch so that he could get an idea of where they were.

"Nothing," said Max "My foot tripped on something and I felt a hard, round stone-like thing under my hand, then my ankle cracked on something and the wall moved." Sam shone his torch ahead of him; they were standing on the edge of a slim staircase. "Blimey," he said, "everyone stand still." The steps were bare stone and looked slippery and worn with age.

"We must be in the West tower," said Lucy. "You can see a turret shape from the outside of the school, but I thought it was just for decoration, I didn't think there was anything here."

"It looks like a secret passage leading somewhere," said Sam, "just in the nick of time as well." The police sirens outside got louder and they heard Mr. Hawksclough move off, his steps ringing out as he shuffled back down the iron staircase.

"Ha ha very funny," said Andrew, laughing, "nick of time, very good." Sam looked at him as if he had gone mad "Well, I thought it was funny," he said.

Sam shone his torch ahead of them. The stairs descended steeply into the darkness below.

"This place looks kind of familiar," said Andrew. "It reminds me of the tunnel at Coombe Bay."

"Yeah," said Sam distantly.

"Do you reckon they join up?" Lucy asked, looking wide eyed, in front of her.

"I don't know," replied Sam "but as we can't go back that way, I guess we will find out." "I could have guessed you would say that," said Max.

"Well, has anyone got any better ideas?" asked Sam raising his voice and shining the torch so that he could see the others' faces.

"No," came the chorus.

"Right then," he said, "follow me."

They slowly made their way down the stairs. There was no rail to hang onto, just the wall to lean on.

"I don't like this," said Lucy stumbling slightly and bumping into Andrew.

"Everyone, take their time," instructed Sam.

"This is killing my leg," said Andrew. The stairs soon flattened out into a passage. It went straight for a while then started to slope downwards. In places it was completely pitch black. In others a vague bit of streetlight filtered in through long forgotten cracks in the rock. Down the path wound until in some parts steps had been hewn in the rock to make the slope more manageable.

They walked in silence, lost in their own thoughts. Off to the left there was a loud bang as if a door was being slammed shut and they heard raised voices. Sam thought he just caught a man's voice.

"I can't see anything, Mr. Hawksclough," the voice said, "and it doesn't look like anything has been taken but the back door is unlocked, and the alarm is off." He heard a muffled response but couldn't make out the words. They carried on until the tunnel opened out into a large chamber. The four spread out and using their torches started searching around the place.

It was dark and creepy, cobwebs hung from the walls and ceiling. There were wooden crates stacked in one corner but on inspection they were all empty.

"This is probably just an old storeroom or something," said Andrew shining his torch up onto the ceiling. "Judging by the cobwebs no one has been down here for ages, maybe years."

"There won't be any rats down here will there?" asked Lucy scanning the floor around her feet, "I hate rats."

"I doubt it," answered Sam. "There has to be stuff to eat before you get rats."

"What about skeletons?" she asked, feeling sick at the thought of running into a pile of old bones.

Max had wandered off to the other side of the chamber. He was ferreting around behind a pile of crates thinking that finding a rat or another skeleton would be a great idea, just to see Lucy's face. He shone his torch across the wall, then down onto the floor. "Hey, come and look at this," he called. The others went to see what he had found. On the floor was what looked like a loose flagstone. Sam bent down and ran his fingers around the crack that had been partially covered by dust over the years.

"Help me move this," he said putting the ledger down and getting hold of a crate that was half sitting over the square. Andrew helped him drag the crate away. Sam dug in his pocket for his penknife and scraped around the stone trying to get a leverage point. Andrew worked with his fingers trying to loosen some of the dirt. Sam jammed his knife into a spot that had become weaker and tried to get his fingers in underneath the stone. "Get your fingers in here, Max," he instructed his brother. Max bent down and tried to get a hold on the stone. Slowly, but surely, they scraped away enough dirt to reveal the lip of the stone. Sam rammed his knife down and there was a hiss of air from the side of the stone as if a valve had been let off. Max jumped back at the tingle that ran up his arm "Ouch," he said, "that was the strongest one yet." Andrew moved round to help the boys and Lucy got down on her knees to help too. Surprisingly it shifted more easily than they had thought.

"It was being held in place by some sort of vacuum or something," suggested Andrew as the sound of stone scraping on stone filled the chamber. Sam shone his torch into the black pit the stone had revealed.

"What's down there?" asked Max trying to see over Sam's shoulder.

"I can't see," answered his brother, "shine your torch down." Max shone his torch and the light revealed what looked like a very old wooden crate. The wood had started to rot away and the lid had slid half off. A black skull and cross bones marked the side and the lid and the words 'Onyx' had been painted crudely under it. The hole they had found was just big enough to hold the crate.

"Let's lift it up," suggested Sam and they each got hold of a part of the chest and heaved it up onto the floor of the chamber. The lid broke away as it banged against the top of the hole as it was dragged out.

They stood in silence for a moment, Lucy looking from Sam's face to Max's then to Andrew's. She nudged Andrew and he looked up to see the same awe-struck glow on the Forshaw boys' faces. Then Sam slowly knelt down by the chest and reached inside. His hands clasped something hard and cold; he pulled it out and saw that it was a gold candlestick. The light from the torches gave it a faint glow.

Chapter 37

The Golden Candlestick

Henry tossed and turned as he slept. He writhed around, his subconscious trying to tell him something. His legs got tangled around his duvet and he felt like he couldn't breathe. He lashed about wildly, trying to escape, his mind full of fear. Then a vision appeared across his eyes. A dark passage, four people hunched over something, the faint glow of something golden. In his dream he felt his chest tighten and the anger rise in his gut. He watched helplessly as he saw Sam Forshaw lift a golden candlestick from a hole in the ground and turn to smile.

"No," Henry screamed out loud, sitting bolt upright now fully awake. "Noooo," and he turned face down into his pillow and cried and cried.

Chapter 38

No Proof!

Sam reached into the crate again and brought out another candlestick, then a silver goblet. Other stuff lay wrapped in hessian on top of other things, which Sam knew now to be the contents of the hold from Black Heart's ship. He carefully lifted each piece out and laid it gently on the floor.

When the crate was empty he shone his torch all round. "It must be here somewhere," he said under his breath.

"What must?" said Lucy staring at the gold and silver pieces in front of her.

"The log, stupid," said Max, "he's looking for the log." Sam felt all round the inside of the crate wondering if it had stuck to the side somehow, but all he could feel was the rough texture of a jagged wooden box. He peered back inside the hole where the crate had come from and looked all around to see if anything had been left behind. Nothing, he couldn't find anything.

"It's not here," he said standing up suddenly.

"But it has to be," said Max staring up at his brother.

"Well it's not," said Sam. He walked off and sat down on the other side of the chamber with his knees curled up and his head resting on his arms. "Where is it?" he murmured under his breath, "where is it, you've brought us this far, help me."

"Who's he talking to?" asked Lucy, starting to feel extremely uneasy.

"Black Heart," said Max and he went to join his brother across the chamber. Andrew and Lucy exchanged glances and sat down where they were waiting for Sam's next move.

They didn't have to wait long. Sam lifted his head as if in a dream.

"Come on," he said, "there must be a way out of here, start looking for a concealed door or a hole in the rock that someone could squeeze through." Not liking to argue they all stood up and started searching the walls for any sign of an entrance, but they found nothing.

"It looks like the tunnel went this way once," said Andrew walking over to a huge pile of assorted rocks that had fallen in from the roof. He shone his torch up and down the debris. "But there's been a land slide or something. Any way out this direction was blocked a long time ago."

"I bet that passage joined up with the one leading from Coombe Bay," said Sam, joining Andrew with his torch. "It doesn't make sense that there are two separate passages." After a while Andrew said, "Perhaps we should just go back the way we came. I bet no one knows about the entrance in the library. We could sneak out that way and back to the gym."

"But the police are there," said Lucy, panicking, "and they'll have re-set the alarm by now. If we go out there we'll set them off."

"What choice do we have?" said Sam "We can't stay here all night."

"What if we get caught?" wailed Lucy.

"We'll just have to tell the truth," said Andrew. "That the Forshaw boys keep getting secret messages from their long-lost pirate Grandad who's shown them the way to some buried treasure."

"Sarcasm will get you nowhere," said Sam turning away from Andrew. "If we're lucky we can open a window or something and sneak out that way."

"What shall we do with this stuff?" asked Max staring at the treasure.

"Let's put it back until we are ready to tell people about it," said Sam. He had a strange sense that soon everyone would know about Captain Black Heart's loot. He just hoped he could find something to restore his great Grandad's honour, but at the present moment he felt very gloomy indeed.

Chapter 39

Max, Not just a little brother!

They set off back the way they had come following the passage back to the steps that led to the wall that led to the library. Sam pushed at the wall, but it didn't budge.

"There must be a lever or something like the one Max found on the other side," he said. They all started searching running their hands over the wall and down on the floor.

"Here's something," said Max his foot tripping up against what looked upon further inspection like a wooden lever.

"The door must be on a hinge somehow," said Andrew shining his torch over the doorway. "Whoever built this passage knew what they were doing," he said. Max kicked the lever and they felt the stone underneath their feet rotate bringing them back into the darkness of the library, the entrance hidden by the huge tapestry.

Everything was quiet and dark. Mr. Hawksclough had gone for his cocoa a while ago, the place was deserted. They crept forwards and down the spiral stairs and crossed the room to the great oak door. Andrew got there first and slowly turned the handle to let them out. The door wouldn't budge.

"Oh no," he said, "it's locked." They looked around for an alternative exit, but this was the only door into the library.

"Try the windows," said Sam, striding over to the wall. The windows in the library were not just any old windows;

on this level they were made of beautiful stained glass, they depicted the scene of St. Betha crossing the Irish Sea and laying claim to Lord Netherfield's land. As with all stained glass they were lead-lined with only a very small part that opened. They tried them all along the back wall but none of them budged.

"They've probably been sealed shut," said Andrew. "They did that to the windows in the Priory a few years ago, it stops the damp getting into the lead and ruining them."

"There's only one thing for it," said Sam standing tall. "We'll have to break one and make a run for it."

"Oh, we can't," said Lucy, tears welling in her eyes, "these windows go back centuries, they are part of our heritage." The tears started rolling down her cheek.

"Well, which do you prefer, Lucy," said Sam harshly, "to stay here all night and get found in the morning by Mr. Hawksclough who will send for the police straight away and get done for breaking and entering, or be safely back in your bed out of the way?" Lucy didn't answer. She stood quietly, tears rolling down her cheeks.

"Right," said Sam, "I've seen this done in the movies." He took off his sweater. "Find something hard I can use like a brick or something." Max looked around and saw an iron doorstop resting against the wall.

"Will this do?" he asked picking the thing up with an effort.

"Perfect," said Sam. "I suppose you do have your uses after all, little brother," he said sarcastically.

"Pleased to be of service," said Max.

"Just get on with it," Lucy snapped.

Sam took his jumper and wrapped it around the doorstop and with a mighty thrust hurled it through the nearest window. The glass shattered and there was a thud as the iron weight landed onto the ground outside.

"Give me your jumper, Max," he said. Max pulled his jumper over his head and Sam wound it round his arm and broke off the pieces of glass left sticking out of the window. "Andrew, you go first and help the others down," he instructed. Andrew climbed carefully up onto the window ledge.

"There's over two metres to drop here," Andrew said as he hesitated on the ledge.

"Can you hold onto anything?" asked Sam panic rising in his voice.

"Wait a minute," said Andrew feeling round the outside of the building. "There's a drainpipe here. If I can just swing my leg over and grab hold," he said straining to reach the pipe. He got a firm hold as best he could with his bad leg and dropped lightly onto the ground outside. He stood up hobbling momentarily as the pain returned to his injured leg, but it subsided and he took up position ready to help the others. Lucy went next, sobbing softly into the sleeve of her jumper. Andrew helped her as best he could. When she was out, Sam helped Max climb onto the windowsill and watched him drop down. Then with a wistful look behind him he too climbed up onto the ledge and swung round to catch the drainpipe. He dropped down onto the soft earth below with a thud.

"Is everyone OK?" asked Sam as he unfolded himself from the floor.

"Yes, yes, yes," came the whispered replies.

"Good, let's get home," he said. Without another word they scurried away. Lucy peeled away into the shadows, still sobbing. She darted across the road and slunk into her back garden. The three boys ran as fast as they could up the Main Street.

"Wait for me," said Andrew, his leg clearly causing him some pain.

They saw no one and as they reached Andrew's house he turned and whispered, "See you tomorrow," and limped off to his back door. The two Forshaws stuck to the houses. Eventually they reached their own house and slid silently in through the back door. They crept up the stairs and into their rooms. Sam leant against his bedroom door gasping for breath. He started to take his clothes off when he heard the sounds of his father getting up next door. He held his breath waiting for his dad to come marching in and for all hell to break loose, but he gently let out a slow sigh as he heard his father cross the landing to the bathroom. He jumped into bed as quickly as he could and finished getting undressed under the covers. He checked the alarm clock - 3:45pm. "Oh well," he muttered, "better than last time," and he fell into a deep sleep.

Chapter 40

Grandad Collapses – Pirate Secrets

When Sam went downstairs the next morning his mother was on the phone. He stood in the hallway listening to the conversation.

"What do you mean it's his destiny, it's just a load of old garbage and you should know better than to fill the head of a young dreamer with such ideas." She banged her coffee cup down and it slopped over the edge onto the side. She reached for a cloth and started scrubbing the spill with a fierce intensity. "I don't care," he heard her say. "There is no such thing as ghosts as well you know, you'll have the lad scared half to death. No dad," she continued, "I have not felt the slightest bit strange recently and you are not in any way related to a pirate. No, I am not the odd one out here and no, I don't think it has skipped a generation. Now can we change the subject, please?"

Just then Max came crashing down the stairs.

"What's for breakfast, mum?" he called as he swung past Sam. "I'm starving." Sam gave a jump and pretended he had been just about to go through. His mother gave him a stern look.

"Sam, your Grandad wants to talk to you," she scolded handing Sam the phone. He took it slowly off her.

"Hi Grandad," he said in a quivering voice.

"Are you alright, lad?" his Grandad asked.

"Yeah," lied Sam. He felt far from all right.

"Keep going, you mustn't give in," his Grandad sounded out of breath.

"Right," said Sam trying to sound chirpy.

"I mean it," said his Grandad. "You must find the treasure; you must get there first, there is another." His voice trailed off and Sam heard his Grandad gasping for breath.

"Grandad, Grandad," Sam said loudly. "Are you okay?"

"Son," came the raspy voice again. "Watch your back, there is another. He will try and get there first, Sam." Sam heard a muffled noise and then silence on the other end of the phone. "Grandad, Grandad!" he screamed. His mother, filled with terror, snatched the phone out of his hands.

"Dad," she yelled, panic choking her words. "Dad, are you there? Dad answer me." Then Sam heard a woman's voice come on the line.

"Mrs. Forshaw, I think you should come over immediately. Your father has collapsed; I'll ring for an ambulance, please hurry."

"Oh Dad," cried Mrs. Forshaw as she put down the phone. She turned to look at the boys. "Your Grandad has collapsed," she said wiping the tears from her face. "I've got to get over there."

"I'm going, too," said Sam standing up and moving towards the door.

"No," said his mother, "I don't know how bad he is; you should stay here and look after Max."

"I'm coming with you," he said firmly. "I'm not letting you go on your own. Max will be all right won't you, Max?" he said, turning to face his brother.

"Yes," said Max through a shaky voice. "I'll be okay, Sam should go with you, mum. I'll stay here and ring Dad. Anyway, Jet will need a walk soon." Mrs. Forshaw was in such a fluster that she just nodded meekly and grabbed her coat.

"Come on then," she said and followed Sam out of the door.

"It's going to be alright, mum," Sam said as they climbed into the car. His mother turned to look at him her eyes bleary with tears. "It really will, mum, don't ask me how I know but it will."

"Yes, of course, dear," she said. "Oh, if only I hadn't shouted at him, him and his silly pirate stories." Sam kept quiet; he knew better than to put up an argument at a time like this.

The roads were unusually busy for this time of day. They got stuck in road works and it seemed nearly every set of traffic lights was against them. It seemed like an eternity before they even got to the outskirts of Whitefield. Sam wasn't sure his mother should be driving, the state she was in, but eventually they arrived. Sam read the board that stood outside the gates of the home, 'Beech Wood House, Luxury Accommodation for the Elderly.'

There was a lady in a nurse's uniform waiting outside. When she saw them arrive she ran over to the car.

"Mrs. Forshaw, I'm so glad you made it. They've taken your father to Whitefield Hospital. They think he's had a heart attack. Nurse Hunter has gone in the ambulance with him. If you don't mind, I'll jump in with you and help you cut through the red tape the other end." She jumped in the back seat and they set off for the Hospital. It was an experience that would stay with Sam for a long, long time.

His Grandad had been taken to the cardiac ward. There were only four beds arranged in a square. Surprisingly none of the other beds was being used; there was just his Grandad lying still on his bed. His eyes were closed and he had a mask over his face to help him breathe. A nurse greeted them and showed them across to his bedside. His mother was in floods of tears and ran over to her father's side. A nurse pulled up a chair for her. She flopped down and held onto her father's hand, sobbing into her hanky. Sam stood by her shoulder choking back the tears.

His Grandad looked really frail and old. He seemed to have shrunk since the last time he had seen him and his skin looked sallow.

"How is he?" asked Mrs. Forshaw in a shaky voice.

"He's poorly but stable," said the nurse. "We think he's had a heart attack but we're not sure why he won't wake up. We are running some tests which should help determine what is wrong."

"Is he going to die?" she asked, choking back the tears.

"It's too early to say," said the nurse resting her hand on her shoulder. "He just seems to be sleeping. There are no obvious signs of a stroke or anything else wrong with him; he just seems to be resting. That happens sometimes," she went on, "when the body has had a shock it can close down sometimes, and people can fall into a deep sleep. It's the body's way of saying, stop world, I need to take five." She smiled at them. "We have made him as comfortable as we can; now it's just a waiting game."

"Right," said his mother.

"I'll fetch you a nice cup of tea," said the nurse. "Would you like one, young man?" she asked, turning to Sam.

"Erm no, no, thank you," he said not taking his eyes off his Grandad.

"Here son, you sit with him for a while," said his mother, "I'll go and ring your father." His mother got up and went to find a phone.

Sam sat down and reached out to take hold of his Grandad's hand. With the other hand he reached up and touched his Grandad's face. As he touched his skin he felt a tingle run up his arm. He heard his Grandad gasp for breath, and then a bright light flashed all around him. His head spun and he felt like he was falling. He felt the beads of sweat form on his Grandad's forehead or, was it his head? - he couldn't tell. He shut his eyes tightly as his head spun.

"Oh no," he muttered under his breath not knowing whether he was awake or dreaming. "Not again, what are you going to show me this time?"

Sam heard the waves crashing onto the rocks. He knew that sound, he heard it nearly every day. Only this time it was loud, really loud and he felt the sea spray splatter onto his face. His head stopped spinning and he saw that he was standing on the rocks at the bottom of Sea Cove Head. In front of him were two boys busy scrambling from rock to rock. The one in the lead jumped his way boldly across channels that the sea had made around the cliffs. The second boy followed more carefully often using his hands to stabilise himself. From what Sam could see they both looked slightly older than he was. He knew instantly who the first person was.

"Grandad," he sighed. But the second person he didn't recognise. Through his dream Sam racked his brain to think of someone his Grandad might have mentioned growing up, but nothing came to him.

The boys slowly made their way round the head and ducked out of sight into the caves that cut underneath the Head in places. Sam followed and listened to the conversation that was taking place.

"Well it must be here," he heard his Grandad say. "This is the place I saw in my dream. We should check the back wall to find a secret door."

"Do you think it's going to be that easy?" asked the other boy apprehensively.

"Of course, Spode, you idiot," his Grandad replied, "I've seen it all. Black Heart showed me." Sam froze.

"Spode," he repeated under his breath in disbelief. "Grandad was friendly with a Spode!"

"Come on," his Grandad said, imploringly. "We need to be off the rocks before the tide comes in or we're goners. Get looking."

The boy called Spode edged his way to the back wall and gingerly ran his fingers over the rocks. To Sam's amazement his Grandad reached into his trouser pocket and pulled out the knife he had given to him. He flicked up the blade and started scratching at the rock, trying to find something, anything. Sam caught the look in his Grandad's eyes. He knew that feeling; it was a desperation the like of which he had felt himself. He recognised the hunger in his Grandad's eyes, the deep need to find a clue, an answer to the Black Heart mystery.

"But you're looking in the wrong place," he heard himself say.

His vision flickered for a moment and he saw the shadow of his Grandad lying still on his hospital bed, a tense look fixed onto his face. He blinked and watched as the boys tracked across the wall, looking for an entrance to a passage that he knew wasn't there. Ages passed and Sam heard the roar of the sea as the tide turned slowly making its way in again. He watched his Granddad's anguish as realisation dawned on him that he wasn't going to find anything.

"We have to go," came Spode's voice over the roar of the waves.

"But it has to be here," he heard his Grandad almost wail. "It has to be. I have to do this; I cannot pass this burden on." His hand reached up to his throat and he grasped the half coin medallion that hung on a brown leather cord. "Don't you feel anything, Will?" he shouted at Spode, "Nothing at all?"

"No," Spode shouted back and again to Sam's amazement Spode reached inside his shirt and pulled out the other half coin necklace. He held it up so that it spun in the wind. "Ever since you gave me this I have felt nothing. I don't know what you mean when you say it makes you tingle. It was a nice gift, mate, don't get me wrong, but that's all. I don't feel anything else. We have to go, now." Sam watched in amazement as Will Spode tucked the medallion back inside his shirt. "Come on," he said. "Forget it. It's just a dream, a story. It sounded good up until now and I've gone along with it because I'm your best mate, but, Sam, it really is time to go now." Sam gasped at the sound of his name. Then slowly let his shoulders relax.

"Of course," he said almost mockingly, "Grandad is called Sam as well. That's who I'm named after."

Will gripped his Grandfather's arm and dragged him towards the entrance. His Grandad's feet moved as if in a dream. They reached the cave mouth and the sea spray whipped up and covered them in salty water. The wind howled and the boys were forced backwards trying to catch their breath as the wind tried to steal it away. Sam felt a shiver run down his spine and he felt himself tense.

As he watched he saw the glow in his Grandad's eyes. He saw his Grandad turn to face Will and saw the look of pure hatred on his face. Will jumped back in fright not knowing what was happening to his best friend.

"What's the matter?" Will asked nervously. "What's the matter with your face?" Sam watched as his Grandad walked forward. His hands reached down to his waist and he looked like he was pulling something out from his side. He held it up in front of him and Sam thought he saw a glint of light on metal.

"Stop it, mate," Will said, his voice shaking. "You're scaring me."

"Well, good," said a deep voice that came from his Granddad's mouth. "This is the second time I have tried to find what is mine, Spode, you evil murderer, and yet again it seems you have thwarted my plans."

"What," said Will backing into the cave wall, "I don't know what you're on about, mate, but this isn't funny." Sam's Grandad laughed a deep, chilling laugh and raised the thing in his hands towards Will.

"You see this sword, Spode?" he said raising his arms higher.

"What, have you gone mad?" Will shouted, but Sam saw the look on Spode's face as the light shining through the sea mist caught the edge of something metal. "Oh my," Will muttered, terror hanging on every word. "Sam, what is happening?"

"This body is strong," Sam heard his Grandad say, "but perhaps not strong enough. I cannot see the way. I cannot see the entrance. I fear the time is not yet right." Sam watched as his Grandad faltered, but what ever was going through his head passed quickly. Sam watched in horror as what must have been Black Heart regained control and moved closer towards where the petrified Spode was quivering against the hard rock.

"This isn't happening," Will cried as the spray flew into his face. "Sam, please stop it." Sam raised his arms as if holding a heavy weight. Sam could see a sword in his Grandfather's hands and watched helplessly as he slowly brought the tip down over Will's heart. "Sam," sobbed Spode, "Sam, come back. Get a grip, Sam, don't do this. What ever happened in the past, Sam, is in the past. This is me, your best mate, please Sam stop it." His Grandfather hesitated again and blinked as if to get something out of his eye. It was enough. Will threw himself at him launching all his weight into the attack. The two boys rolled over the rocks, neither able to get a grip of the other, each slipping and sliding over the seaweed that gripped the rocks, the incoming tide making things worse.

"Get off me," Sam heard his Grandad say. His voice had returned to normal. "What are you doing, you idiot? You'll drown us both."

"Oh Sam," Will gasped releasing his grip. "Thank goodness, it's you."

"Well who else would it be?" his Grandad said in a sarcastic voice.

"You mean you don't remember?"

"Remember what?" his Grandad replied impatiently. "Let's get out of here before we're cut off." He rolled onto his feet and made his way slipping and sliding out of the cave onto the rocks that led back to the safety of the beach. Staring after him in disbelief Spode gathered himself together and followed.

Sam opened his eyes and realized that he was staring into his Grandad's eyes and they were staring back.

"Grandad," he said looking around him. He was in the hospital. "Of course, where else would I be?" he scolded himself. "Are you all right?" he asked.

"Aye lad," his Grandad rasped weakly. "It takes more than a dickey heart to keep a pirate down," he said with a glint in his eye.

"Oh, dad you had us all so worried," said his mother rushing over.

"Don't fuss, love," Grandad said, "I'm all right; I just had a funny turn."

"You look so pale, dad, how do you feel?"

"A bit fuzzy in the old brain box but no damage done, I don't think. I'm sure I'll be on my feet in a few days."

"We'll see about that," said the nurse coming back over. "You should rest now Mr. Black, you've been through enough excitement for one day." She turned to Mrs. Forshaw, "Perhaps you should go now, we'll take good care of your father. He needs to rest now. Come back tomorrow and well have him up in his chair."

"Right," said Mrs. Forshaw. "If you're sure, dad."

"I'm sure, love, I'll see you tomorrow." Mrs. Forshaw turned to go but Sam lingered by his Grandad's bed.

"Son," his Grandad said quietly. "I told you. I tried but failed. I wasn't strong enough. I wasn't the one. Now you have to reach the treasure before Spode does."

"Spode," said Sam. "You mean Henry Spode; he is the other one looking for the treasure?"

"Oh, Sam, my boy, sometimes I wonder what fills that space between your ears. Of course, Spode, Henry is it? Who else would it be? He is the direct descendant of the man that killed Black Heart. He is Will Spode's Grandson. One hundred and fifty years, Sam, this is the last chance to lay Black Heart to rest, do you think the ghost of Spode would just sit around and let things all get sorted out after what you just saw?"

"No, I suppose not," said Sam feeling a right idiot. "That explains a lot of things," he said as he turned to walk away. Then he stopped and turned back. He leaned close to his Grandad and whispered: "I've found it, Grandad. I've found the treasure, but it's no good. I need to find the logbook." His Grandfather's face illuminated for a minute.

"You've found it, where?"

"Buried inside the school. I'll explain everything when we get you out of here, but it's no good. It doesn't prove anything. I'm going to keep looking." Then he turned and followed his mother out of the room.

"Good luck Sam, stay strong," his Grandfather called as Sam disappeared out of the door.

"What was all that about?" Mrs Forshaw asked him as they walked down the corridor.

"Oh, nothing, mum," he lied. She stared at him knowing there was something going on. Sam felt like he would burst and came very close to telling her everything, but he just smiled and walked on. Mrs. Forshaw drove home feeling a lot better than she had on the way.

When they got home, Max was out playing with his friend Nolan. Sam didn't feel like doing anything in particular and spent the day moping around, watching telly and playing on his computer. Max and Nolan came rushing in at one point and headed upstairs to get something from Max's room. Sam noticed that as they passed his room Nolan seemed to stare at him. The boys seemed to be doing a lot of whispering.

"Hi Nolan," he called knowing that the boys were standing right outside his room.

"H.. Hi Sam," came Nolan's scared voice.

"What are you two up to?" he asked.

"Oh nothing," Max piped in a voice that sounded very suspicious to Sam. "Come on, Nolan," he said, "let's go." Sam had a feeling that they were up to something.

"Max," he said coolly. Max poked his head back around Sam's door. "Please tell me you haven't told Nolan anything, have you?"

"No," said Max hurriedly and ran off down the stairs before Sam could say anything else.

"Max, this is important," he yelled as Max disappeared out of sight. There was no reply "The little rat bag," he muttered and turned back to his game. That evening Max seemed to Sam to be all of a sudden very helpful to his mother, it was almost as if he was trying to keep away from him. "I'll kill him if he's told Nolan," he thought to himself. Then thought, "Maybe it doesn't matter. What harm can it do?"

Chapter 41

The Pirate Curse – The Last Stand

The next morning Sam's father came in carrying the paper.

"There was a break in at the big school the other night," he said peering over the top of the Sea Cove News. "One of the original stained-glass windows was smashed, police think, from the inside. It says here that Mr. Hawksclough the Librarian thinks it was a group of young boys whom he had chased off the premises earlier that day."

"Was anything stolen?" asked his mother putting down a mug of tea in front of him.

"It says nothing was stolen and nothing seems to have been disturbed," read his father. Sam caught Max's eye and looked straight back at his plate.

"What are you boys up to today?" Mrs. Forshaw asked.

"Not much," said Max diving into a piece of toast and marmite.

"What about you, son?" she asked Sam.

Before he could answer the doorbell rang. Mrs. Forshaw went to answer it and came back smiling. "It's for you," she said. Sam got up and went to the door.

"Oh, hi Lucy," he said and pulled the door too behind him. He lowered his voice, "Did you get back in okay?" he asked.

"Yeah, no problems, both mum and dad are sound sleepers," she said. "Look, I've been thinking," she said excitedly, "I reckon I know where the logbook is you've been looking for." Sam stared at her.

"Where?" he asked, trying to conceal his excitement.

"I heard my dad talking at breakfast about the break in at the school and he started talking about all the valuable stuff that's in the place. You know old stuff. He said that over the years they must have accumulated millions of pounds worth of stuff. Then he went onto say that he heard a story when he was a boy about smugglers operating off the Sea Cove coast, he said they used secret passages that they dug into the rocks that brought them out into the monastery that used to be on the site the school is now on. He said they had a secret way of opening the entrance to the tunnel and only those blessed with the knowledge could make it work." Sam looked into Lucy's eyes.

"Blessed with the knowledge," he whispered, "but how does Mr. Collins know about the entrance?"

"Well I was thinking," she continued. "The Priory used to be part of the old monastery so maybe the tunnel you followed was the original one that came out in the school; well you know, the monastery then. And because you are related to Black Heart you were able to open the tunnel."

"Oh no," thought Sam "what else has she worked out?"

"But what about the log?" Sam asked checking over his shoulder that nobody was listening.

"Well dad said that some stuff is kept in the Priory to this day, you know stuff the monks kept, mainly papers, writs from ships and monastery stuff. He says a lot of it was destroyed in the fire back in the 1800's but some of it is still there, maybe the log you're looking for is in there somewhere."

"Come on," said Sam, grabbing her arm. "Let's look." Before Lucy could open her mouth to complain she found herself running down the street trying to keep up with Sam.

They sprinted down Main Street and only slowed up as they approached the Priory grounds. Sam looked over towards the school. There was still a police car parked in the school car park, its lights flashing. He caught sight of an Officer walking round the outside of the building and guessed there would be more inside. Lucy came gasping up behind him. She too had seen the police car but thought it best not to say anything. They caught their breath and walked into the West door of the Priory trying to look like they belonged there. Sam tensed as he walked past the worn sandstone columns that supported the old roof. He knew this building was old but now he felt it in his bones.

"Let's try over here," Lucy whispered as she walked down the side aisle.

A lady kneeling down silently praying at the front of the church looked up and smiled at the youngsters. Sam nodded at her and followed Lucy to the glass covered display cases that lined one side of the top of the church. They bent their heads and searched across the old papers and scrolls that were laid out for visitors and those interested in local history to see.

Nothing sprung out at them as Sam had hoped. The lady praying got up and made her way out of the big doors at the back. Sam looked around him. The west side of the Priory seemed older than the east side. He walked across and stared at the stained-glass windows that lined the wall. They were beautiful and Sam noticed how the light shone through them like a prism making patterns on the stone floor. A pang of guilt hit him as the realization of what he had done in the library dawned on him. It was then that he heard a scuffling sound coming from the corner. He looked round but couldn't see anything.

He walked up towards where the noise had come from and heard a muffled noise, almost like someone trying to speak but being stopped by someone else's hand over their mouth. He stopped in his tracks and waited; a dark feeling came over him. "Spode," he whispered to himself. A large white marble statue stood out half across the aisle marking the end of the main part of the church from the side wing and a thick purple velvet curtain was drawn across the aisle. Sam took a deep breath and sprang round the curtain.

"Got you, Spode, you murdering traitor," he was shocked at the sound of his own voice it sounded rich and deep.

As if in a dream, he went to pull his sword from his belt. He knew there was nothing there, but his arm felt heavy as if he really was holding a sword. He looked down and the light from the window glinted off metal for a split second.

"Ah Black Heart, so we meet again," came an oily voice from the shadows. Henry Spode stood up, but he had a strange look in his eyes. "I thought I had got rid of you once before, you wretched man, now it seems I'm going to have to do it again." He reached down to his side and seemed to pull something out of his belt and wielded it at Sam. Sam hesitated, "this can't be happening" he tried to tell himself, but he could feel an anger welling up inside him. He saw Henry lunge at him and he sprang back. He felt the tip of something sharp touch his stomach. He held his sword up as Henry came at him again, this time whipping his sword up and down, trying to get at Sam's body. Sam parried the blows and thrust back towards Henry. His head felt dizzy, he tried to think straight but he felt out of control. A red mist had descended over his eyes and he felt angry, really angry.

"What are you two doing?" came a voice from the shadows. Tezz hiding in the corner tried to stand up but Henry pushed him back.

"Get out of the way you idiot. This has nothing to do with you."

"Henry, what's the matter with your voice?" he asked backing away from his best friend.

"We have business to attend to, child," Sam heard himself say, "leave now while you still can."

Tezz stared in disbelief from Henry to Sam, then scuttled round the statue and ran down the church desperate to get away from the madness that was happening behind him. In his confusion he wasn't looking where he was going and bumped straight into Lucy who was just walking up the aisle looking for Sam.

"Hey, watch it," she said angrily. "What's the matter with you?" she asked taking hold of Tezz's shoulders. "What are you running away from?"

"They've gone mad," he spluttered tipping his head towards the side wing, "they're fighting with imaginary swords only their voices have changed."

"What are you talking about, is this some sort of joke?" she scolded crossly.

"I'm not joking," he replied, "I'm getting out of here."

"What? You can't, wait," she said trying to hold onto him, but he pulled away and ran out of the back door.

Lucy turned and heard the sound of steel clashing on steel.

"Oh, my goodness," she muttered, "what is happening?" She ran to the front and crossed over to the side wing. She nervously peeped round the statue and couldn't believe her eyes. There were Sam and Henry glaring at each other. She noticed the intense look in their eyes, it was pure hatred. Both boys were sweating profusely as they circled cat-like around each other. Henry spat at Sam's feet and Sam lunged at him.

"I won't let you get away with this," Sam's voice rasped out. Henry laughed a horrible evil laugh.

"I already have, Captain," he said in a voice that was full of spite, "I ran my sword through your black heart once and I will do it again now." He lunged at Sam again, but Sam was too quick for him and leapt out of the way.

"You are scum, Spode," Sam yelled at him "I will not be caught this time, you murdering fool. Did you think I would let you get away with this? My time has come. I go to the land of my father's where your soul cannot go. You are banished, Spode, as well you know and I will be caught in this purgatory with you no more."

They circled each other again. Henry lunged but Sam knocked the blow aside and thrust upwards. Henry jumped backwards into the curtain. Lucy gasped and jumped out of the way as Sam's sword stabbed into the space she had just filled. Sam stared at Lucy; he was vaguely aware of her standing there. "Get a grip," he heard a voice in his head say, "hold it together, what is happening to you?"

"Sam," Lucy cried staring at him. "Sam, what's going on?" Sam opened his mouth to reply but a wave of emotion rolled over him.

Lucy thought that his eyes darkened and when he spoke it was a voice like thunder that made her bones tremble and her skin shiver.

"I am Black Heart," she heard him say. He turned to face Henry; his sword raised in two hands above his head. "I am Captain Black Heart of the mighty vessel, The Onyx." He strode towards Henry, a fire burning in his belly. "One hundred and fifty years I have waited for this moment." Henry backed up against the wall, his sword gripped tightly in both hands. "The others were not strong enough, they tried to help me, but they couldn't, the time wasn't right." He advanced on Henry who edged further back. He somehow seemed smaller. "This body is strong." He loomed over Henry. "You will pay, Spode," he raised the sword and pointed the tip at Henry. "You will pay right now, you scum." He swung the sword round and Lucy heard a loud clang of metal on metal. Henry caught the blow with his sword, but the sheer force made him fall over. He rolled again and again trying to escape Black Heart's mad lunging.

"Stop him," screamed Henry. This time it was Henry's voice. Lucy stepped forwards into the chamber. "For Goodness' sake, Lucy, stop him. It's Black Heart, he's taken over Sam's body, help me." Black Heart swung again and this time Henry didn't move fast enough. Black Heart brought the tip of his sword down and rested it against Henry's heart. Henry stopped wriggling and froze on the spot. His breathing was hard and fast and he could feel the steel tip pressing against his skin.

"Please," he sobbed, not daring to move, terrified at the sight in front of him. "Please Sam don't." Black Heart raised his sword. "Go to meet your Maker, Spode, rot in hell."

"No," screamed Lucy. She sprang at Sam knocking him out of the way. They rolled over in a desperate struggle.

"Sam," she called through her tears. "Sam come back. Sam, it's me Lucy." She felt his body relax, his muscles released their grip on her and he rolled over onto his back staring up at the ceiling.

He gasped for breath trying to understand where he was and what had just happened. He turned his head and saw Lucy lying next to him tears streaming down her face, then he saw Henry backed up against the wall trembling with fright.

"What just happened?" he managed to squeak out.

"I don't know," said Lucy, "I think Black Heart and Spode were here, they took over your bodies and you were fighting." Sam rolled onto his knees his head was banging. He looked over at Henry.

"Are you, all right?" he asked trying to shake the fog that seemed to be clouding his vision.

Henry didn't say anything. He slowly stood up and edged his way to the curtain.

"You're mad," he said trying to hold back the tears, still visibly shaking. "I had a dream the other night that some idiot called Friar had hidden the precious logbook you are looking for in here somewhere. Then I heard your brother talking yesterday to his mate about how desperate you were to find it because it might tell you where the treasure is hidden. I came here to look; I thought if I found it first I would be able to find the treasure."

"How do you know about the treasure?" Lucy asked getting to her feet. She looked from Henry to Sam and back again.

"I know because I am Spode's last remaining blood relative, you idiot. Lover boy here isn't the only one who has pirate ancestry. Plus, I've seen him find it in a dream," he said pointing savagely at Sam.

"You mean you are great, great, however many it is, Grandson of the man that killed Black Heart?" she asked in amazement.

"Yes, he is," said Sam standing up. He leaned heavily against the wall. "He was supposed to stop me finding the treasure," he said, still winded from the battle he had just fought.

"Well you haven't found it yet have you, Forshaw?" Henry said laughing through gritted teeth, "and I reckon you've just about run out of time." With that he turned on his heels and ran down the main aisle and out of the church into the bright sunshine.

Lucy turned to Sam. "Are you, all right?" she asked not knowing whether to fling her arms around him or what to do.

"Yeah, I'm fine," Sam replied despondently holding onto his side. "I guess that's it then, Spode was right, I've failed Black Heart." He turned his head hanging low and headed back through the curtain.

"We'll see about that," said Lucy striding past him.

"What are you doing?" he asked. "It's over, Lucy, can't you understand that, it's over? I failed, it's done, finished, let's just go home and forget any of this ever happened."

Lucy ignored him and marched over to the glass case they had looked at before. She dug her hand into her jeans pocket and pulled out a penknife, which she carefully inserted into the lock that held the glass in place.

"What are you doing?" Sam asked horrified at what she was doing.

"I saw this in the movies once," she said, smiling at him. The lock clicked and the glass cover opened. She reached inside and took a battered leather journal from its resting place at the back of the cabinet. "This looks like the oldest thing in here to me," she said and started flicking through the pages.

It was some sort of list of names. "Probably the people who used to come here to worship," she said as she reached the middle of the book. She flicked to the end. "There must be something here," she said, sounding a little too desperate as she started going through the book again. Sam watched in silence as page after page of swirly writing floated past his eyes. She reached the end of the book again and was just turning over the back cover to close the book.

"Stop," Sam said. Lucy froze as if a deadly snake were about to bite her. "Give me your knife," Sam instructed.

She obediently handed over her knife, which he took in his trembling hands. He laid the book onto the flat surface of the adjoining cabinet and very carefully ran the knife round the edge of the book. He lifted the paper to reveal a small, creased and very yellowed with age, brown leather book that had fitted snugly into the inside cover of the journal.

"Oh, my goodness," said Lucy squealing with delight, "that's it, isn't it? That's it." Sam silently eased the back away from the book with the knife and gently took hold of the fragile log in his fingers. He stooped down to read the words on the front cover, they were barely visible.

'This be the true account of Capt. Black Heart, Pirate, and the journeys made by the Onyx. May who ever finds this treasure use it well. It was signed *Capt. Black Heart.*

He turned to the first page. The ink had smudged and he couldn't make out the words. The next few pages were stuck together and there was a sheet missing on the next page. Sam could see the jagged edge left by the fold in the middle. His heart skipped a beat, was there anything in here, had he come this far for nothing. His breathing had become shallow and strained; he turned over the next page and read the swirly text in front of him.

'And so it was, that we boarded the stricken vessel and found there not more than 10 poor beggars still alive, all moaning and writhing in pain close to death. Those that were dead already, from starvation and disease lay rotting where they fell. The storm was rising as if to send that miserable ship to its unhappy end. The stench on board was revolting. My crew retched at the sight of those poor bastards sent to their doom by the fat Lord Blaney. The worst sight, which I shall never forget till my dying day, was the sight of two young 'uns, all skin and bone lying huddled together at the

bow of the ship. Dead from cold or starvation, it was hard to tell which. I knelt down and prayed to God for the souls of the innocent to be redeemed. I had given up hope of finding anyone capable of telling the truthful tale of their woeful voyage, when I heard a moan from the Captain's Cabin. There, moments away from death, himself lay the head of the household. His name I discovered was Patrick McClinty, his papers said he once owned a large number of potato fields back in Ireland, but plague must have struck and rendered him and his family homeless and penniless.

As he lay dying on the mattress he begged me to take his hoard, to smuggle it somewhere safe, to keep it away from that greedy vilain back home. Before his last breath I swore an oath to take it and take it I did.'

Sam read on:

There are those who would take that treasure and claim it as their own, "I bet he meant Jake Spode." thought Sam to himself '*John Friar be the only man I trust now amongst the crew, only he knows the entrance to the passage that leads to a place where the hoard will be safe. If I meet my Maker before he does he has sworn an oath to hide the treasure and this log for my son or his son to find so as they may know that Captain Black Heart was a God-fearing man who did what he had to do, to right wrongs. To take from those that had plenty and give it to those who needed it most.*

May those we came across today find peace with the divine Maker, may God rest their souls.

Underneath the text it was dated *Thirteenth Day of September in the year of Our Lord 1854.*

Sam turned the page; someone else had added a note at the back of the book. It was in a different style to Black Heart's writing, the ink was lighter and it had almost faded away to nothing. He could just make out the words, it said:

'There is not much time. I know I am a dying man. I am parched and I can feel my strength leaving me, but I have done it. I have hidden the treasure where Black Heart said. God rest his soul and curses on the one who sent him to his early grave. As for this log, if my last wish is carried out it will be well hidden, until the rightful heir finds it. Then all will know that Spode was a double-crossing murderer and Black Heart a good man. May the entire world know that Spode killed Black Heart in cold blood and ran the Onyx aground. Black Heart's body will rest for now, but his spirit will not be at peace until the pirate death code is enacted." It was signed *'John Friar, first mate and last remaining friend of Capt. Black Heart.'*

Sam felt like a heavy weight had been lifted off his shoulders. He looked up tears filling his eyes and smiled at Lucy.

"This is it, this is what I've been looking for, now I can set the story straight and he can rest in peace finally." As silent tears ran down his face, the church door opened, and the Vicar strolled in. Next to him was an elderly lady that seemed to be asking him lots of questions about the place, probably a tourist.

The Vicar looked up and smiled at them, then his face turned to a scowl as he saw the glass case open in front of them and the book lying as he said later 'desecrated' on the cabinet. "What on earth are you doing?" he glowered his cheeks bursting with pompousness and turning a vivid purple colour. He marched down the aisle to where Lucy and Sam hung their heads.

Chapter 42

Police Sirens

Sam said later that he thought about running away but he knew it was over, he had been caught and now all he could do was tell the truth. He felt his energy had completely drained away and his legs felt heavy and lifeless. Thinking quickly, he slipped the book into the back of his trousers and pulled his t-shirt down over it, he wasn't going to give that up easily until he really needed it. The Vicar ranted and raved at them for a while then sent the old lady out to get the police. Sam let most of what he said wash over him, but Lucy was in floods of tears next to him.

It wasn't long before they arrived. Two policemen entered the Church and had a hurried conversation with the old lady who seemed to be going to great lengths to tell them what young hoodlums they were and how they had been caught in the nick of time before they could do who knows what untold damage. The two friends found themselves being led away to two separate police cars.

As he was climbing into the first car a voice behind him said, "Dear me, have we been a naughty boy then?" Sam turned and glared at Henry who was delighted to have been able to help the police with their enquiries. The policeman beckoned Sam to get into the car, which he did quietly. As they pulled away he could hear Henry shouting some sort of abuse at him, but he didn't care. He had found what he was looking for; he would deal with Henry later.

Ten minutes later they arrived at Sea Cove Police Station and were led inside to separate interview rooms. Sam was hoping to see Lucy before she was led away to tell her to tell the truth, but he guessed the state she was in, she probably would anyway. He was shown to a small room, which was painted completely white with a blue door. There was a table in the middle of the floor with two plastic chairs placed either side. On the table was a tape recorder with a spare tape sitting on top of the machine. A water dispenser sat squat in the corner. The room looked clean but sparsely furnished. Sam supposed you didn't need a lot of pretty furniture in a place like this. He was shown to a seat and two Officers sat down opposite him.

"Would you like a drink?" asked one of the men removing his helmet.

"No, thank you," said Sam sheepishly.

The Officers went out and Sam was left alone for a while. His head spun and he felt sick at the thought that he might get his friends and Max into trouble. He paced the floor wondering what was going to happen next.

He didn't have to wait long before the door opened and two Officers showed Sam's father into the room. He glared at Sam and sat down in the chair next to him.

"Mr. Forshaw," said one of the policemen, "I'm pleased you were able to join us."

"What's this all about?" he asked removing his jacket and loosening his tie. "I have had to come out of an important meeting for this. It better be good." He looked hot and flustered and tiny beads of sweat were running from his forehead down the side of his face. The policeman ignored him.

"For the record please state your name and address to the tape," said the other Officer looking at Sam.

"Sam Forshaw, 5 High Views, Sea Cove Bay" he said speaking to the tape.

"This is PC Meadows, and I am PC Fox," said PC Fox. "We are going to ask you a few questions about the vandalism caused at the Priory Church Sea Cove, today 15th August 2004 and about the vandalism that occurred at Sea Cove school the night of 13th August 2004."

"Good grief, Sam," his dad said in an exasperated tone, "what have you gone and done now?" Sam sat silently waiting for the questioning to begin.

"Sam, we have reason to believe that you wilfully damaged a very expensive and irreplaceable stained-glass window at Sea Cove school the other night whilst trying to exit the premises."

"That's ridiculous!" blurted Mr. Forshaw. Sam was at home all that night; in fact, he was in his room.

"Are you sure about that, Mr. Forshaw?" PC Meadows asked, staring straight at Sam. Mr. Forshaw looked at Sam but the words failed to materialize in his mouth. "Let me make this easier for you, Sam," said PC Fox. "The reason we believe you were involved in the vandalism the other night was because we found your jumper wrapped round an iron door stop that had been thrown through the window."

"Well how do you know it was Sam's jumper?" said Mr. Forshaw looking from PC Fox to PC Meadows and back to Sam.

"Because Mr. Forshaw, it had Sam's name sewn into the collar."

"Oh mum," thought Sam, "why do you have to do that to all of our clothes."

"We also found a jumper belonging to a Max Forshaw with shards of glass all over it, your brother I assume, Sam?" PC Fox said looking from Sam to Mr. Forshaw.

"He is being brought in for questioning as we speak," he continued.

"Sam, what have you done?" said Mr. Forshaw losing some of his huff and puff, "you haven't gone and got Max involved in this as well, have you?" Sam had heard enough. "I'll tell you exactly what happened," he said in a voice that was surprisingly strong and clear for the circumstances. "A great man called Captain Black Heart has been contacting me for help. It started when I saw the map in Mr. Clayton's history class last term," Sam started explaining what had happened to him over the last few weeks and how Max had got involved as well.

He told them everything, all that he had seen and heard and smelled, all about his dreams and the midnight trips to Coombe Bay and the Priory and to the big school. The three men sat wide-eyed silently listening to Sam's story. PC Fox made notes on an A4 pad as Sam talked. He told them about the graveyard and the conversation with his Grandad and the story Lucy's dad had told her at breakfast. He talked and talked, feeling that if he didn't tell every detail he would burst. He went on to tell them about finding the skeleton in the tunnel and the ledger in the Priory and opening the case to get at it. Finally, after an hour and fifteen minutes of solid talking he leant forwards and pulled the battered log from the back of his trousers. It's all in there he said flinging the book down on the table. "Now please can I have a drink of water?"

PC Fox slowly moved his chair away from the table and fetched Sam a plastic cup full of water. The machine continued to bubble as he sat back down again.

His father was sitting trance-like in the chair next to him and PC Meadows clicked the tape recorder off, ejected the tape and walked silently out of the room. A few moments later he came back in.

"Right," he said a shade gingerly, "I think that will be all for now. Mr. Forshaw you may take Sam outside to the waiting room, Mrs Forshaw and Max will be out shortly."

"What happens now?" Mr. Forshaw asked, his voice sounding very meek indeed.

"Now we review the information Sam has given us and compare it to that which Max and Miss Collins have provided," said PC Fox staring at Sam. "We will of course be asking Master Johnson to share his version of the story with us, I understand he has voluntarily come down to the Station with his father and is sitting outside." Sam kept his face blank but knew he couldn't have kept Andrew out of the story if he had tried, even though the thought of getting Andrew into trouble as well filled him with horror.

Sam and his father walked out of the interview room and were shown to a bench in the waiting area. As he sat down Andrew and his father were led past. Andrew winked at Sam and Sam managed a brief smile before they disappeared into the same room Sam had been interviewed in. Not long after, Max and his mother appeared from a door further down the corridor. Max's face was red and his eyes looked sore. He had been crying all the way through his interview. Mrs. Forshaw looked pale and was visibly shaking as Mr. Forshaw took her hand and ushered them to sit down. They sat in silence, Sam staring at the floor, Max quietly sobbing into his handkerchief.

They all looked up when the door to Andrew's interview room opened about half an hour later. PC Fox and PC Meadows emerged and went into the room further down the corridor. Sam risked a glance at his brother then down the corridor to see if he could see any sign of Lucy, but she was nowhere to be seen. Ten minutes later the Policemen appeared and PC Fox approached the Forshaw's.

"You may take the boys home now," he said directing his comment at Mr. Forshaw.

"Right," said Mr. Forshaw jumping up. "Are you going to charge them with anything?"

"Not yet," said PC Fox. "We will need to discuss the matter with Mr. Bainbridge the Headmaster at the school and of course with the Reverend Oakes at the Priory. We will be investigating the story and we will be in touch with any decisions that are reached about the boy's futures. It is likely," he continued, "that Mr. Bainbridge and the Reverend Oakes will want to press charges. Some extensive damage has been done to both buildings and the crimes are made more severe by the age of the buildings and the damage done." Mrs. Forshaw sighed deeply and started crying. Mr. Forshaw reached into his pocket and pulled out a handkerchief, which he handed to her.

"Come on, boys," Mr. Forshaw said and he led his sombre family out of the Station.

Chapter 43

The Wait

The next few days were like a dream to Sam. He and Max stayed in their rooms and were only allowed down at mealtimes. When Mr. Forshaw was out at work Mrs. Forshaw allowed the boys to go into each other's rooms. They consoled each other by playing cards or taking it in turns to read out loud from a book. Occasionally one of them would mention something about their adventures but the conversation soon petered out as their minds would instantly turn to what the consequences of their actions might be. Sam was desperately worried about Lucy and Andrew. He remembered the look on Lucy's face when they had been discovered in the Priory; it was as if her whole world had ended. He knew this was entirely his fault. Each night when he went to bed he went over and over in his mind the things that had happened, the things that had made him believe Black Heart was talking to him and needed his help. If only he hadn't got so hung up on the idea that there was a pirate in the family none of this would have happened. Yet just as he was on the brink of sleep, he knew that he had been right to help. He knew that Black Heart's spirit or ghost or whatever you wanted to call it had called to him and he had answered.

Neither Mr. nor Mrs. Forshaw mentioned anything about the events of the last week when they saw the boys. Mr. Forshaw went around in a permanent bad mood and Mrs. Forshaw would keep bursting into tears all the time. She hadn't been out of the house much since Max and Sam had been questioned for fear of what people might say. Sea Cove was a small village and word got around fast. She couldn't face the whispered conversations or the snide looks that she received when she did nip out to get something from the Village Shop. On the fifth day following their arrests the family was sitting down to breakfast when there was a knock at the door. Mr. Forshaw looked up from his paper at the boys.

"What now?" he said exasperatedly and went to the door. He returned shortly followed by PC Fox. Both Sam and Max instantly stood up and Mrs. Forshaw started flapping around the kettle.

"Sit down, boys," said PC Fox.

"Have you come to arrest us again?" squeaked Max going pale, his eyes filling up.

"No," said PC Fox, "I've come to tell you that neither Mr. Bainbridge nor the Reverend Oakes will be pressing charges."

Mrs. Forshaw gave a huge sigh and dropped the teacup she had in her hand. Sam and Max looked at each other in amazement. Mr. Forshaw went to stand at his wife's shoulder and put his arm round her.

"Please do sit down," said Mrs. Forshaw, all flustered.

"Thank you," said PC Fox taking off his helmet and sitting down at the table. "It appears," he said with a smile at Mr. and Mrs. Forshaw, "that your boys here might well turn out to be local if not national heroes. I sent some of my best men to see if the story you had told me was true," he said turning back to face Sam and Max. "They found the entrance at Coombe Bay as you had described it, it was blocked but some TNT soon shifted the rubble. They found the skeleton halfway along, then they searched the library for the secret passage and after several of them trying they finally found out how to open the door and found the hidden treasure. Mr. Bainbridge has had all the treasure dated and it is indeed believed to be from the early 1800's of Irish origin and worth thousands and thousands of pounds."

"I knew it," said Sam sitting back in his chair, a gleeful look on his face. "And what about the skeleton?" asked Sam. "Have you any idea who it was?"

"Well, from the account in Black Heart's log we believe it might be the remains of John Friar," said PC Fox. He stood up and walked around the room with his arms behind his back. "We think he may have collapsed on his way back from hiding the logbook in the Priory, it's just a guess but it's as good as any other theory anyone can come up with."

"But what about the damage done at the school?" Mrs. Forshaw asked wearily. "The window alone will cost thousands to repair."

"Mr. Bainbridge appears to be so overwhelmed that there are tunnels and hidden passages in his school that he didn't know about and that date back to the height of the pirate smuggling days, that he has decided to reward the boys rather than punish them.

"Oh," said Mrs. Forshaw, a smile returning to her face for the first time in days.

"He has decided there will be a ceremony at the school next Saturday with Sam and Max here along with Lucy Collins and Andrew Johnson as guests of honour. He has also apparently agreed with Reverend Oakes," he said turning to look at Sam, "that the remains of old John Friar will be given a decent burial up at the Priory."

"Great," said Sam smiling, "but what about?"

"And" said PC Fox, interrupting him, "the Reverend Oakes has said that there is still a wrong to right with regards to one of the graves in the Priory graveyard." Sam took a deep breath. "He said that if there is a spirit not yet at rest in his grave yard then something should be done about it, so after the ceremony at the school everyone will be invited to the grave for prayers for Black Heart's soul to find peace."

Sam sat down heavily on his chair; he couldn't believe it. Not only had he found out the truth about Black Heart but also, he had somehow got away with the damage he had caused at the school and the Priory and so had his friends. Max laughed out loud and Mrs. Forshaw ran across the kitchen and flung her arms around her boys squeezing them tightly. Sam felt a surge of emotion welling up inside him. He burst into tears and sobbed and sobbed into his mother's arms.

Chapter 44

I Hate You Dad!

Since Sam's arrest Henry had felt marginally better. His archenemy was in real trouble and he had helped to put the icing on the cake when he bumped into the policeman outside the Priory. Now though he felt empty and more alone than he had ever felt before. He knew deep down that he had failed, that he wasn't good enough to beat Sam Forshaw and that made him feel sick to the bone. He couldn't be bothered going out. Tezz and Pike were no company. He just sat in his bedroom re-reading the letter he had received from his real father.

He was just in the middle of the second page again when he heard a noise outside his door. Before he had time to hide the letter his father burst in with a verbal tirade about leaving a mess downstairs again for his mother to tidy. He stopped short when he saw the letter in Henry's hands, he recognised the writing instantly.

"Give me that," his father shouted, storming across the room and snatching the letter.

"No," screamed Henry hanging on for dear life, "that's mine." His father pushed him back hard onto the bed and ripped the letter from Henry's hands. Henry heard the pages tear as he fell backwards. He sobbed into his hands as he watched his father's face as he held the torn bits of paper together and read the letter. When he had finished reading he turned to Henry lost for words.

"You don't believe any of that do you?" he asked his voice stilted.

"Yes, I do," Henry screamed at him, outraged that he had read his private letter. "I especially believe the bit where it says you are not my real father." Henry pulled himself off the bed and faced his father, "I hate you," he said, venom in his voice that shocked even him. His father had an intake of breath and lashed out at Henry. Before Henry realised what was happening he felt the full weight of his father's hand across his face and he fell onto the bed.

"Never ever speak of this again," his father said menacingly as he stood over the cowering form of Henry. Then he turned and stormed off down the stairs and out of the house slamming the door behind him.

"Good riddance," Henry shrieked after him holding his cheek as it throbbed with pain. Then he vowed to himself that as soon as he could figure out a way he was getting out of this place.

Chapter 45

The Ceremony – Treasure Re-united

Saturday dawned bright and fair, there wasn't a cloud in the sky as Sam got up and went down to breakfast. Max joined him but was interrupted by a loud knock on the door. "I'll go," he said, through a mouthful of cornflakes. When he came back to the table his cheeks were red and his chest seemed somehow more puffed out.

"Who was it, dear?" asked Mrs. Forshaw coming down the stairs in a pretty floral dress ready for the ceremony.

"It was the Press," said Max, "there are about ten photographers on the lawn, mum."

"Oh my," said Mrs. Forshaw going into the front room to see for herself. Sure enough, people were spread out on the lawn, some behind tripods, others holding cameras on their shoulders. "Hurry up and get dressed," she instructed the boys excitedly as the boys left the table to get changed.

They each put on their best suits they wore for family occasions. Mr. Forshaw emerged in a light grey suit with a paisley patterned tie. "Ready?" he beamed as he put his hand on the door latch to open it.

"Ready," said Mrs. Forshaw smoothing down her dress.

"Ready," said Sam and Max together. Mr. Forshaw opened the door and the flash bulbs started instantly.

"Sam, Sam," came the first question "How does it feel to have psychic powers?"

"Mrs. Forshaw how does it feel to have a pirate ghost in the family?"

"Mr. Forshaw what do you think about the events of the last few days?"

"Can you describe how you feel now, Sam?" came another question. Sam stood frozen to the spot, words trying to form in his mouth. Mr. Forshaw ushered his family into the car before anyone could say anything and they set off for the school.

"Charming," said Max. "No one bothered to ask me any questions," he said sulkily.

"Don't worry, Max," said Sam. "You'll be grateful by the end of this." Mr. Forshaw drove down the street and looked out amazed at all of the people lining the pavements to try and get a look at Sam and Max. It seemed like the whole village had turned out to see what was going to happen.

The car rolled up outside the school and Mr. Bainbridge came flapping down in his black gown and mortarboard to meet them. More photographers were waiting at the school and he posed for the cameras as the Forshaws climbed out of the car. He ushered them to a white marquee that had been erected on the lawn and invited them to sit in the chairs that were placed in a line at the top.

"This is like a wedding," Sam joked to Max behind him. Already sitting in their seats were Andrew and his parents, and Lucy with her parents. Everyone beamed at each other as the Forshaws took their seats. Sam winked at Lucy who he thought, was looking particularly pretty with her hair done up and a pink summer dress on.

Sam looked at the people filling the seats in front of him. He noticed a burly set man in the front row. He was wearing a dark green corduroy jacket, with a gold cravat and grey trousers. He had a mop of curly brown hair on his head and his face looked weathered and sun kissed. He looked up and Sam saw he had the most vivid green eyes he had ever seen. Sitting next to him was a stocky lady wearing a tweed skirt and jacket. She had a frilly white blouse on and shiny black shoes. She had a kind smile on her face that also had a tanned complexion, one that you get from working outside a lot, rather than from a sun bed. She caught Sam's eye as he looked at her and beamed at him. Sam smiled back wondering who they were.

Just then Mr. Bainbridge moved to the lectern that had been placed in front of the chairs. There was a tapestry hanging over the front with the school shield and motto embroidered on. He turned to face the hundreds of people that sat in the rows and rows of chairs in front of him. More people were standing at the back craning to get a look at the four youngsters. Sam felt himself going red as his cheeks took on their familiar glow. The crowd went quiet.

"Welcome, welcome all of you," he said in a loud, proud voice, "and in particular our four guests of honour, Sam and Max Forshaw, Andrew Johnson and Lucy Collins." There was a round of applause from the crowd and the press flashed away with their cameras. Mr. Bainbridge was just about to speak again when there was a disturbance at the back of the marquee, everyone turned to see what all the fuss was about. Sam's face broke into a wide grin and he left his seat and ran down to meet his Grandad hobbling up the side, two walking sticks as an aid.

"You weren't going to start the party without me, were you?" he said beaming, pretending to cuff Sam round the ear.

"No Grandad," laughed Sam. "We were just warming the crowd up ready for you to take centre stage."

"Ah, that's what I like to see, my boy," he said. "As long as you're enjoying yourself that's all that matters." Sam helped his Grandad up to the top of the tent and Mr. Bainbridge flapped to one of the teachers standing near the front to bring another chair. Mr. Bainbridge almost bowed as he took Grandad's hand and shook it heartily. "Well,

well," he said bustling around, pride swelling in his chest, "the great grandson of a pirate, who would have thought it, here in our school." Grandad chuckled as he sat down and made himself comfortable. As Mr. Bainbridge started off again, Grandad leaned across to Sam and whispered in his ear, "Well done lad, you certainly have a gift there. I'm surprised you haven't noticed it before. You know this may only be the start of the spirits, you may be able to help find the rest they are searching for." Sam shivered. He somehow felt different. He looked out at the sea of faces listening to Mr. Bainbridge and relaxed back into his chair. Maybe he did have a gift and there would be other ghostly spirits that called to him, who knew? His attention was brought back when the crowd began clapping. Mr. Bainbridge was calling forward the man and lady in the front row Sam had seen before. They stood up and came across to the lectern. The man was clearly very shy and not comfortable to be facing so many people; the lady on the other hand seemed to be revelling in the spotlight and was beaming broadly at everyone.

"Mr. and Mrs. McClinty," said the Headmaster giving them both a hearty handshake. "We are honoured that you were able to join us on this momentous occasion." Sam couldn't believe his ears.

"Mr. McClinty," he thought, "as in Mr. McClinty's treasure!"

"It must be wonderful to have your family heirlooms returned safe and sound after all these years," he babbled on. "Would you like to say anything?" he asked stepping back from the microphone leaving Mr. McClinty no choice but to step up to the mike.

"Well, yes, I, I, I mean, thanks and well, erm," he choked on his words, his thick Irish accent making it hard to determine what he was saying.

"What he means to say," said Mrs. McClinty in an equally broad Irish accent brushing her poor husband aside, "is that we are delighted to be here and wouldn't have missed it for the world. We would like to say a big thank you to Sam and Max Forshaw for finding our family treasure and to Lucy and Andrew for their help. It's always good to have friends you can rely on," she said giggling at Lucy and Andrew. "We are very proud to be part of this story and to be able to take some national treasures back to Ireland. That is the treasure, I mean, not poor Sam and Max here," she giggled again waving a perfumed hand at the boys. "And we should be honoured if the children here would accept a small donation from the hoard in reward for their perseverance in this matter." And with that she nudged her husband in the ribs sharply with her elbow.

"Oh yes, right," he said and dug in his pockets bringing out four small black purse bags drawn together at the top with black silk.

"Please, take this as a token of our thanks," he said shyly handing each of them a bag. "It's just a few coins from the treasure we thought you might like as a keepsake," he said and winked at them.

"Wow." said Max. "Thanks, that's brilliant, real pirate treasure." Sam, Lucy and Andrew laughed and all thanked Mr. McClinty.

The crowd clapped heartily again. Then Sam felt Max nudge him on his other side and gesture him to stand up.

"Come on Sam," said Mr. Bainbridge, "don't be shy." Sam stood up and walked over to the lectern. "Would you like to say a few words, Sam?" Mr. Bainbridge asked him. Sam's face froze in terror; he hated public speaking at the best of times.

"Erm, well," he said, "Yes, actually I would. I would just like to say that I'm very sorry for the damage that we caused. I didn't mean to get my friends involved, it just sort of happened, and well, some of you may think I am crazy but Captain Black Heart did speak to me to show me the way, I know he did. I know it sounds strange and I can hardly believe it myself but it's true. Apart from that I just want to say 'thank you' to a brave little brother who happened to turn up just when I needed him and to the best friends anyone could have in the world, Andrew and Lucy. Erm that's it."

There was a pause then the crowd erupted into applause again and people started getting to their feet to clap even harder. Sam went scarlet from ear to ear. Only one person in the crowd wasn't clapping - Henry Spode who was sitting near the front on the end of a row.

"I guess he doesn't like the fact that his family name is associated with a double-crossing murderer," thought Sam as the clapping died down. "Well, that's his problem," and he flashed Henry an extra special smile just to rub it in a little. When the clapping had stopped, the general background noise increased as everyone gathered their things and started to move out of the tent. "Now for the important bit," said Grandad wobbling a bit as he stood up.

They made their way over the road and into the graveyard at the Priory. Sam walked on one side of his Grandad whilst Max walked on the other. The sun was high in the sky and the graveyard was bathed in glorious sunshine. Only the walls were in shadow where the leaves cast their shade onto the ground. Reverend Oakes led the way carrying a large cross and a black prayer book and climbed the grassy slope to where the grave stood, a new stone cross erected at the head of the grave. Sam noticed that the marking he had seen last time he was here had vanished.

Next to the cross was a fresh pile of earth where John Friar had been buried next to his friend. Mr. and Mrs. McClinty walked round and stood next to the Reverend and everyone else gathered round to see where they could. So many people wanted to attend this part of the ceremony that the crowd stretched down the hill and round to the Priory door. Some climbed onto the wall around the graveyard to get a better view, whilst youngsters were hoisted up onto dads' and brothers' shoulders to get a glimpse of history in the making. The Reverend Oakes opened his prayer book and began reading from it. He held up his hand over the new grave first and there was silence from the crowd.

"Lord God Our Father," he said in a loud voice so that the people at the back could hear him. "We ask that eternal rest be granted here today to John Friar, a loyal friend to one in time of need. May he find the joy of ever lasting peace with you in heaven and bring him home to your kingdom this day. Amen."

"Amen," chorused the crowd. Then he raised his hand over Black Heart's grave and said:

"Lord God, Our Father, the time has come for you to welcome another of your own. The soul of one of your family has been wandering in the wilderness for too long. Hear the prayers of the faithful and open the gates of Heaven to this soul, the soul of Captain Black Heart, who sailed under the pirate flag but was an honest and good man. Hear this prayer, oh Lord, may the soul of this faithful departed now rest in peace, Amen."

"Amen," came the chorus again. Sam closed his eyes. He knew what was going to happen next and he braced himself for it. He felt the shiver run down his spine and the hairs on the back of his neck stand on end. He felt the tingle in his hand and felt it run up his arm, he felt the lightheaded sensation he had felt so many times before and just on the edge of hearing, heard a breath of air rush past him.

"Thank you," said the wind as it circled round him. He opened his eyes to see his Grandad and Max both standing still as statues with their eyes closed, he glanced at his mother and she too had her eyes closed.

"So, it does run in the family," he thought to himself. As he regained control of his senses a black rook hopped on to the grave, gave a bow and then took off in flight to a tree top overlooking the grave yard where it stayed for a moment or two and then flew into the sky circling higher and higher before it became a black dot on the edge of vision.

Sam didn't know whether he had a special gift or not. He didn't know whether the spirits of those yet to find their rest could really speak to him in order to get his help. All he knew was that he had helped lay his great, great Grandad to rest and that was enough for now. He felt somehow different, almost older and wiser, even though it had only been a matter of weeks since this whole thing began. He turned round and caught Henry Spode giving him a venomous look.

"Maybe," he thought to himself, "maybe I will get another chance to help some other lost Souls find peace, but I reckon Henry Spode might be involved somewhere along the line as well." He turned and headed back down the hill. As he passed Henry he jingled the coins in his pocket.

"I'll get you, Forshaw," said Spode angrily under his breath. "One day, when you least expect it, I'll get you."

"Right," said Sam. "I'll be sure to look out for you," he said, making a mockery of Henry's words.

"You might have made some new friends here today, Forshaw," said Henry in a fierce voice, "but you've made an enemy as well, and I'll settle the score. Just you wait and see."

Sam frowned knowing somehow that his fate was tied with Henry Spode's, whether he liked it or not. Then he turned and headed off with his family to enjoy the party that was being thrown in their honour.

"Maybe," thought Sam, "maybe, but I'll be ready for you Henry Spode."

Milton Keynes UK
Ingram Content Group UK Ltd.
UKHW021115030324
438552UK00007B/54

9 781835 380710